I0825303

Social Animals

Also by Camille Perri

When Katie Met Cassidy
The Assistants

Social Animals

A NOVEL

Camille Perri

G. P. Putnam's Sons
New York

PUTNAM
— EST. 1838 —

G. P. Putnam's Sons
Publishers Since 1838
An imprint of Penguin Random House LLC
1745 Broadway, New York, NY 10019
penguinrandomhouse.com

Book design by Silverglass Studio

LIBRARY OF CONGRESS CATALOGING-IN-PUBLICATION DATA

Names: Perri, Camille, author
Title: Social animals : a novel / Camille Perri.
Description: New York : G. P. Putnam's Sons, 2026.
Identifiers: LCCN 2025038696 (print) | LCCN 2025038697 (ebook) |
ISBN 9798217181759 (hardcover) | ISBN 9798217181773 (ebook)
Subjects: LCGFT: Fiction | Novels
Classification: LCC PS3616.E768 S63 2026 (print) | LCC PS3616.E768 (ebook)
LC record available at https://lccn.loc.gov/2025038696
LC ebook record available at https://lccn.loc.gov/2025038697

Printed in the United States of America
1st Printing

The authorized representative in the EU for product safety and compliance is Penguin Random House Ireland, Morrison Chambers, 32 Nassau Street, Dublin D02 YH68, Ireland, https://eu-contact.penguin.ie.

Social Animals

Prologue

It's a lonely life, being a stray.

Did you know feeling lonely activates the same part of the brain that processes physical pain? That's why rejection hurts as bad as it does. Because the need for connection and belonging is evolutionary, stemming from a past where isolation meant increased vulnerability to danger. Today, isolation is differently dangerous—but no less so.

For a dog with enough time spent alone, without anyone to trust, starving for kindness, a change happens and that aloneness becomes a personality. You see this clearly at the park, the extroverts running around, kicking dust into the eyes of the introverted loners looking on from afar.

Of course, not all who are solitary are unhappy, but the fact is once an animal's been socialized, it's tough to change it, whether they're happy that way or not.

People are no different. That's my opinion, anyway. Bring a stranger into a group, one who doesn't play well with others, and the dynamic shifts, new packs form. Sometimes a fight breaks out, sometimes someone gets hurt. So, what happened at Hamilton Dog Park came as no surprise to me.

I was there. I saw it all. And for months I'd been telling anyone who would listen: Someone here is going to end up dead.

CHAPTER 1

The little beast glared at Val from the doggy car seat, ears back, round eyes intent on expressing her profound displeasure.

"I'm sorry I didn't let you eat my earbuds," Val said as she pulled out of her assigned parking spot at the apartment complex. "But you need to let go of all that unhealthy anger."

In response, Cash emitted a low, discontented growl that over the past forty-eight hours Val had come to know well.

"It's a beautiful day!" Val said, though five thirty p.m. was technically evening. "There's not a cloud in the sky. You're about to make a bunch of new friends."

Cash snorted to indicate that she knew Val was full of shit and turned her head in protest.

"I know, friends are overrated." Val continued onto the road that led to Hamilton Dog Park. "But sometimes you have to fake it."

Last week at this time, before accepting this job, Val had been secure in her identity as a person who would no sooner talk to an animal than to a kitchen appliance. In fact, in the case of a missing container of leftovers, say, she would have been far *more* likely to speak to her refrigerator—something reasonably rhetorical, like "Did I already eat those mozzarella sticks and forget?"

Now look at her. Having entire conversations with this speechless creature. Clothes covered in hair. A plastic poop bag in one pocket. In the other, a damp, half-chewed stick processed from God-only-knows which body parts of what. She probably stank like dog, but who could say for sure? You can't smell yourself, and she had no one in her life close enough to tell her.

The absurdity of chauffeuring around this self-important little animal, propped up like a diminutive princess or a tiny, furry Miss America, in the back of her beat-up Nova, was not lost on Val. She still found it hard to believe car seats for dogs existed, but they were a "small-dog safety necessity," according to the lady at PetSmart, who also managed to upsell Val on the booster model that would give Cash a better "out-the-window view."

A 1970s muscle car was never intended to cater to such refinement, which made the contraption a challenge to install. As she MacGyvered it to the Nova's bench-seat lap belts, Val tried to remember if she'd had a safety seat as a baby.

Yeah, right. She would have been rolling around on the back floormats with her father's every haywire turn, or else clinging to her mother's lap for dear life up front, getting ashed on.

But only the best for this precious cargo. Along with the booster seat, Val was the baffled new owner of a doggy harness, because a regular collar would apparently be "too hard on the neck," as well as a doggy travel water bottle for proper hydration on the go, and—most mind-blowing—a doggy dental hygiene kit. When did people start brushing dogs' teeth? And what was next? Professional whitening? Incisor veneers? Was Val supposed to lay out a few grand to get Cash braces before sending her off to middle school?

This job had started out with so much promise. The man on the other end of the phone was courteous. His voice was direct, but unaggressive, when he said, "Hello, may I please speak to Valerie Caruso?" Phone etiquette was a huge tell.

She asked her standard question: "How'd you hear about me?"

"You did work for a friend of mine last summer," he said. "Out on the east end of Long Island."

Cha-ching. That Long Island job had been a goldmine.

And so, Val agreed to meet the polite and probably wealthy man at the waiting area of Penn Station, where he'd be arriving on the Acela from DC. His name was Silas Kennerson and he told her to meet him at the Blue Bottle Coffee kiosk, which spoke volumes to Val considering the Starbucks just across the hall. With its minimalist aesthetic and meticulous brewing methods, Blue Bottle was a luxury brand for those seeking a premium experience over convenience and common sense.

Reputation-conscious much? Val thought as she cased the surroundings, watching Silas from afar. She already knew what he looked like, thanks to the internet, but now she could get a real sense of him. He was about five foot nine, medium build, suit and tie, more handsome than the average man, with a sweet, wholesome face that could be dangerously charming. He was in his mid-forties and was well-groomed, but with floppy hair that made him seem younger, like a mischievous schoolboy. Val disliked him immediately.

Beyond the fact that she always viewed attractive people with suspicion, Val also noted that even though Silas didn't make a purchase at Blue Bottle, he claimed one of the few customer chairs for himself. He also removed his black laptop bag from across his chest and placed it on the chair beside his. Meanwhile, two poor schlubs who had just paid out the wazoo for espresso drinks and pain au chocolat were struggling to sip and eat while standing. Clearly the man was selfish, self-absorbed, and lacked a conscience.

Val made her approach, set and ready to take this jerk for all he was worth.

He stood when he saw her coming and shook her hand, palming her a hundred-dollar bill. "For your discretion," he said.

It was a solid start if Val had ever seen one.

Silas reclaimed his bag so Val could sit beside him, also coffee-less.

This close up, Val was struck by Silas's baby blue eyes, but to her nose he smelled more sadistic than most of her clients. This gave her hope that—for once—she would be tasked with something less humdrum than digging up dirt on a jealous husband's wife.

Silas got right to the point: He wanted to hire Val to spy on his wife.

Ho-hum, humdrum it would be—finding evidence of an affair—but at least this guy had resources and was joyously quick to throw money at a problem. He would double her usual rate for the inconvenience of having to relocate to Bethesda, Maryland, and offered to pay for her lodging before she even had the chance to feign hesitation.

Val let her gaze wander to the bearded, cap-wearing barista, who was carefully pouring hot water over coffee grounds in a filter. It was a precise and deliberate process that allowed her to calm her elation over this sudden great fortune.

"And you're going to need a dog," Silas said.

Wait. What? The dollar signs fell from Val's eyes. The dog park was apparently where Silas's suspicions were rooted, and he would not be convinced that she could capture all the nitty-gritty from afar. She had to get up close. And the only way was with a dog.

"Nope," Val said. "Sorry. That's a deal-breaker. Dogs are not my thing."

It had not been a negotiating tactic when she tried to get up and walk away, and yet even this turned to Val's favor.

"Give me a number," Silas said. Such extravagant, reckless, self-destructive words to utter to someone with Val's skill set. "What would make it worth your while?"

Val wondered now, as she parked her old beater alongside shiny Mercedes and Lexus SUVs, each one more massive than the next, if she should have held out for a luxury car stipend. Perhaps she would call Silas tonight and ask.

"Okay. You ready?" Val locked eyes with the ten-pound fur monster in her temporary care, this bossy, mini-tyrant called a Brussels Griffon. What a stupid, stuck-up-sounding name for a breed of dog. She had to practice saying it aloud all morning to stop cringing.

At the animal shelter, Val had initially heard it wrong. After perusing the sorriest array of neglected strays and street dogs, she had just about settled on a mild-mannered Muppet-type mix when someone cried out, "Is that a grift?"

Val's inner grifter startled at the accusation. Had the twenty-something volunteer working the counter seen right through to the empty black hole at her core?

Then Val noticed the other twentysomething volunteer, who had come from the back. In her arms, she held what appeared to be a baby monkey wrapped in a blanket, or maybe a swaddled ET plucked from Elliott's bicycle basket. While the two adult women goo goo–ed and gaga-ed over the thing, Val realized it was "Griff" they were saying.

"As in Brussels Griffon," the first volunteer said when Val asked for clarification. "We rarely get these in here. I've never even seen a smooth-coated red Griff in real life before."

"Only two years old and a purebred, too," the other volunteer offered.

They went on this way long enough for Val to pull out her phone and search the important-sounding keywords spilling from their mouths. She mangled some of the spelling, but the numbers came up nonetheless, confirming her suspicion: the average resale value of this little bundle of joy was upward of three thousand dollars.

The adoption fee was $150, and only a suggestion, so Val paid $75.

It was beyond a good bargain—it was a steal.

A steal, Val reminded herself at dawn the next morning, with the dog standing on her stomach, barking directly into her face. *The quickest three grand I'll ever make.*

Since then, she had come to better understand why a person might be driven to give away such a high-value animal.

Val's first full day serving as Cash's custodian came with unexpected challenges. Being followed to the bathroom, for example, was a new experience—made worse by Cash's disturbingly human-like eyes. Val flushed and washed her hands, then searched the internet to see if toilet-ogling was normal or if it were possible for a dog to be a pervert.

What she discovered online was bone-chilling.

Griffs are not like other dogs. They are affectionately known as

Velcro dogs because they attach themselves to a person and need to be with them 24/7.

This was from the American Brussels Griffon Rescue Alliance, an organization that appeared to really know their shit.

It only got worse from there.

They want to sleep in bed with you. If you are standing at the sink, you may find your Griff sitting on your feet. When you sit down, your Griff will be in your lap. Can you handle that as part of your lifestyle?

Who could handle that as part of their lifestyle? Val wondered. What kind of person could have anything stuck to them twenty-four hours a day and not flick it away like the pest it was? Did Griff owners have no appreciation of independence? Did they dislike freedom? What had Val gotten herself into?

Later that night, as Cash whimpered and cried and barked *I hate you!* from inside her crate across the bedroom, Val knew she had no one to blame but herself. She had conducted her breed research too late.

It wasn't Cash's fault that she was wired to be anxious, excitable, and annoying as hell. Genetics were a cruel lottery that couldn't be rigged, and if that weren't enough, the environment she was raised in had not done her any favors. There was no telling what Cash had endured before being abandoned. Who understood this lethal combination better than Val?

As her state-sanctioned social worker once said, *Nature loads the gun, but nurture pulls the trigger*, which Val's adolescent mind rightly took to mean *There's no hope for you, kid.*

Val tried to remember this while silently counting backward from one hundred to keep from wringing Cash's howling neck.

This is an intelligent breed, but sensitive, the Rescue Alliance website had said. *The Griffon will not respond to rough handling, hitting, or excessive shouting. They will, however, respond well to guidance given with kindness, consistency, and love.*

Eventually Val lost her nerve, releasing Cash from the crate and placing her onto the cloud-soft, circular pillow bed the PetSmart lady called a "Poof."

"Happy now?" Val failed at her attempt to sound calm and collected. "From here I can watch you sleep, and you can watch me sleep, quietly."

Cash clenched her little jaw around the Poof's downy fuzz and thrashed it about like enemy vermin. She wanted in on Val's bed, which she communicated by growling and standing up on two legs with her front nails gripping the top of Val's mattress.

"Absolutely not." Val considered having a dog in one's bed to be in the red zone of the grossness scale, but Cash persisted, hopping up and down, begging, pleading.

It went on this way long enough to become mind-bending, especially because Val was certain Cash could have made the jump onto the bed with minimal effort if she tried.

"You're being ridiculous," Val said when the clock on her nightstand flipped to three a.m. "You don't need my help."

The repetition had become relentless. Over and over, Cash would back up, false-start, false-start, lose her nerve, whimper, growl, begin again.

"You can do it!" Val shouted, against her better judgment and contrary to her own desired outcome. "I've seen you jump twice as high!"

Exhausted and worn down by the need to be proven correct, she said, "If you figure it out on your own, I'll let you stay up here."

It was only the next morning, after waking up with Cash curled like a baby fox in the bend of her knees, that Val recognized how marvelously she had been conned.

In fact, if Val learned anything from those first forty-eight hours with Cash, it was that she had underestimated the role of manipulation in the dog-to-human social contract. But this was a challenge she was determined to see through. The amount of money Val could make on this Silas Kennerson job might be enough to take the rest of the year off, travel a bit, go someplace warm for the winter, see another country, or even another continent. Val had been next to nowhere beyond a handful of US states—she just didn't have the means, but she did have the vision. And she was not about to give anything up on account of one badly behaved dog, whether that dog was an evil genius or not.

"Ready?" Val stepped out of the Nova, careful not to nick the door of the BMW X5 she'd parked beside.

Cash was up and alert in her car seat, recognizing they'd arrived someplace significantly grotesque by the faint odor in the air.

Leash clipped to harness, Val set the dog onto the pavement and steered her across the parking lot toward the double-gated entryway to the park.

One whiff of the assembly beyond the gates and Cash charged ahead, pulling Val along with the strength of a miniature bull.

"Don't you dare embarrass me, now," Val said, shocked to hear her mother's threat of choice fresh from her own mouth. She noticed, too, the tight grip she had on the leash, how she'd unconsciously wound it around her hand, braced for a bare-knuckled tug.

This was what she had to fight against—her own inclination toward impatience and violence, learned from her parents or inherited. Such a pet-rearing approach would not fly with the dog lovers

Val was tasked with winning over, and the only way to successfully embed herself in their group was to be convincing as one of them.

With her next foot forward, she inhaled a calming breath, unclenched her fists, and let the leash unravel to a more merciful hold.

There was a sign on one of the front gates designating the field to the left as the "small dog area," defining *small* as under twenty-five pounds. Another sign read NO BARKING, which, in context, was as perplexing as a riddle.

Cash, confident in her supersized ferociousness, strained toward the section for big dogs.

"No! This way!" Already Val was yelling.

Once inside the proper area, she secured the latch on the gate behind them and reminded herself that she was not to scold this dog in front of these people. This would be a crowd that fed their animals organic raw diets, got them groomed at pet spas, and bought them seasonal wardrobes.

Right on cue, a furball in a pink princess dress came over yap yap yapping as Val released Cash from her leash.

Unsure of what to do next, Cash eyed the princess with skepticism.

"Go ahead." Val urged her forward. "You can play."

Cash took a seat, dubious.

"Don't be scared," Val said, just as Cash got body-slammed by one of those whatever-doodles—a curly, white lunatic clearly over the twenty-five-pound limit that should have relegated it to the "big dog area."

"Chester! You say you're sorry right now!" A woman came Val's way. She was wearing natural-looking makeup and understated diamonds likely worth a tidy sum. Her shirtdress was the embodiment of chic comfort, but she added a touch of sophistication by cinching her waist with a belt.

"You'll have to excuse Chester," she said. "He doesn't like dogs with smushed faces."

This was supposed to pass as an acceptable, and in no way politically incorrect, explanation?

I don't like your *face*, Val wanted to say to this woman she had already pegged as the park's resident popular girl. *And your cocker-doodle-doo is an asshole.*

Cash seemed to recover fine once Chester was out of sight.

"You must be new. I've never seen you here before." Popular Girl wandered back toward the clique of women from which she'd emerged, not bothering to check if Val was following her.

Val did follow her, because she already recognized one member of the hive as June Kennerson—the Wife. She was about five foot nine with long blond hair pulled back in a ponytail. Like Popular Girl, June was wearing a dress, but hers was a brightly colored sundress with a flowery print, which she had paired with strappy sandals. She looked summer-ready even though it was only mid May, yet the sun did seem to shine with more radiance over her than all the others.

"What *is* your dog?" Popular Girl asked over her shoulder. "A pug mix?"

"A Brussels Griffon," Val replied in her practiced pronunciation.

"Boy or girl?"

Val had done her homework before arriving. Statistically, this affluent DC suburb was the best-educated city in the US, which meant these people weren't just rich, they were also supposed to be smart. Yet, as she introduced herself to each of the park regulars, she was asked the same question—"Boy or girl?"—countless times. A few even asked a second time, rephrasing it to "Is Cash a *he* or a *she*?" The confusion, Val finally realized, was that Cash was a girl dog with a gender-unspecific name, wearing a blue collar. No one, it seemed, could get their brains around this.

No one, except for June. The first question she asked was "Is her namesake Cash, as in Johnny?"

It was Cash as in cold, hard. But Val answered in the affirmative.

"She must be great at walking a line." June laughed in an embarrassed way at her own corniness, and then, as if to double down, she added, "I bet she still hasn't gotten over the fact that her coat isn't black."

The husband—Silas—had said June was beautiful, but most men willing to hire a PI to keep tabs on their wives thought they were beautiful, even if they were total frogs. In this case, the husband was right. June had the physical glow of a California Dream Girl and the unassuming inner warmth of the girl next door.

Val could immediately see how they worked as a couple, with June's bordering-on-intimidating good looks tempered by her goofy sense of humor, and Silas's dreamy boy-next-door quality humanized by an awkwardness that came off as self-deferential. He was overeager to please; she was easily delighted. They were a match made in heaven. Except for the fact that June lacked the sinister quality Val had picked up on in Silas. He had a definite ick factor beneath the surface, whereas June gave off a simple, friendly, what-you-see-is-what-you-get kind of vibe.

Val was finding it hard to imagine June cheating on Silas, but all sorts were unfaithful. Years of PI work had taught her nothing if not that.

Meanwhile, Popular Girl was body-shaming Eloise the miniature dachshund. Val wasn't too secure in her ability to identify dog breeds, but she was certain about this one because Popular Girl's exact words were "There is nothing miniature about that mini dachshund."

"I think she may have actually lost a pound," said the older woman who had the inexplicable confidence to wear an ecru pantsuit and high heels to a dog park. Her sharply cut shoulder-length hair was the exact shade of gray as her schnauzer's fur.

This was Paisley's mom. (*Don't say owner,* Val observed. *Human is fine, but never owner.*) After two decades working in government, Paisley's mom founded her own lobbying firm, which explained her aura of smarmy self-satisfaction.

"Paisley! Get out of there!"

The gray-furred schnauzer ignored her hair twin's command and continued sticking her robust snout into the stream of Chester's urine as he peed.

Already, Val had a special loathing in her heart for Chester—how he pranced around like he owned the place, lifting his doodle leg on everything in sight.

"What is that new dog again, a pug mix?" Paisley's mom asked Popular Girl in a stage whisper loud enough for Broadway. "And is it a boy or a girl?"

Val pretended not to hear as she scanned the park, having lost sight of Cash for a few minutes. She found her sitting alone on the outer periphery, observing the action from afar with the slouched posture of the iPhone monkey emoji.

Of course Val would end up with the weirdest, most socially inept animal ever to walk on four paws. How could this have gone any other way?

Over the next hour, Val listened more than she spoke. She would leave here tonight with a solid feel for the personalities and politics that defined this subculture. How Chester's mom may have been the queen bee type, but Paisley's mom was the powerhouse whom everyone feared. How the topographical superiority of the "big dog side" was a hot-button issue best left unmentioned. How it was a social normality to discuss your dog's bodily functions and fluids, as well as those of anyone else's dog, present or in absentia.

What Val wouldn't leave with tonight was the slightest lead on June Kennerson's infidelity. Not a single hint of flirtation, no shared suggestive glances. If there was a special someone, they hadn't shown up here. Maybe tomorrow Val would have better luck.

"I think Cash is trying to tell me she's had enough for one day," Val said to no one in particular.

The hypervigilant nugget watched Val's long approach across the damp grass, sitting still as a statue, but when Val got close enough to pick her up, she leapt a few feet out of arms' reach.

"Come on, Cash." Val tried to sound amused. "Time to go home." She reapproached slowly, then lunged for the dog, prompting her to take off with Usain Bolt–level speed.

Who knew she could run so fast? Not Val, and not every other dog in the park, all of whom stopped whatever they were doing to take chase. What did the newbie have? A treasured stick? A ball? Or nothing whatsoever; had Cash herself become the prize?

This was the "small dog area," sure, but enforcement of the supposed under-twenty-five-pound rule was lackadaisical at best. Among the pack gaining on Cash's tail was a German shepherd (about a hundred years old, but still), a boxer (shockingly fleet-footed considering it only had three legs), and a Labrador retriever (who was blind, but whose sense of excitement was clearly intact).

"Do they think she's a squirrel?" someone asked, alerting Val to the fact that all the humans in the park had also stopped what they were doing to watch the spectacle. "Or maybe a rabbit?"

Val should have known what to do in a situation like this, whether she was supposed to let the animals work it out for themselves or risk life and limb to intervene, but she found herself frozen—as if her feet took root in the mud while her mind separated itself to another place, a different time.

Often, Val's memories from childhood came to her in black and white, like an old TV show. She was raised in the 1990s, but for her old-fashioned, Italian parents it may as well have been the 1950s. This memory, however, arrived in stark color: Val was trackside, up on tippy-toes to see over the railing, excited to watch the horses speeding around the bend, while her father hurled expletives at their backs. Except, instead of going to see the majestic horses at the Aqueduct, her father had brought her to a dog race, where skinny greyhounds lusted after a terrified bunny.

Gianni's anger was loud in her ear. *It's not real!*

Her gullibility embarrassed him; he'd raised her to be tougher and smarter than this. *It's a piece of metal some guy's working like a remote-control car!*

That rabbit was mechanical. But this dog was a living thing—ten tiny pounds, with warm blood and a beating heart.

It was a Jack Russell terrier who caught Cash first—who she promptly smacked across the mouth with a catlike swipe of her paw.

Next came the boxer, who could learn a thing or two from Cash's jab-cross combination.

The German shepherd might have gotten the best of her if she hadn't launched herself through the air, smack into the haven of June Kennerson's open arms.

Val fully returned to her own body as she made her way toward them on shaky legs, but she was more uncertain than ever about how to behave. Was she supposed to scold her unruly pet or show it love?

June hugged Cash close to her chest, cooing into her ear, "You're okay. You're safe. I've got you."

This is a dog person, Val thought. Whatever it was in June's brain or soul—whether her actions and reactions were the result of nature or nurture—Val was missing those parts. And they couldn't be faked.

Cash wiggled in justified protest to June handing her over. Val had to hook her thumb beneath the dog's collar to keep her from fleeing again.

"I'm so sorry," Val said, though she wasn't sure to whom she was apologizing.

"It happens to the best of us." June gave one last reassuring pat to Cash's back, then rested her warm, blue-green eyes on Val and said, "You're doing fine, you know."

Val was unsure how to respond to a statement so kind and vastly untrue.

"She's your first, I take it?" June asked.

"First and last," Val said.

June threw her head back and laughed like Val was the funniest person she'd ever met. "It'll get easier. You should keep coming back. The socialization will be good for her."

"Same time, same place tomorrow then?" Val asked.

"I'll takc that as a promise." June smiled.

As she dragged Cash toward the exit gate, Val was feeling pretty good about herself. The day wasn't a total loss. Forging a friendship with a target the first time out was a boon, but was June this affable to everyone? If so, it was possible she was having one hundred affairs.

Val was halfway to the parking lot when she caught sight of the figure lurking near the east side of the fence. Tall, with dark sunglasses and a ball cap, generic clothing. Val knew a shadow when she saw one. And whoever they were, they were watching.

It was possible that Silas Kennerson, after hiring Val, had also hired this other person to keep an eye on her. Paranoid employers had done this before, as a test.

If Val were being tested now, she was confident she would pass. A spy would not rattle her. Cash would not break her. And if June had a secret lover, Val would uncover them in due time, collect her bonus, and go on her merry way.

By the time Val started the Nova's engine, she was already counting her money and imagining herself in a tropical locale, and so she ignored this early glaring sign to walk away from this job while she still had the chance.

CHAPTER 2

June pulled the boning knife from its woodblock and contemplated its razor-sharp blade. Her "Happy Songs" playlist was already blaring from the portable speaker on the counter, a necessary distraction any time she had to hack through the raw meat of a once-living animal. Tonight, it was a Flintstone-looking chunk of rib-eye steak.

"I'm sorry and thank you," June whispered to the poor cow that gave its life to this meal, then took the cold flesh in hand.

The sensation of cutting through the meat was awful, terrible, but so much was good. She loved her kitchen, how spacious it was, how it shined. It was three times the size of the one she had growing up, where she and her sisters would bump elbows while serving as their mother's sous chefs, slicing garlic, dicing onions, fighting over who got to use the good knife. They really did only have one effective chopping knife. Even today, if she opened her mother's kitchen drawer, it would be there among all the other crappy ones, also still there.

Here and now, all of June's knives were good. Silas had given her the same kind professional chefs carried with them in leather satchels, and she was thankful—truly, she was—to have all this and to live such a blessed life.

The blessings were what she continued to focus on as she felt her way against bone, peeling meat back as she worked across it. It didn't even take much effort. She just let the blade do all the work.

From the living room, June heard the ecstatic clang of Willow's ID tag knocking against her collar as she shook off her nap. A moment later she galumphed into the kitchen, wagging her long fluffy golden-retriever tail and sniffing expectantly.

"Do you smell something delicious or something disgusting?" June asked.

Willow sat and offered up her paw, which was her go-to way of saying *Can I please have some of whatever you have?*

June took comfort in the simplicity and predictability of her dog's desires. "This is for Daddy," she said as she cut some excess fat from the steak's edge. "But I bet you're ready for your *dinner*."

The word *dinner* alone could send Willow into hysterics. Color it with a note of enthusiasm, and she full-on lost her mind, panting and jumping for joy the way a person might if they won the lottery or the World Series. It was hard to believe Willow was nine years old. She still behaved like a puppy. Every single night, this much excitement. Over kibble! And every single night, June got to enjoy witnessing it.

To stretch out the fun, June made a game of it, scooping the kibble into a clean bowl but not setting it down right away. Instead, she tossed pieces, one by one, across the kitchen and living room floor while yelling "Find it!" It was half entertainment, half training exercise, and a useful method for preventing Willow from wolfing down the entire serving in two mouthfuls.

But tonight's fun came to an abrupt end when Silas stepped through the front door just as Willow charged in that direction, a runaway happy train with no brakes, pummeling him against the doorjamb.

"Really?" Silas took off his jacket and made a show of checking it for dirt, or June didn't know what, exactly.

"You're home early." She set down Willow's bowl.

"Would you like me to leave and come back later?" Silas draped his jacket onto a hanger and placed it in the foyer closet.

On nights Silas came home with his floppy hair chaotically tousled and his necktie knot yanked halfway down his shirt, June knew there was no use taking his harsh tone to heart. Eight years of marriage had taught her to grant him the time he needed to release whatever aggravation he'd brought from the office.

For a man who claimed to love his job, it mystified June how miserable and stressed he seemed just about all the time, but what did she know? She had never worked behind a desk. If she did, maybe she too would be a short-tempered grump.

"I just didn't have a chance to tidy up yet," June said as she made a quick visual sweep of the house. There were three items out of place: the muddy pair of sneakers she'd kicked off in the entryway and failed to return to the shoe rack; the dog leash she'd tossed onto the credenza instead of hanging it upon its hook; and—most egregious to Silas—the empty mug she'd left on the coffee table since midmorning.

As expected, Silas went right for the mug. June often wondered if he had always been so particular about his surroundings, or if it was something that worsened over the years. Was he this cranky when she chose to spend the rest of her life with him, or had he kept it hidden? Either way, somewhere along the line, he had given up trying to at least appear a little lighter when he was in a dark mood.

Silas picked up the forgotten mug, examined its insides, and placed it quietly into the kitchen sink. Sometimes he would call her names or connect her poor organization to a lack of intelligence, but tonight his silent countenance of disappointment spoke for him.

June also refrained from saying what she was thinking. *So what if the coffee cup gets stained brown on the inside? It's a COFFEE CUP. That is its intended purpose in life!*

But she understood that, to Silas, the staining was a mark not only on her character, but on his. If a guest were handed that cup, say, and saw its blemishes, it would be a shameful revelation of laziness and imperfection that exposed him as a man with poor habits, unclean and unconscientious.

The part that really baffled June was that it wasn't just Silas's self-consciousness that made him this way because, on the flipside, if he were a guest at someone else's home and given a stained mug, he would react similarly.

Would you look at that, he might say to June later. *He doesn't have it together enough to control his own home; how could I trust him to run an entire department?*

June had to remind herself that in the larger scheme of awful things people dealt with in their marriages, where one stood on mug rinsing was a minor issue. On the important stuff, she and Silas were of one mind, right?

Well, June wasn't so sure. This big fancy house, for instance, their luxury cars—in truth, June had no desire for any of it. She dressed up on occasion because Silas liked her to, and because he often bought her dresses that he wanted to see her in, but she actually preferred simple, practical clothing and couldn't care less about jewelry.

Even their basic worldviews differed, when June really gave it thought. Silas was a striver who saw the world in black-and-white, made up of winners and losers. More than anything, he needed others to view him as impressive, while all June wanted was a humble, quiet life surrounded by animals and maybe, one day, a kid or two.

But what was June supposed to do about all these discrepancies now? After she had already invested so many years and made so many sacrifices. And anyway, she believed wholeheartedly in making the best of things.

While Silas went upstairs to change, June sprinkled some finishing salt onto her side dishes and flung together a quick arugula salad doused with oil and vinegar. Then it was time to face the steak.

The sizzle of raw meat against hot pan brought Willow back around the stove. June avoided her curious snout while holding her own breath as best she could to keep the scent of cooking flesh from entering her nostrils.

She urged her thoughts elsewhere to the unexpected novelty of the day. Not one, but two new people at the dog park. The first, Val, seemed friendly enough, maybe a bit too cool in that motorcycle jacket and those tough-girl black boots. She was probably pushing forty, a good five years older than June, and yet she seemed younger. Maybe because she was on the short side, or because her jeans were fashionably ripped, as if she were a surly but style-conscious teenager. Regardless, she'd lost all her edginess getting run around in circles by that high-strung little Griff.

June hoped they would return tomorrow, Val and Cash. They were the most amusing development to hit the park since the lady who showed up with her tabby cat on a leash and tried to pass it off as a Shiba Inu mix.

Silas returned from upstairs just as June slid his crackling steak from pan to plate.

They sat down to eat.

It was the same as always. Silas held his steak knife in his right hand and his fork in the left. He made a deep cut in the middle of the meat to observe its color on the inside and determine its level of over- or underdoneness. With a satisfied nod he then proceeded from the middle, slicing against the grain of the flesh, one bite at a time. The string beans and potatoes were an afterthought. The salad wouldn't be touched until after he wiped every trace of bloodlike grease from the plate with a potato.

For herself, June had warmed up some leftover vegetarian chili from yesterday. She asked Silas the usual questions about his day, which was like winding him up with a turnkey and watching him go.

June understood the basics of his job at the EPA, but she had long lost track of who was who above and below him, the allies versus nemeses. She took it as flattering that he assumed she could follow the chemical names that rolled off his lips—a complex, multisyllabic nomenclature of similar prefixes and suffixes—when she couldn't even remember if Bill was friend and Brian was foe, or if it was the other way around.

"The exposure levels are negligible," Silas said. "These guys want to lower the cutoffs, run the calculations for each chemical individually, which is insane. We use thresholds, that's how it's done. We can't just stop applying them or change how we do our assessments. We tested the dialkyl sulfate. Genotoxicity isn't a concern. It's diluted in the air."

June nodded along, thinking again of Val. When Val and Cash left the park, June had watched them walk away, wishing they would stay a little longer—and that was how she first caught sight of the mysterious figure between the tennis courts and the eastern side of the park.

From June's perspective, the moment Val disappeared, this new person emerged, linking them in her mind as two parts to some whole.

The ball-cap-and-sunglasses-wearing woman was lingering where passersby often stopped to watch the dogs through the chain-link fence. Sometimes they were parents with small children, who would crouch and point, asking *See the nice doggy? Do you know what the doggy says?* Sometimes they were teenagers with their phones aimed at catching a meme-worthy moment. (Wait till they got a load of Val's little maniac.) And sometimes it was mourners. These were the people whose sorrow June could feel from across the field. Half here in the present and half somewhere in the past, longing for something long gone. This new person was one of them, June was sure of it.

Willow, who could catch the scent of sadness like a day-old piece of fish, noticed it, too. She scampered to the fence to better assess the situation.

June watched the woman remove her sunglasses at the appearance of the busybody pawing at the chain-link barrier, snorting and whimpering.

The cap-and-sunglasses combo was a sartorial pairing that always reminded June of her high school soccer coach, whose colorful collection of hats and lenses had inspired a cultlike following of young impersonators, including June, for a while. Whether one's ponytail should be kept inside or pulled out from the back of the hat to sway in the wind was a point of contention among June's friends. She was on Team Free Pony, whereas Coach K and the woman before June now were fans of the stuffed pony look.

Perhaps it was this resemblance to Coach K, along with a similar tall, athletic build, that made June feel like they had met before, though this woman's eyes were a striking shade of green that June would have remembered, so perhaps not.

Still, to be safe, June hedged her uncertainty like she did with Silas's colleagues at work events, with a just-familiar-enough "How are you?"

Her casualness in tone was meant to provide cover if they had met before, and would only make her appear friendlier if they hadn't, but it seemed to backfire.

The stranger before her reddened from the tops of her ears to the bottom of her neck, as if she had been caught doing something unseemly. "I was just walking by," she said, sounding apologetic and defensive.

"That's okay." June felt compelled to reassure her, put her at ease. When she introduced herself, she tried to seem extra welcoming.

Alex was her name. Again, June tried to place her. Maybe they had played against each other at some point? Or participated in the same camp or summer league?

Willow went up on her hind legs and stuffed her nose through an opening in the chain link, trying every tactic she had to get a pet from this human.

Alex took a step back. "Is she a full golden, or mixed with something smaller? Maybe a Cavalier King Charles?"

Aha. So she did know dogs.

"We think she's got some corgi in her, or maybe some Cavalier. We aren't sure." June took charge of Willow, calmed her to a whimpering sit. "But I'm certain she wants you to come inside."

"I don't have a dog," Alex said. "I did. But not anymore."

"Oh, I'm sorry."

"No, it's not—" Alex paused. "It's not as morbid as that. I'm recently divorced. My ex-wife got the dog."

"How awful!" June's strong reaction got a smile from Alex that seemed to melt away some of her reticence. Soon after, June had convinced her to walk around to the park entrance, where June unlatched the gate and guided her toward the others.

"Ahem." Silas interrupted her thoughts. "Are you alright?"

June returned to the present, where she was near the bottom of her bowl of chili. "Of course. Why wouldn't I be?"

"It's like you're sitting here, but your mind is someplace else. Are you bored?"

"Don't be silly."

"Are you unhappy?"

June began clearing the table to give herself something to do. "Silas, where's this coming from?"

"You would tell me, wouldn't you? If you didn't love me anymore?"

June remained very still. *He knows.*

Silas began to rise from his chair, then thought better of it and remained seated. "Because I'd rather you be honest with me." The look of pain on his face was brutal. "I'd rather you just come out with it, rather than try to deceive me."

Only just recently had June considered divorce for the first time. She'd gotten as far as some rudimentary online research, but she'd quickly gotten spooked and closed it all down.

"I love you as much as the day we met," she said. "You know I do."

She had been careful not to leave a trail, but she must have missed some dumb little thing.

Silas stared deep into June's eyes, looking as hurt as she'd ever seen him. His expression reminded her of Willow's heartbreaking confusion when June would take away something sweet and wonderful that Willow picked up from the sidewalk, something June could not explain to her was also poisonous.

It did not help matters that Silas had the disarming, winsome charisma of an American Hugh Grant in his *Notting Hill* era, whom everyone always said Silas resembled.

Part of June wanted to tell him the truth, that it was a moment of weakness and frustration after he'd scolded her for something stupid, that it meant nothing. Because ultimately June did still love Silas as much as the day they'd met; she just loved him differently. It no longer felt like the pink valentine heart kind of romance, but it was childish to expect to swoon in her thirties. Adult life wasn't rose-colored glasses, kissing and hugging, feeling perpetually giddy over her sweetie-pie soul mate.

The thought had crossed June's mind that maybe Silas wasn't her soul mate after all—or maybe soul mates weren't even real—but either way, it didn't matter; he was still her husband.

Does Silas cheat? Does he drink too much? Take drugs? Gamble? These were the questions June imagined a divorce lawyer might ask. *Has he ever hit you or threatened you?*

Nope. But it got to June sometimes, all the correcting of her behavior, Silas's constant refrain of *How many times do I have to tell you. Glasses go on the top rack of the dishwasher. Don't walk around while you're brushing your teeth. Push in your chair. Close the cabinet.*

How many times did he have to tell her, June wondered, before he would stop telling her?

"You've read one too many romance novels," June's mother once said, before June stopped going to her for advice. "Husbands can be grumpy and a little bit bossy. Welcome to real-time married life."

There was no doubt something more complex going on with Silas. Undiagnosed obsessive-compulsive disorder, perhaps, coupled with a fear-based need to control his surroundings. Both of which were serious issues that deserved sympathy and a gentle touch. It was June's problem—not Silas's—that she was having more and more trouble finding that sympathetic gentility within herself.

Now, their staring contest ended with a stalemate. Enough time passed that Silas turned away, sulking. He picked up his water glass and took a long sip. Longer, longer, so parched he was by her failure to admit the truth.

Then some distant intrusion too slight for human detection startled Willow to her feet. Someone out on an evening stroll or riding by on a bicycle. Whatever it was, it was June's cue.

"Willow has to be walked," she said, heading for the leash still resting guiltily on the credenza, instead of the hook specified for that purpose.

Silas followed close behind. "But we're in the middle of something."

"Do you want to explain that to her after she pees on the floor?" June wrestled her feet into her sneakers, grabbed her house keys. At times like this, when Silas was hell-bent on having a fight, she could not escape the house fast enough. There was no other way to defuse him.

Fortunately, Silas was too in his own head to notice any of

Willow's highly predictable needs and wants. He was oblivious to the simple fact that June usually let Willow out into the backyard for her after-dinner potty.

Willow, though, was quick to catch on to the exciting surprise of a bonus walk. She jumped and snorted, unable to stay still as June knelt to attach her leash to her collar. Once it was connected, she beelined for the door. Then she lost faith for a moment, as if this rare delight might be too good to be true, or maybe she was confused into thinking Silas was joining them because of the way he was hovering. Who could say for sure what the reason was? Dog logic was unreliable at best, but something made Willow double back, turn, launch forward again and figure-eight around Silas, tangling him up in her leash and disarming him like one of the robbers in *Home Alone*.

"For heaven's sake!" Silas unwound one calf at a time. "How many times do I have to tell you? Hold that leash closer in. One of these days you're going to get somebody killed."

CHAPTER 3

Alex surveyed the poorly lit living room, its synthetic-fiber couch and veneer wood tables, its contractor-grade fixtures, and walls the color of a compromise between beige and gray. It was perfect. Exactly the sort of apartment this other Alex would call home while she got her life back on track. Even-keeled, unremarkable Alex Miller, who drove a sensible sedan and shopped at mid-tier department stores, and who, despite her recent troubles, was smiling wide in her extremely convincing Maryland driver's license photo.

Alex may have gotten a little carried away with the fake ID, but it felt good to be so committed to something, to disappear herself so completely that even the toiletries in the bathroom medicine cabinet weren't her favorites. Considering the breeziness of her first encounter with June Kennerson, Alex had overprepared to an almost embarrassing degree. June didn't seem the paranoid type. Still, it was always best to be on the safe side.

It was nearly five thirty, time to get a move on.

Yesterday, June said to come back today for happy hour, which was park-regular shorthand for the interval between five thirty and six thirty p.m., and likely stretched to seven. The moniker had no relation to alcoholic beverages and didn't necessarily correlate to a shared quitting time, as it appeared most of them didn't have jobs. The hour was *happy* simply because it was when they were all there together. The quaintness of this filled Alex with the hopeful, wholly unexpected belief that she might actually like these people, and that there was something fundamental and uncomplicated she could learn from them.

She didn't even have a dog with her! And still they welcomed her into the group as one of their own. Alex's plan remained the same: to forge a friendship with June strong enough to move beyond the realm of the park—ideally, ultimately, into her home. But the dog park itself was turning out to be a far less daunting first hurdle to clear than she'd expected.

From her recently organized closet, Alex chose a white pair of sneakers, then switched them out for a brown pair of boots. She plopped the same ball cap from yesterday onto her head, then changed her mind and decided to go hatless.

Every detail mattered. Even the most trivial components had a cumulative effect on the subconscious. Someone may not be able to verbalize it or point to a specific characteristic and say *There! That is why I believe I can trust so-and-so*—but they feel it. When Alex first read this information during her weeks of preparation for this project, she mistook her sudden shortness of breath for an anxiety attack, but no—it was exhilaration. Finally, the freedom to obsess over what others would consider minutiae.

The excitement Alex felt now, scrolling through the bullet-pointed list on her laptop, was not the nauseated, sweaty-palmed variety she was accustomed to; this was the pleasant kind.

She closed all her documents and put her computer to sleep. The essential facts were already committed to memory. June Kennerson had been a full-scholarship soccer star, fresh out of the Midwest, when she met her future husband at Stanford. From there, the bright points on her timeline dimmed to his: the well-documented upward trajectory of his career; the strategic return here to his hometown of Bethesda; the DC handshake photo ops signaling future political aspiration. June was in some of those photos, standing in his shadow, with glassy eyes and a vacant stare that was nothing like the ferocity caught candidly on the archived sports pages of their college newspaper.

Alex uncapped her orange prescription bottle of Xanax, but then, newly cocksure, decided against securing one of the tiny white ovals deep into the pocket of her jeans. She was moving more smoothly than usual, with a lighter step than she had back at her New York apartment, or anywhere else for that matter.

On her way out the door, she stopped short at the sight of herself in the plastic-rimmed, full-length mirror she had bought from Target and attached to the wall. Her reflection in the crooked glass was pleasingly unfamiliar, not in outward appearance as much as in spirit and conviction.

Yes, Alex Miller knew how to live, how to enjoy friends. She laughed easily. Alex Miller was happy.

"I swear this mud will be the end of me."

Paisley's mom made this announcement with conviction so foreboding that everyone in earshot bowed their heads.

Val nodded somberly. It had rained buckets overnight, leaving the patchy grass soft and wet. In some spots water had accumulated and pooled into murky puddles, which was especially disgusting considering the field was essentially a wide-open bathroom.

Popular Girl, who today was wearing a loose-fitting, potato sack–shaped smock dress that she somehow still made fashionable, rubbed the back of the sharp-bobbed older woman. "Meryl's worked tirelessly to try to get the county to do something about the ground's drainage problem."

Aha! Paisley's human's name was Meryl.

"Half my life in government politics," Meryl said, while monitoring her schnauzer's proximity to an exceptionally large pool of filth. "You'd think I'd have enough sway to get one dog park renovated."

"Not even one. Half of one!" Popular Girl waved her manicure in the direction of the drier, superior big-dog side. Like yesterday, her makeup was perfectly applied and her jewelry sparkled like her Colgate smile. Val imagined what life must be like as a former mean girl, now in her thirties, with no high school to vote her Best Dressed or Best Hair, or hell, why not Most Likely to Succeed—but she did have this soggy little dog park and its student body of weirdos to boost her ego.

"Thank you, Kennedy, for the belittling correction." Meryl stared down her younger second-in-command with the unmistakable authority of a K Street power player, and then said to Val, "Don't let Cash drink that muddy water. She'll end up with giardia."

Kennedy. Popular Girl was named Kennedy, and if she was the superlative queen of the park, Meryl was its real control center, the classy, influential, gray-haired king in a sharply tailored pantsuit.

Unsure if she was supposed to express thanks to Meryl for the fetid piece of advice, Val perused the sea of mudpies for Cash. She found her seated upon solid ground next to the stoic German shepherd, who—until yesterday's high-speed chase—Val could have mistaken for a wax sculpture.

Where the hell is June? Val wanted to know, just as Kennedy said, "Oh my god, look. Alex is back."

Meryl turned to the park entrance. With a suggestive smile, she asked, "Did Alex and June come together?"

Aha! Val thought. *First sight of the man June was having an affair with.* She followed Meryl's gaze to the entryway, where June was hanging Willow's leash on a gatepost.

Clearing the anticipation from her throat, Val asked, "Who's Alex?"

"She doesn't have a dog," Kennedy said. "But don't mention it. She's in mourning."

"Her dog isn't dead," Meryl corrected. "Her ex-wife got it in the divorce."

"Were we allowed to repeat that?" Kennedy asked. "I thought it was supposed to be a secret."

"How much of a secret could it be if she told all of us?" Meryl said. "And besides, secrets don't make friends."

Val watched June's careful approach across the soppy field. Close by her side, mirroring her every step, was the mystery person Val had seen in the parking lot the day before.

So June was sleeping with a woman. Wait till Silas got a load of this.

"Val! I'm so happy to see you again." June's face emitted an unambiguous glow. "I don't think you've met—"

"Alex." About five foot ten and fit, with light brown hair that fell onto her shoulders in expensively cut layers, she offered Val a handshake.

Her skin felt soft when Val shook her hand, properly moisturized.

"That rain was absolutely biblical." The group was going on about the mud again. "And all that pounding thunder?"

Paisley needed a trazodone dipped in peanut butter just to get through it. Chester required drugging as well as a white-noise sound machine.

"How did your little Cash handle the storm?" June was asking. "Was she afraid?"

Actually, every time Val jumped from the crashing thunder, startled against her will, Cash had looked at her with mockery, as if to say *Really?* This from a dog who ran for cover at first sight of a broom.

"She has particular tastes when it comes to fear," Val replied, leaving unmentioned Cash's sociopathic lack of empathy.

To soothe Eloise through the night, Regina (whose name Val just figured out) gave her a food-dispensing toy and streamed her favorite show—the Australian cartoon *Bluey.* Ava sat with Popcorn in a soundproofed, aromatherapy-infused closet designed specifically for this purpose.

"Which one's yours?" Alex posed the question with a smidge too much curiosity to Val's ear.

"Mine's the one who looks like a Dobby the Elf lawn ornament sitting beside the German shepherd statue."

June chuckled. "It's so cute that Cash made friends with old Virgil."

"And even-older Mrs. Pearlberg," Kennedy said. The German shepherd's equally sedentary owner was positioned on the wooden bench to his left; she could have been anywhere from seventy years old to a hundred ten. "You don't have to worry about Cash stepping out of line on her watch."

"Are you implying that my dog lacks discipline?" Val asked, with overt sarcasm that no one picked up on.

"I just meant because Mrs. Pearlberg is a retired school principal," Kennedy stuttered. "She was mean. Everyone was petrified of her."

"Now she's the one who's *petrified*," Meryl said. "Like a prehistoric forest."

This cheesiness they laughed at, Alex a bit too loudly. Her manner was agreeable enough, and Val could see how June might fall for someone with Alex's easy good looks. She was objectively attractive, making what Val guessed was a nearly ten-year age gap between Alex's fortysomething and June's thirtysomething a nonissue. But to Val's eye, Alex didn't add up. Her styleless clothing, for example, struck a discordant note with the discernible care that went into her hair, physique, and skincare. And, though she maintained a confident posture, her anxious eyes and tense jaw told another story.

"Virgil's kind of big to be on this side, isn't he?" Alex asked.

"The separation is more about nice dogs and nasty ones," Kennedy said, in clear defense of whopping Chester's rightful place among the twenty-five-pound-and-under crowd.

"No," Meryl interjected. "It's about safety."

A heated enough debate ensued for Val to act. "Whoops!" She took a misstep with an assist from the slippery ground, bumping into Alex, covering all her angles. It was a work of art. Zero sightlines, a perfectly executed pincer-finger dip.

Moments later, Val patted her jeans and jacket. "Oh shoot, I think I forgot my phone in the car."

No one cared. Still, she said to no one in particular, "Keep an eye on Cash for a sec? I'll be right back."

Trekking across the field, out the gate to the parking lot, Val fondled the object in her pocket. By feel alone, she was certain the wallet was new. It was stiff and thin, not broken in at all. Inside her car, she sunk down low in her seat, pretending to search for her phone on the floor, while rummaging through its contents.

What she found was less astounding than what she didn't: not a single credit card, no receipts, no photos, no dirt or sand or library cards or smoothie punch cards. Just some cash and a driver's license. Val snapped a photo of the ID. It, too, appeared newly acquired and felt rigid in her fingers. She examined it closer, assessing its security hologram, reconsidering its heft. It was high-quality work, but a fake, nonetheless.

Val shoved the ID back in place and scrambled out of the car with only her phone in hand. What kind of person, she wondered, carried a decoy wallet to a dog park?

Her heart began to pound, sweat dripped down the back of her neck. She knew it. She knew it! From the first moment she saw her creeping around the edges of the park yesterday. Alex must have been working undercover for someone—maybe for Silas, or not. Her relationship with June could be part of the act, or not.

The possibilities were endless, and as Val unlatched the first gate to reenter the park, her mind raced through the full range, from harmless to deadly. It didn't help that she was standing in the espionage capital of the United States.

Thousands of spies lived in the suburbs surrounding Washington, DC. Some worked at an embassy or for the government. Others were students, professors, or businessmen, hiding in plain sight among the shopping centers and strip malls of towns like this one.

Because, as it turned out, the suburbs were a perfect place for hiding.

Val secured the first gate closed and unlatched the second. During her prep research she discovered that Montgomery County, Maryland, had a rich history as a locale for KGB meetups. Bethesda itself was a covert favorite, situated as it was, just northwest of the nation's capital.

Val took stock of the anonymous suburbanites along her journey back to the park regulars with new eyes. How many of them were government employees with high-level security clearances? Who among them had undergone elite training?

This innocuous, waterlogged field, unlikely to attract much attention from the community at large, took shape in Val's mind as a backdrop for clandestine meetings, signals, and secret codes, the underhanded exchange of encrypted messages.

She observed Alex observing June. *Now*, she told herself. This was no time to hesitate.

Do not wuss out on me. Her father's voice was loud in her ears. *That's why we drill and drill and drill, so when the moment comes on game day—bam—full confidence, zero doubt, it's automatic.*

By *game day*, of course, Gianni meant the successful execution of any number of minor crimes. Growing up, some kids did Scouts or Little League. Val went to pool halls, the racetrack, and barroom card games, where she learned how to bet, hustle, and shark. According to family lore, which came with fifty-fifty odds of being completely made up, Gianni first recognized Val's vocation as his God-given apprentice when he brought her, at six weeks old, to bargain down the seller of a used window-unit air conditioner.

His sob story—that he needed the air conditioner because the baby had bad lungs, but he couldn't afford the asking price—was getting him nowhere until, as if on demand, his newborn prodigy let out the most delicate of coughs. Then she began to cry, and then proceeded to wail, red-faced and kicking, until the seller accepted the lowball offer just to get them out of there.

This kid was born a swindler, Gianni told Rosetta when he returned home. *Her instincts are out of this world. She's a natural.* By the time Val was in kindergarten, he had her staging accidents, feigning broken bones. Her weekends were spent dealing three-card monte on the boardwalk at Coney Island. Small potatoes, as far as Gianni was concerned, compared to what they were building toward. Because his little girl was the full package. She had been gifted the charm and brains necessary to master the ultimate big-ticket score: a high-net-worth long con. This, he assured her, was her destiny.

He'd be burned to learn Val had ended up a PI, of all things. *Nearly as rotten as a cop*, he'd say.

But not nearly as rotten as a criminal, Val might respond.

Alex's wallet was back in her pocket before anyone even noticed Val had returned.

Then Alex turned to her, looked her dead in the eyes. "So you found it."

If Alex were a pro, she might have known. Only a fellow specialist could have been wise to Val's lightning-fast hands.

"Yup." Val held up her phone. She checked to see if Cash was still sitting in the same line of three with Virgil and Mrs. Pearlberg.

"Cash hasn't moved a muscle," June said.

Val wasn't sure what to make of June now, whether she was a victim or perpetrator. "Yeah, Cash only likes to run when I try to take her home."

"There she goes again." Meryl's authoritative timbre caught their attention. "Every frigging day."

Along with the others, Val located the offender as Meryl cried out, "Popcorn is pooping!"

Indeed, Val confirmed, the puffball Pomeranian had popped a squat.

This was something Val was still getting used to about the park crowd. When they weren't shit-talking each other's dogs, they were talking about shit. Its size, shape, consistency, frequency. They used terminology they may have coined themselves to describe their pet's fecal habits, like the "poopwalk," the "poop-and-run," the "recreational poop," and the most serious: "poop karma," which was the cosmic force generated by the human action of picking up *or not picking up* a dog's poop.

June had explained the concept in layman's terms yesterday. "If you don't clean up after your dog," she'd said, "then you're destined to step in poo. It's sort of like take a penny, leave a penny, but with messier shoes."

Popcorn's mom, Ava (who styled herself exactly as one would expect from a woman in her forties who accessorized her dog with a tiara), was infamous, apparently, for letting Popcorn poop about while she flirted with one of the few men who frequented the park—a well-built guy with a shock of gray and white hair, who Val knew only as the Silver Fox.

"Doodie calls!" Meryl shouted.

Val wondered how many times, for how many years, she had been using that same punny homophone for a cheap laugh.

Ava responded to the public shaming just as she had yesterday, with feigned surprise and a wave. "Thanks, Meryl!" she said, in a voice loud and high-pitched enough to bend steel, as she slow-jogged toward her crappy comeuppance.

The repetitive predictability of this place, which was apparent after only a day, would be mind-numbing if every single one of these oddballs hadn't begun appearing to Val as potential KGB or CIA. Or NSA, or FBI, or some other acronymic agency Val didn't yet have the letters for.

Alex was trying too hard to appear comfortable, to blend in. She fidgeted. She chewed unconsciously on the inside of her mouth. Her fixation on June was palpable. All of which begged the question: If Alex were a professional of some kind, wouldn't she be better than this? She would, at the very least, have a dog with her. Even Val knew not to show up here without the applicable props.

Just then, Cash stood up, sniffed a 360-degree circle, and squatted.

"Shit," Val said.

"Yoo-hoo," Meryl gave Val a wiggle-fingered wave.

Faking a smile, Val waved back a thank-you. "Good eye," she said as she pulled a poop bag from her pocket.

The spot Cash chose to conduct her business was way too close to an effluent sinkhole for Val's comfort. She planted her feet firmly into the soft ground, as far from the pool as possible, then stretched her arm nearly out of its socket to palm a plastic bag over the turd. The sickening sensation of holding actual poop in the palm of her hand, protected by nothing more than a thin sheet of plastic, was something Val had not yet become used to—and she hoped she never would.

Cash was amused enough by the gymnastic feat to follow Val back to the group. She went directly to June, who bent down and clapped her hands, excitedly asking, "Who's a good girl? Are you a good girl? Yes, you are!"

Cash bowed her head and wriggled her rump in a cutesy ploy for more of June's attention. She was not a dog who liked to be picked up, and yet there she was, up on two legs, twirling for June like a monkey-faced ballerina.

June scooped her up and Cash licked her face with a joyous affection Val almost couldn't stand to watch.

It would be absurd for her to be hurt by the cuddlefest on display, to feel slighted by an animal she considered a short-term investment.

"Do you want in on this?" June offered Cash to Alex.

Alex shook her head, took a vehement step back. "No, that's okay."

"Oh, come on," Val shouted. "But she's so lovable!"

What made Val react this way? Her aggression went beyond what was normal or acceptable when she swiped Cash from June's arms and shoved her into Alex's chest.

Alex appeared stunned, like she'd been tased by Cash's body against hers. She tried to speak, but no words came out. When her eyes filled with tears, Val knew she had made a grave error.

"I'm sorry," Alex was able to say, finally, placing Cash on the ground. "I have to go." She took off toward the exit.

June chased after her, kicking up splashes of mud behind her with each stride, leaving Val at the mercy of the others.

"You. Should. Not. Have. Done that!" Meryl pounced first.

"You made her cry!" Kennedy was nearly crying herself in commiseration. "I told you she was in mourning. What the heck is wrong with you?"

A lot. So, so much.

But Val knew that already; she didn't need to be told. And these people didn't need to like her, so forget them! All Val needed was to find answers—she hadn't come here to make friends.

"I should go try to apologize." Val strained to catch sight of an Alex or a June shape in the distance.

"I think you've done enough." Meryl stepped a few ostracizing feet away.

If Val hurried, she could probably still catch June and Alex in the parking lot. If they left together, she could trail them to their next location. Now where did Cash run off to?

"Would you believe it? There goes another one." Meryl's wrath was thankfully averted from Val's failings.

"Popcorn again?" Kennedy asked.

"Eloise." Meryl pulled a plastic bag from her pocket.

At least it wasn't Cash, who Val located back at her favorite spot beside Virgil.

"There's no point in even trying with that one," Meryl said, meaning Eloise's mom. "She is permanently off doodie."

Val groaned and plotted a quick strategy for getting ahold of Cash without inciting a high-speed chase while Meryl, the martyr, made a big show of trudging across the field to pick up the poop of someone else's dog.

The crux of Val's plan for absconding with Cash was to approach with indifference, entice her with the hamburger meat just released from both Val's pocket and its odor-proof wrapper, and then, with the same *now you see it, now you don't* method of misdirection used by magicians and card sharks everywhere, scoop her up with a swift, unseen hand.

This was where Val's focus was when—

There was a scream.

Val turned just in time to see Meryl mid-stride—with her right white-pantsuit leg ahead, and her left white-pantsuit leg behind—straddling a brown puddle-lake of disgustingness. She had lost her footing trying to clear the obstacle, which was the cause of the scream, then made it across and lost her footing again.

All eyes were on Meryl now as she struggled, legs apart, arms out to her sides, like a professional surfer in corporate attire. When both her feet slid forward, they did so parallel, of their own volition. Then her front-right Jimmy Choo (in a color formerly known as ecru) continued onward while the rest of her body tilted diagonally back into a wobbly triangle pose.

Gone went the left foot's Jimmy Choo, lost in the depth of the river's brown, while the right one floated sideways on the surface like a dead whitefish. And Meryl was dancing barefoot, heading for a spin (as the great Patti Smith once sang). She spun so ceaselessly. And then, *splash!*

The bystanders screamed. Meryl went flat out, face down in the mud. She thrashed and kicked, tried to worm herself to drier ground, all to no avail.

As a kid, Val had an inordinate fear of quicksand. As an adult, she questioned whether it existed in real life. But now here it was, the nightmare of panicked movement only sinking a person deeper, manifested before Val's eyes.

Kennedy, ever the loyal queen to her king, was the first person to run to Meryl's aid—and the last—given the way she, too, skidded into a yawning fishtail before being swallowed by the roiling mud. The dogs were also no help at all. In fact, eager to be part of the game, they darted back and forth and in wild circles, their paws slinging sludge and muck and feces into the faces of the screeching humans.

Finally, someone said, "Find a stick or long branch!" But there were no sticks or long branches in sight.

"Toss them a leash," someone else said, but no leash was long enough.

"Connect two leashes together!" was Mrs. Pearlberg's innovative idea, which she called out from her bench seat, without fanfare, taking everyone by surprise.

"It's the obvious solution," she said to Virgil. "It seems they know nothing about how to think during an emergency."

Virgil responded with a resonant bark and wagged his long tail in agreement.

The Silver Fox then took the lead on the extraction operation, using the suggested two-leash method, while Ava cheered for him from afar.

Meanwhile, Val snuck up behind Cash and scooped her into her arms—a first-try success she was proud of—but too much time had been wasted. They reached the parking lot too late. June and Alex were already off somewhere together, out of reach.

"It's okay," Val said to Cash while buckling her into her car seat.

The picture of what this job would entail was becoming clearer, and she was ready for it. She started the Nova's growling engine, gripped her dried mud–encrusted hands to the steering wheel, and backed out of her parking spot.

"Don't you worry your little frowny face," she said to Cash in the rearview mirror, accelerating toward the road, shifting into second gear, then third. "We'll catch them next time."

CHAPTER 4

"Alex! Wait!"

In her state of alarm, Alex mistakenly searched the parking lot for her Porsche, then her motorcycle—then she remembered the used car but couldn't bring to mind which midsize make and model she had chosen, only that it was silver.

"Hey." June caught up to her. "Are you okay?"

Alex could not say that she was.

"Val shouldn't have forced a dog into your arms like that." June was furious on Alex's behalf. "Of course that was upsetting to you," she said. "Under the circumstances."

Which circumstances again? Alex couldn't recall. All she could focus on was getting away from here.

"Alex, you're shaking."

She was. And sweating. She also felt dizzy and sick to her stomach, as if she'd just come off a roller coaster or was trapped on one, speeding upside down, out of control.

"It's just a panic attack," Alex said.

Just. As in only. As in, *Don't be afraid of my intense, debilitating fear. I'm not going to die here before you, I don't think, but if I do, please let me go ahead and do so by myself.*

June told Alex to breathe. She said, "I understand how what happened back there was triggering for you."

"Please go away," Alex replied. She despised that overused, infantilizing word—*triggering*—as much as she resented its accuracy.

Because it did feel mechanical, like the firing of a gun, how a simple action—a dog pressed to her chest, its warm head nestled on her shoulder—could release a violent explosion of feelings and dormant memories.

A wet snout nosed at her ice-cold fingers.

"Willow, off!" June commanded. "I'm sorry," she said to Alex. "That's probably the last thing you need."

Alex brought her hands to her knees, leaned forward, tried to inhale into her belly the way countless therapists and doctors had taught her. Any one of them would have said this episode was her own fault. For over twenty years she had never left the house without a Xanax in her pocket, on standby, for times like this.

She was in character, she had told herself. Alex *Miller* wouldn't be riddled with so much irrational social anxiety that she would need a pill stashed somewhere on her person just to make it through the day. Like someone was going to, what? Somehow discover the two-millimeter tablet and start asking questions?

"I'm fine," Alex said. "Really." She centered her vision on June. "I just need to go home."

"You can't drive like this." June reached for Alex's shoulder, and the gentleness of this spontaneous, non-transactional physical contact was startling. Alex was usually only ever touched by people she employed—her masseuse, her acupuncturist, her fitness trainer.

"Come here." June wrapped her arms around Alex and held her close, like a lifelong friend.

Alex had to choke down tears but, finally, the spinning blur of thoughts and sensations began to slow, and her mind inched back to reality.

June let go, allowing her to take a fresh breath of air deep into her lungs.

The worst of it was over.

"There you are," June said. "Thank goodness. The color's back in your cheeks. I thought I was going to lose you there for a second."

Alex was surprised to hear herself laugh. "Sorry, I know that can be frightening to watch. I'm better now. Thanks."

June fiddled with her phone and Alex feared she had called an ambulance and was now trying to cancel it, but it turned out she was texting someone.

"Can I take you somewhere?" June asked.

"Now?"

June's phone vibrated with a return text. "Yes, right now." She began typing on her phone again.

Alex was relieved that June seemed unfazed by her utter meltdown, but she was also confused as to what exactly was happening now. In therapy she had learned to ask herself in moments of uncertainty, *Is this a cognitive distortion? Am I thinking clearly?* Instead, she asked June, "Where do you want to take me?"

June shoved her phone back into her pocket. "I'm afraid if I tell you, then you won't come."

"Well, that's convincing."

June smiled. "You'll have to trust me."

"How do you know you can trust *me*?" Alex said. "I could be a murderer for all you know."

June shrugged her shoulders. "I guess I'm feeling daring. It's not every day I get the chance to make a new friend. Why let a little thing like potential murder ruin it?"

"I like how you think." Alex followed her to her SUV.

There was some commotion back at the dog park field, distant screaming and yelling that went silent with the closing of her passenger-side door.

June backed out of her parking spot and only then did the reality of the situation truly hit. Alex had bumbled her way into June Kennerson's car. Never had her nerves betrayed her to such a welcome end.

When they merged onto the highway, June said, "We don't have to talk about it if you don't want to, but I think I understand what happened, what got you so upset."

Alex stayed quiet. She couldn't wait to hear this.

"You miss the dog you lost to your ex." June paused to glance at Alex's face, which Alex kept neutral on account of there not actually being an ex, or a dog, for that matter.

"And I know you don't feel ready for another dog just yet," June went on. "But maybe you should consider the fact that your other one—What was his name?"

"Buttercup," Alex said. Christ. Really? That was the best she could come up with? Buttercup was so obviously a horse's name. She was really going to have to get better at thinking on her feet if she was going to pull this off.

"Maybe you should consider," June continued, "that Buttercup is alive and well and would want you to be happy."

June, sweet June, trying to be so careful and understanding.

She was making this too easy. Why should she care whether Alex was happy, which she was not, or if she ever had a dog.

At one time Alex wanted a puppy, sure. As a kid she ached for one.

But you have a Thoroughbred, her mother had said. *Multiple Dutch Warmbloods. What do you need with a silly dog?*

"Alex?" June said, changing lanes. "You can talk to me. It would help make this little trip feel less like an abduction. Please do me the favor. I've been starving for some good conversation with anyone other than Willow."

"You're lonely." The revelation came to Alex as a surprise so pleasant that she accidentally declared it aloud.

"I've never thought of myself that way," June said. "But I suppose I am, maybe a little. My husband, Silas, he works a lot."

Just like that, June introduced Silas as fair game for discussion. "What does he do?" Alex asked, as if she didn't already know every detail of Silas's résumé, along with the complete timeline of their courtship, marriage, and major life decisions to present.

"He works in government," June said. "Like everyone else within commuting distance to DC." She checked Alex for a reaction. "What consulting firm did you say you work for again?"

Alex hadn't. Yesterday, when they were exchanging the small-talk bullet point summaries people use to get acquainted, Alex only said that she was a consultant, which was a usefully nebulous job title, common around these parts, that in most other places would leave a person mystified.

"I'm freelance," Alex said to add to the blur. "Management consulting, mostly. I help businesses improve their operations."

Ha. As if anyone anywhere would hire Alex to give advice on anything. Having never worked a real job, despite a pristine degree from Wharton, or accomplished anything of substance in her life—unless spending gobs of her family's money qualified as an achievement—what could she possibly be an expert on? She did have a knack for filling the hole in her soul with luxury impulse buys and international travel, so perhaps she could give out hot tips on that.

June kept her attention on the road. "You mean you're the person who comes in to a company and lays everyone off to cut costs?"

Alex was taken aback by the heartfulness of this response, her sensitivity toward the common workingman, though considering what she'd thus far observed about June's character, she shouldn't have been.

"No," Alex said, "that's not my style. I like being able to sleep at night."

Again, ha. Like she would ever sleep at all without her tranquilizing pharmaceutical cocktail.

"I specialize in risk and compliance." Alex was on a roll now. Her nerves had dissipated, her five senses were again functioning at full capacity. "I help companies and people adhere to regulations, ethical practices. I ensure they're following the rules." Technically this was not a lie, even if it was more of a recent hobby than an occupation.

June could look at Alex again without disfavor. "You're an enforcer," she said. "Of order."

Yes, come to think of it, Alex was.

"I love it." June changed lanes, speeding ahead. "We need more of you in this town. My husband is also an enforcer of sorts, a real stickler for rules. I bet you two would have a lot in common."

Bite your tongue, woman. Alex tried to decipher a fissure in June's facial expression or a crack in her voice as she went on.

"Silas was a science guy when we first met," June said. "Before he shifted focus to public service."

Alex had been working under the assumption that June was privy to all the grime beneath the squeaky-clean surface of Silas's CV. The corrupt double-dealing, the bribes, his absolute lack of sympathy for the common man when it came to allowing carcinogenic chemicals into the air they breathed and the water they drank. Because how bad were a few million cases of cancer, really, when his upward trajectory was at stake?

Yet, she began to wonder. Could it be that wide-eyed June, with her soft smile and easy-breezy demeanor, was genuinely oblivious to her husband's despicability?

No. The wives always knew. It was an insult to their intelligence to assume otherwise. The Ruth Madoffs and Carmela Sopranos of the world—to underestimate their self-serving ability to calculate and compartmentalize was downright unfeminist. That was why Alex chose June to begin with.

"Is your background in business?" June asked. "Or politics?"

She was asking an awful lot of questions, wasn't she?

Alex replied that her background was indeed in business, but she did not mention her family's dirty money or their infamous surname.

She didn't explain that she had everything and could buy anything, yet she remained stuck in a losing battle with herself, uncertain how a person with her extreme privilege was supposed to live responsibly in the world.

"What about you?" Alex asked, to direct the conversation back onto June. "What do you do besides dog mommying?"

"Silas and I have talked about starting a family. We tried for a while . . ." Her voice trailed off the way voices tend to do when a person doesn't want to say more. "We'll try again. But lately I've really been missing having a career, or at least some kind of job."

"What would you want to do?" Alex asked.

"Back in the day, I was a total jock. There wasn't any sport I didn't love." June left the byway they'd been traveling and drove onto an unpaved rural road. "Tennis was my whole world for a while. Then I homed in on soccer. I played in college, D-1, I almost went pro. Then my life took a turn in a different direction."

"What direction was that?"

"So, listen." June clicked on her turn signal, even though there wasn't another car on the road, forward or back, for as far as the eye could see. "You're under no obligation here."

Alex looked around. How long had they been driving? It didn't feel like much time, but the local landscape had gone full country, transforming into a panorama of rolling hills and agricultural fields.

"Where is *here* exactly?" Alex asked.

They turned left onto a long gravel driveway with a steep incline. "This is my friend Terri's place."

The large ranch house that came into view was rustic but well-maintained. Willow was up and excited in the seat behind them, pawing at the side window, whimpering with anticipation.

The sound of another dog barking—no, multiple dogs barking—filled the air.

"You didn't," Alex said.

June cut the engine. "Try to keep an open mind."

"You brought me to a dog breeder?" Alex shouted. "How could you possibly think this was a good idea?"

"Terri's not a breeder. She's a professional handler and trainer." June opened the driver's side door and stepped out of the truck.

Alex took a breath and tried to remain calm. The sun was low on the horizon, casting rays and shadows between the trees. The air smelled woodsy clean, of nature and well-being. Like June said, Alex was under no obligation to do anything she didn't want to do, so there was no reason to panic.

June freed Willow, who made a frantic beeline from the backseat for the woman approaching the driveway. This must be Terri. She was wearing mustard-colored overalls, and she had the tough, ruddy face of someone accustomed to the outdoors. Her hair was tied back in a long, silver-gray braid.

Willow received a proper greeting before Terri gave June a hug hello.

Alex was still seated in the passenger seat of the truck, and considered staying put, while June and Terri whispered about her amongst themselves.

Terri was eyeing Alex through the window like she was some creature in a cage, or maybe one of the more skittish dogs under her care. Then she knocked her knuckles hard against the glass and said, "Come on around back" in the no-nonsense tone of a person whose job it was to bend animal will to her own.

Alex did as she was told.

The land behind the house went on for acres, divided into spacious, fenced-in sections and multiple agility courses. In one segment, a trainer coached a terrier through a sequence of obstacles—a jump over a low bar, across an inclined plane, in one end of a blue vinyl tunnel and out the other.

Noticing Willow barreling her way, the trainer opened the gate for her entrance.

Terri led Alex and June to a covered porch at the back side of the house. "Have a seat," she said. "Help yourself to some sun tea if you'd like."

Alex sat on one of the long wooden patio benches that were arranged for conversation, but she declined refreshments as June poured herself a glass.

Terri remained standing. "I'm not sure how much June told you—"

"Not much at all," Alex said. "We barely know each other. She basically kidnapped me to bring me here."

Alex took a breath. She needed to calm down.

Terri shot a stern but amused glance at June. "I work for a family with a long history of breeding top show-ring dogs," she said. "Champions. AKC title winners." She seemed to be examining Alex, inwardly judging the reticence and resentment that must be emitting from her every pore.

Terri and June exchanged another silent communication.

"Well, anyhow," Terri said, giving in to June's unspoken urging. She opened the screen door to the house and, fingers to lips, produced a shrill, high-pitched note.

Out came running a floppy-eared bundle of four-pawed energy, delighted to have been summoned.

"This is Bruce," Terri said. "He's thirteen inches, sturdy, solid, beautifully proportioned. Everything a beagle should be."

Alex's knee-jerk reaction was to shoot up from her bench and back away.

Bruce looked up at her with large brown eyes and a pleading expression. Terri gave him a signal, and he came to a sit.

"He's got a pedigreed lineage, a title-holding bloodline," Terri said. "Appearance-wise, he's an exemplary model of the breed, and even his manner, as you can see, he's cheerful, obedient. But . . ."

Terri hesitated, as if she didn't want to speak ill of Bruce while he was sitting in floppy-earshot.

Alex's heart began to race.

". . . Part of my job is to recognize what's hardwired and innate to a dog and what can be trained and taught." Terri surveyed Alex for a reaction. She was looking for something, or perhaps already saw it.

"Some things you can shape and change," she said. "Others are traits you need to accept. All you can do is learn how to manage and work with them."

Alex understood perfectly. She observed Bruce from a safe distance. No way was she about to touch him. *Poor thing*, she thought. On the outside, he was near perfection, but something inside was flawed. *You can try and try and try*, she wanted to tell Bruce, *but it's no use, you're a lost cause.*

"There's not a thing wrong with him," Terri said, as if Alex had spoken aloud. "For a house pet. He's just not right for competition. I know he can't win."

June watched Alex with an odd expression. Could she hear her pounding heart? Could she smell the sweat bleeding through Alex's shirt?

"Bruce is a good dog," June said. "And he needs a new home. You're a good person and you have a home to give. I thought this might be an appropriate match."

She had no idea how appropriate.

"I didn't mean to overstep." June turned to Bruce to give him a scratch in an obvious attempt to give Alex a bit of space.

"This is no charity case," Terri said in a sharp voice. "Do you know what some people would give to have a dog like this? I have no interest in handing him off to anyone with halfhearted interest."

Great, now Alex had insulted them both.

"No, forgive me. That's not why I—" Alex's voice caught in her tightened throat. She choked back the unanticipated emotion.

Then came the black hole and she was falling, falling, her vision blurring. Red-hot went her face, her neck. She tried to locate the porch railing, but she was staggering in the dark.

Maybe, she thought, if she didn't try to speak or move a single muscle, the panic could pass without anyone noticing. But Bruce was up, nosing at Alex's hands and nudging her torso. He barked: *Alert, alert*!

The sudden alarm and shocking feel of Bruce's warm coat against Alex's skin jolted the world back into focus. She found her patio bench and lowered herself onto it.

Bruce followed her, put his head and two front paws upon Alex's lap, and stayed there.

Alex looked up. June was standing over her, awestruck. Terri, beside her, beamed with pride and appreciation of Bruce, a marvel to behold.

"Was he trained for that?" June asked.

Terri shook her head. "He hasn't had any service dog training, if that's what you're asking." To Alex, she said, "Can I get you anything? Glass of cold water?"

So much for getting by without anyone noticing. "I'm fine, thanks."

Alex assumed Terri had been briefed on her emotional fragility prior to her arrival, but she still thought she had some explaining to do.

"I have an anxiety disorder," Alex said, leaving out the part about her co-occurring, on-again, off-again relationship with depression, because admitting to both always felt like giving someone too much to bear.

In Alex's experience, people tended to react better to anxiety than depression, probably because almost everyone had experienced the physical signs of extreme nervousness in some form or another, but the degree of sadness, despair, and loneliness that came with being depressed was harder for the unaffected to fully comprehend. And so, talking about one's own depression, somewhat ironically, gave others anxiety.

Not that Alex ever talked about hers, because the most incomprehensible part of a depressive disorder was that it was entirely disconnected from your station in life, and no one wanted to hear about how sadness didn't discriminate on the basis of wealth and class. It seemed like it should; Alex agreed. Anyone as grossly fortunate as she was had nothing justifiable to be sad about and no right to complain.

"I'm usually in better condition than this," Alex said. "I had a slipup with my medication today."

Terri gave Bruce a pat. "I won't pretend to know much about all that, but he seems to get it."

"He's incredible." June sat down close to Alex's side. "Alex, isn't he incredible?"

Bruce picked up his head and appeared to be waiting for an answer along with everyone else.

The beagle is an intelligent, friendly, people-oriented dog and loyal companion. The facts Alex had memorized as a kid, back when she yearned for a puppy, started coming back to her like the lyrics to a song she hadn't heard in twenty years, but could still sing along to, word for word. Descriptions from the American Kennel Club, summaries from Encyclopedia Britannica, anything and everything dog-related she could get her hands on. *The beagle is a solidly built, small hound who is full of life and fun to be around. Beagles make wonderful family pets. They make both canine and human friends easily.*

Alex still had not allowed herself to touch Bruce. His paws may have been resting on her legs, but her arms were drawn back, fists at her side.

She was unsure how to proceed.

"He's obviously a really special dog," Alex said.

Emboldened by this acknowledgment, Bruce hopped fully onto Alex's lap, licked the side of her cheek, sniffled in her ear, and curled up under her arm.

Alex held her breath and swept a tentative palm over the surface of his coat. His fur was smooth and dense, the skin beneath sturdy and warm. She could feel the life in him, and it made her feel more alive.

June placed a supportive hand on Alex's back. "You don't need to explain feeling a bit raw considering all you've been through. With your ex and losing Buttercup . . ."

In that moment, Alex wanted to chew off her own face. What the hell was she doing here? An impostor among these kind, generous people. The real Alex didn't deserve their benevolence, and they didn't deserve to be tricked.

Guilt had brought Alex here. She was trying to do something good, *be* something good, and yet somehow all she'd accomplished was more to feel guilty about.

Silas Kennerson needed to be taken out, disassembled piece by piece as an example, a warning to the others like him. He deserved to be punished, and Alex had the means to implement that punishment. If the wife ended up serving as cannon fodder—Alex had originally thought—so be it.

Except here was that wife with her comforting hand on Alex's back, offering her friendship, a lifeline, softly stroking the dog in her lap—her dog, Alex's. It ached how much he was already hers.

"What do you think?" June asked. "Did I do right by bringing you here?" A low sunbeam shined on her face.

Alex forced a smile.

None of this would work out well for June—Alex was as certain of this fact as she was tormented by it—but she was in too deep to turn back now. The end would have to justify the means.

CHAPTER 5

The flyer called it a committee meeting of the Friends of Hamilton Dog Park. Kennedy had a stack of the 4 x 6 invites, which were professionally printed in black ink on premium ecru card stock, and she urged one into the hands of everyone coming or going through the gated chamber of the small-dog area.

"Meryl would be delighted if you could attend, and please do bring your dog," Kennedy said in a Stepford-y way when she handed June a card. It sounded like Meryl, who was conspicuously absent, had instructed her to say those exact words and Kennedy was trying her darndest to do a good job.

This was the first June had heard of any committee called the Friends of Hamilton Dog Park.

"Meryl's too embarrassed to come back after her fall," Ava said, with enough volume for the senior citizens on the tennis courts to hear, as she unleashed Popcorn the Pomeranian Princess onto the field. "So she's making us go to her."

Ava spoke in a loud, playful, high-pitched voice that made everything she said sound like a joke. It was her defining characteristic, second only to her ability to work bubblegum pink into every one of her outfits. Many at the park found this quirkiness annoying and surmised—on account of her once being a member of Chicago's Second City improv troupe—that the voice was put on, part of an act to get attention or an easy laugh, but June enjoyed Ava's willingness to embrace the outlandish. What did it matter if she was playing a part or just being herself?

"Meryl doesn't get embarrassed," Regina said, while Eloise the miniature dachshund furiously dug a tunnel hole into the ground. "She gets even."

The Silver Fox agreed. "Of all the people to fall in the mud."

Yesterday's mud incident was a bigger deal than June first realized. She had missed it, preoccupied as she was with Alex in the parking lot, but Regina, who wasn't one to exaggerate, described it to her as "worse than watching a car crash in slow motion."

June thought of Regina, fiftysomething mom to Eloise the miniature dachshund, as Ava's polar opposite. Where Ava was bubblegum pink, Regina was a sensible gray or a modest navy blue, or whatever color was not about to do cartwheels for your approval. Regina was a T-shirt and soft pants–type and most of her clothing had a dog on it or featured a dachshund-related joke, and she didn't care if you thought it was funny or not.

It wasn't until Regina showed June a few photos on her phone that she got a true sense of the mud incident's horror. Then Regina showed her a video, and then that same video set to a remix of Rimsky-Korsakov's "Flight of the Bumblebee," which wasn't a neighborly thing for a person to create or watch, and yet June found herself mesmerized, unable to look away.

"Cocktails and canapés will be served," was Kennedy's new line. "Refreshments for humans and for pups."

"Is this really for real?" Ava asked of the flyer while Popcorn pooped on the grass beside her with no Meryl to point it out.

"Extremely." Regina pulled her flyer out of the pocket of her DACHSHUNDS ARE MY FAVORITE PEOPLE hoodie to peruse it again. Then, echoing the Silver Fox, she said, "Of all the people to fall in the mud."

There was no mention of the word *renovation* on the flyer, but that was the word everyone started throwing around, given Meryl's past efforts and uncharacteristic failure so far.

"Maybe this was what needed to happen," June offered, trying for a positive spin, "to make a park renovation possible."

"Maybe she called the town and threatened to sue," Regina said.

Ava, miraculously noticing Popcorn's poop herself, bent down to snatch it with a flamingo-colored bag. "Maybe Meryl called the President," she screeched. "Doesn't he owe her a few favors?"

The Silver Fox shook his distinguished dreamboat head. "That's no party invite Kennedy's shelling out. Bring your wallets, folks, because this is about to be the most expensive free pup cup you'll ever get."

Everyone had their own theory on what to expect from the Friends of Hamilton Dog Park committee meeting. There was a certain mystery to the flyer—no image, just the black-and-white, bare-necessity details in a chic but strong font. June didn't know much about the psychology of typography, but it didn't take a design person to understand this one meant business, much like Meryl herself.

June snapped a photo of the flyer with her phone and texted it to Alex. *Everyone is heading to Meryl's straight from the park*, she wrote. *I don't think you're going to want to miss this.*

In the time that had passed since she and Alex had exchanged phone numbers, just after their trip to meet Bruce the beagle, June had texted Alex three times, which was probably three times too many.

Whether the reason was desperation or a lack of practice, June knew she was trying too hard to attach herself to Alex. She felt stupid when it came to many things in general—trying to do math in her head, recalling basic world geography, remembering the pronunciation of foreign foods on menus—but nothing made her feel as clueless as trying to make friends as an adult. And unlike math or geography, there was a time when she had been good at friendship. As a kid, a teenager, right up to about her early twenties, it was one of her greatest skills. Why then, she wanted to know, did this ability go so wrong with age?

It was the paramount mystery of her thirties: How had she become this socially inept, forgetting how to talk to people in groups, at parties, or even someplace as dorky and unintimidating as a suburban town dog park?

June and Alex had to leave Terri's yesterday without Bruce so Terri could put together the necessary paperwork for the official adoption, but he was basically already Alex's, and on the drive back to Bethesda, June couldn't stop smiling over it. Alex, though, had been cagey and quiet.

She cringed to think of it now, how Alex had dropped out of her car at the end of the evening, tired and emotionally spent. Alex thanked her and said only courteous things, but June could see the exhaustion in her eyes, on her face, in her body, as if she were a citrus fruit June had squeezed dry.

Since then, Alex hadn't responded to any of June's texts—not the one this morning offering to accompany her to PetSmart, or the follow-up offer of some of Willow's unused pet gear, or the one June sent later in the afternoon inviting Alex to meet up at the usual park happy hour, and not to this last pathetic attempt to exploit the intrigue of Meryl's flyer—but could June honestly blame her for being scared away?

"It's time!" Kennedy called out from her post by the small-dog area entry gate. She pointed to her diamond-encrusted watch. "You don't want to be late!"

"Are any of you going?" June asked the huddle of regulars, only to find all of them already making their way to the exit.

It was a mass migration to the parking lot, the way a summer rainstorm could send them all scrambling to their cars at once, except in this case they were all headed to the same destination.

The traffic jam they created along Hamilton Avenue was like a funeral procession for someone universally beloved, June thought, someone who died before their time. An onlooker could have mistaken it for an emergency evacuation, or a misguided attempt to escape inevitable catastrophe.

June's truck was lodged midway in the bumper-to-bumper row of vehicles along the street leading to Meryl's cul-de-sac. Staring ahead, she tried to identify who was in front of her in a Subaru Impreza with a license plate that read K9MAMA and a back window sticker that read MY DOG IS SMARTER THAN YOUR HONOR STUDENT.

In the Jeep Grand Cherokee behind June was Yoshi's mom, who allowed Yoshi to stand on her lap with his paws on the steering wheel. The fluffy black and white shih tzu dwarfed his diminutive human so thoroughly that it appeared in June's rearview mirror as if Yoshi had driven himself alone in the car to the committee meeting.

"Look, Willow," June said to her copilot strapped into the passenger seat, "Yoshi knows how to drive. Would you like to take driver's ed?"

Willow replied with a confused head tilt.

"You're right," June said. "We should start you on a bicycle first."

As they inched closer to Meryl's house, June located the cause of the backup. Just before the turn onto the cul-de-sac, two valet attendants in matching red jackets were taking keys and parking cars somewhere within running distance. Their cardio strength and speed were sights to behold as they alternated driving and sprinting, barely breaking a sweat despite the stiff jackets, which appeared to be an unbreathable synthetic blend.

June enjoyed watching them. They were tireless and unbreakable in the way only men in their late teens and early twenties could be. She tried to tip the one who took her key fob in hand, but he genteelly declined, claiming, "Ms. Bryant is taking care of us, ma'am."

Of course Meryl was.

June attached Willow's leash to her collar and guided her up the slight hill of the cul-de-sac, toward the magnificent but unostentatious house. It may have been considered an estate. June wasn't sure of the qualifying factors, but any home residence with four levels seemed like it should be referred to as more than just a house. Its clay-brick facade and cathedral-like windows reminded June of her childhood church, and at somewhere around six thousand square feet, the buildings were probably about the same size, too. The property lines looked to be about an acre, which wasn't a huge spread, relatively speaking, but in this historic area it was a lavish amount of land to have to oneself.

At the center of the circular driveway, a pair of cater waiters—white jackets this time—were holding trays of wine and seltzer with lime. They instructed the guests to proceed across the threshold of the open front door, into the parlor. June chose a seltzer even though she wasn't a teetotaler by any means. Something told her she had better keep a clear head for whatever was coming next.

In the lawn space between the driveway and the open front door to the house was a secondary welcoming committee composed of more young, energetic twentysomethings. Their uniforms weren't jackets but khaki pants and light blue T-shirts with the name of a doggy daycare printed on the front.

"Heavens to Betsy," unpretentious Regina said, after handing Eloise off to a ponytailed woman who greeted the miniature dachshund by name. "The dogs have their own valet."

"This must be Willow," chirped the next ponytailed woman in the greeting line.

June was stupefied. Were these poor girls given photos of their pets beforehand and made to memorize their names? She had encountered this excessive level of event prep at gatherings with Silas—like when a host she'd never met would chummily ask how her backhand slice was coming along, or if she'd caught the latest National Women's Soccer League game, and even that struck her as unsettling—but this was a whole new tier of overkill.

Separated from their humans, the dogs were led to the backyard, where they were to be feted with allergen-free treats and entertained with games of fetch by hired hands. Willow galloped off to the designated area with her handler, no questions asked.

She was so easily lured, which June understood was the nature of a golden, coupled with the happy-go-lucky personality that June fell for the moment Silas introduced her to Willow. In no universe would June expect her fun-loving, sweet-hearted buffoon to be a keen watchdog. And yet, in a small way it did irk her that as full-bodied as Willow's devotion to her was, if anyone wanted to rob their house or abduct June from right under Willow's nose, all they would need was a cookie or a piece of cheese.

June felt a little lost now, without Willow by her side, as she stepped through the doorway into the grand foyer of the house.

Meryl was waiting just past the entrance, welcoming her guests one by one, shaking hands like a pantsuited politician. She never forgot a name—dog or human. June tried her best to be as conscientious, but even the supposedly helpful reminder notes she kept on her phone said things like *Cavalier King Charles owner, dark hair, big glasses—Carol or Caryn?*

Whereas if June went to Meryl after a conversation with the King Charles spaniel owner and whispered, *Is her name Carol or Caryn?* Meryl wouldn't even need to check her phone to inform June that the woman's name was Karen, she was a vice president and corporate counsel for Marriott International, and married to Paul, a systems engineer at Lockheed Martin.

"Welcome, June!" Meryl sounded genuinely happy to see her. "Please make yourself at home. The mushroom croquets and the zucchini fritters are vegetarian, but the spring rolls contain meat, so steer clear of those."

June thanked her, grateful for the heads-up. She appreciated not having to swallow down any surprise bits of pork or trying to spit gracefully into a cocktail napkin, but where did Meryl store all that personal information? She imagined Meryl's fast-processing brain, alight with cerebral activity, as so different from her own sleepy, dim orb that always seemed focused on the wrong things.

Meryl moved on to her next guest, welcoming them with equally genuine-sounding fanfare, as June proceeded to the parlor.

Was a parlor the same as a living room? What about a sitting room? Was a study different from a library? And what the heck was an efficiency? Meryl's home was said to have all of these, and June wasn't sure how to count them, unlike the fireplaces, which were all simply fireplaces. Current parlor gossip placed the over-under on fireplaces at four.

The wood-paneled room was crowded with about twenty-five people, which should have felt stuffy, but high ceilings and warm lighting provided an air of comfort. A perimeter of temporary folding chairs was set up around a long regal sofa and multiple accent chairs, which appeared to be permanent fixtures, possibly for generations.

June recognized most of the people present. Curiosity had even drawn a few of the keep-to-themselves, non-participatory types. They were probably not the only ones who turned up just to see the inside of this house. Senators, members of congress, and presidential hopefuls had stood on this carpet and most likely snacked on these very canapés from the same caterer. Barack Obama or Joe Biden may have once sipped from the rocks glass in June's hand now.

She took a sip and tried to taste something special. Then she set her purse down onto the first empty chair she saw and sat on the one beside it.

Saving you a seat just in case, she texted Alex, because she could not stop herself.

"May I?" Val shook off her black leather jacket and lowered herself onto the seat beside the one holding June's purse. "Nice digs, huh?"

June nodded.

"You ever been here before?" Val asked. "Wowzah." She ran her fingers through her shiny black hair, which June took to be a nervous habit.

"It lives up to the rumors," June said, for lack of something better to say. She was distracted by a childlike quality to Val that she had missed earlier. Beyond her smallish frame, there was wonder in her big brown eyes, and a helplessness that June found compelling. It was different from Alex's raw, anxious energy, but vulnerable in a similar way.

Was it weird that June felt compelled to reach out to Val and pull her in for a hug? To thank her for being unusual and captivating and outspoken like no one else she'd met in a very long time? June wanted to know everything about Val, to take her to dinner, or go shopping together this weekend. What product did she use to make her hair so lustrous? What was her bold shade of red lipstick called? How had she managed to find the perfect white T-shirt and have it hang from her torso with such hip nonchalance?

June picked at the skin around her fingernail, newly aware of the chipped polish, which made her feel silly and careless, like an adolescent. She considered spreading a fresh layer of pale pink gloss to her lips, but applying makeup in public made her feel self-conscious. Maybe she had a mint or stick of gum in her purse that she could offer up to Val, paving the way for pleasant conversation. She unzipped her bag to have a look.

"Attention, attention." Meryl tapped the underside of her diamond ring to her wineglass. "Hello, friends!"

She stood upon a low riser that served as the fulcrum to the room's seating arrangement, like the center spot of a peppermint candy swirl. "Thank you for coming, and thank you for being a *friend*."

It occurred to June then that the Silver Fox had been right. This was going to be a hard press for monetary donations.

Back home, before she met Silas, a friend was a companion, someone you were attached to by affection or esteem. Sometimes it was a person with whom you shared a group, as in camp friends, or anyone who wasn't an enemy, as in friend or foe.

Around here, friend groups or "Friends of" organizations existed for the sole purpose of raising charitable funds. There were Friends of the library, Friends of museums, and Friends of various schools and institutes.

Coming from Meryl, in their present surroundings, the phrase "Thank you for being a friend" was in no way an homage to the *Golden Girls* theme song. It was a peer-to-peer solicitation intoned with social pressure.

"After yesterday's incident, of which we do not need to speak . . ." Meryl paused and monkeyed a face to let the crowd know it was okay to giggle. "By the way, if I catch anyone playing that video, I'm going to tell you to get the fuck out of my house."

When she broke into a laugh, so did everyone else, in communal relief, like a released pressure valve.

"Seriously, though," Meryl set her glass down and brushed a strand of hair back from her forehead. "The condition of our beloved dog park is no laughing matter."

She was working from a script, June realized. The opening lines were planned, along with her transition to earnestness. Even her wineglass was a prop.

June was fascinated by the show—but just then Alex appeared in the doorway. Her light sweater was misshapen, and her brown hair pulled back into a sloppy ponytail, but she still somehow seemed well put together. Alex was one of those people who could look good wearing anything. Their eyes met and Alex half smiled an apology, for what exactly June couldn't be sure, but she grinned back forgiveness anyway. And then she couldn't stop grinning, so happy she was that Alex had come. Immediately, she felt silly for worrying that she was being rejected somehow, that Alex had been giving her the slip.

We're going to be friends, June thought, or maybe wished. *The real kind*. She would do everything in her power to make it happen.

Alex seemed to know better than to distract from Meryl's spotlight by making her way across the room, so she stayed put and listened from just beside the entryway, but June already felt less alone as Meryl continued her speech.

"As many of you are aware, my past attempts to get the town to agree to a park renovation have all come to naught."

The crowd snickered. Predictions had been made on how long it would take Meryl to utter the secret word: *renovation*.

"I know." Meryl caught the snickerers off guard by acknowledging them. "You're tired of hearing me talking about it. Believe me, *I'm* tired of hearing me talking about it. Which is why we need to do something, together, starting right now."

The room got quiet enough to hear the dogs roughhousing with their handlers outside. June could pick out Willow's *I'm having the best time!* play bark among the pack.

"The problem," Meryl said, "can be solved like most issues. With enough money."

No one chuckled or tittered now.

"We need to discuss how to fund a park renovation ourselves," Meryl continued. "If we come up with enough capital to cover all costs, I have been assured, we can have the improvements we seek. How does that sound?"

It sounded to June like happy-go-lucky dogs outside, and nervous people clutching their wallets inside.

"Questions?" Meryl asked. "Concerns?"

Everyone eyeballed one another, but no one spoke up.

"I'll go first," Meryl said. She turned to one side and raised her hand as if she were a member of the audience. "How much money are we talking?"

Then she was Meryl again, poised and all-knowing. "Excellent question," she complimented herself. "For a simple leveling of the land, to take care of the drainage problem, we may be looking at as little as a low six figures."

"That's it?" Ava shouted out, her voice like a kazoo. "Why didn't we pay for it ourselves years ago?"

"Before any of you grab your checkbooks," Meryl cut Ava off right there. "My contacts have stressed the importance of optics. This needs to be a community effort."

"As a member of the community," Ava said. "I'll put up twenty K just to save me from all the dry-cleaning and new shoes."

June noticed Val's reaction to this statement, how her facial features contorted with disgust. *She must not come from money*, June thought. Her stomach probably turned sour, as June's once had, by being around people for whom twenty thousand dollars wasn't a life-altering sum.

"As much as I admire your generosity," Meryl countered Ava's offer. "We can't just put up the money. This has to at least appear to be more democratic than that."

"Pass around a hat," someone yelled from the back. "We each throw in what? Ten, twelve thousand? Done."

"For that much money we should consider it a membership fee," said the lady seated upon a red brocade accent throne, whom June knew as the barky Maltese's human. "Put a lock on the small-dog area and only we have the combination."

"No pay, no play," Ava agreed.

"We can't privatize a public park," Yoshi's mom said.

June was glad someone said it. How would that be more democratic than one of them, or even a few of them, playing the hero?

Arguments flared, raising the temperature of the room, until Meryl reclaimed control.

"I was thinking more along the lines of a fundraiser," she said. "Something wholesome. An event local politicians can get behind, maybe even provide them with some good photo ops. Everyone in town would be welcome to participate. There can be a suggested donation, pay what you wish, or nothing at all. We could have it right at the park, in and around the dog area."

Meryl had obviously already thought the whole thing through.

"Memorial Day's just around the corner," she said. "If we work hard, I don't see any reason we can't be ready by mid-July. After the Fourth of July holiday but before the treacherous heat of August. That's our sweet spot."

Kennedy, who had hung back at the park to distribute last-minute flyers and crept into the room shortly after Alex, must have been filled in on the idea beforehand. She was bursting with suggestions.

"I'm seeing a mid-summer festival," she said. "Maybe a barbecue.

The dogs should definitely be there, and we can come up with a theme, so we can put them in fun outfits."

Yes. The group liked this.

"And we can have a costume contest!" Ava squealed. Popcorn already had a closet full of options, no doubt.

Meryl nodded, visibly pleased. "We can get local businesses to donate prizes. In fact, we should bring on some event sponsors."

While ideas flew around the room, June found herself watching Alex. She did not appear to be awed by the display of unencumbered wealth, or by this self-centered approach to the greater good.

June's own experience with fundraising was limited to soliciting funds for new soccer jerseys by selling KitKats and Welch's Fruit Snacks in front of Kroger. But this was the DMV—District of Columbia, Maryland, Virginia—where people knew how to *campaign*.

And yet Alex seemed to be more comfortable than June had ever seen her.

The Silver Fox had been quiet up to this point, but he spoke up now to express a lone voice of hesitation. "How much can we really expect to make in terms of funding from something so small-scale?"

"It doesn't matter," Val said in a volume that was almost to herself. Her tone of revulsion was what caught the room's attention. "The whole suggested donation aspect is just a gesture. You call it a pledge drive, but it's still going to be the people here in this room footing the bill. Right, Meryl?"

"Personally, I see an opportunity here." Meryl addressed the room, rather than just Val. She was not about to agree out loud to anything so tacky. Like anyone with her level of media training, she instead replied with a statement that promoted her intended messaging. "If we're going to all this trouble, what's the point in stopping at level ground when we can make our park into something so much better?"

Meryl gave the hushed crowd a moment to decipher exactly what that meant. One could almost see the castle building in their minds.

Ava spoke first. "Do you mean, like, better . . . amenities?"

June heard Val mumble under her breath, "Oh shit, here we go."

Ava held the floor. "Because I have been saying forever that the park needs better shade options, maybe a structure like a pergola or gazebo, even a little cabana."

"Sun protection is an important health issue," Meryl said. "For sanitary purposes I would also add more waste stations and trash receptacles, cleaning supplies."

Regina spoke next. Her idea, like Regina herself, was fairly humble. "What we really need is our own lighting, so we don't have to rely on the ambient glow from the tennis courts to find our way back to our cars once the sun goes down."

Meryl nodded and took notes on her phone. "Lighting is a must for safety and visibility, and it would increase the usable hours of the park, particularly in fall and winter."

"An updated water station," someone yelled out.

"Proper hydration is imperative," Meryl replied.

"Can we add misters to the hydration station?" someone else asked. "What about a splash pool?"

Meryl couldn't type on her phone fast enough. "To prevent overheating on hot summer days? I don't see why not."

"Play equipment," Yoshi's mom said. "A balance beam, a bridge climb, jump hurdles. For better agility."

"But even the children's playground doesn't have those sorts of things," someone said. "It's two swings and a teeter-totter."

Somebody from the back of the room shouted, "Who cares about that? The kids around here are already too spoiled as it is."

"Children don't need as much public running space or exercise," someone else offered. "The zoomies are a dog-only phenomenon."

"And everyone knows most fur babies are more intelligent than the average toddler," a third person added. "Depending on the breed."

"I've been to a park that had a zen zone," the Maltese lady cut in. "For dogs who feel like they need to decompress."

"You know what would be awesome?" Kennedy spoke over her. "A photo booth panel. For social media posts."

This was a crowd favorite that created a stir. Meryl had to quiet everyone down. "Perhaps we should get back to discussing the nature of the fundraising event itself. The more of these upgrades we'd like to see come to fruition the more we'll need to—"

"A ball!" Ava cried out.

Like Meryl, and the rest of the room, June was momentarily confused by the outburst. She thought Ava might still be stuck on the amenities and was suggesting the park provide fetch toys.

Ava clarified. "You were going to say we need to do something with a bit of pizazz, right? Something big-ticket. We should throw a ball."

Kennedy was quick to piggyback the idea. "Or a gala. Like the Met Gala. With a red carpet step-and-repeat."

"A red carpet for us or the dogs?" Regina asked.

"Why not both?" Ava said.

"Optics," Meryl shouted. "Remember? An event by the people

for the people. But you're right that we can go a little bigger. A few add-ons to the festival, within good taste, would make sense. If we keep it somewhat traditional. We can do a sit-down dinner, a silent auction."

"It can be a tasteful gala," Kennedy said. "And the theme can be summer barbecue."

"The Met Gala always has a theme," Kennedy added, but she had already convinced the room.

Val leaned over to June. "It didn't take long for this to spin completely out of control now, did it?"

June concurred. "You're not from around here, are you?"

"I figured that was obvious right from the jump," Val said.

June smiled because it was.

"We should continue meeting like this regularly." Meryl forged ahead with planning and logistics. "But we should also set up subcommittees, each with their own responsibilities and assignments."

"Subcommittees are how we roll," June whispered to Val.

A plan was hammered out.

There was the Auction Committee, tasked with biddable item procurement; the Entertainment and Program Committee, in charge of hiring an emcee, auctioneer, and live performers; the Sponsorship Committee, whose mission was to find local businesses willing to come on board as sponsors and provide in-kind donations of food, drink, or items to raffle off as prizes. The Media and Public Relations Committee would make sure word got out about the event and—more importantly—manage how the event would be covered in local media. Most popular was the Décor Committee, which Meryl said would be held accountable for making the event look "gorgeous but not over the top," whatever that meant.

June volunteered for the Sponsorship Committee because why not? She could use the distraction from her recent troubles with Silas. Since their last argument things had been tense at home, which was to be expected. It would take time and effort for June to repair the damage she had done by researching divorce online—and she would have to make those repairs without ever admitting she'd done the research to begin with, because Silas would never admit to policing her search history. Constant, overeffusive reassurance that she would never, no way, no how, even think of leaving Silas was now her daily reality and would be for weeks to come. *Was this how all married couples managed to stay together?* June honestly wasn't sure.

To her delight, both Alex and Val also joined the Sponsorship Committee. Once everyone was assigned to a subgroup, Meryl had them break up into individual clusters around the room to play a get-to-know-you game.

"Even if you are certain the others in your group, with whom you've been acquainted for years, already know your basic personal facts," Meryl said, "I assure you, they do not. Proceed as if you've just met."

This wasn't too hard of an ask in the case of the Sponsorship Committee, given the fact that despite June's smothering of Alex and her curiosity when it came to Val, the three of them were in fact strangers.

Meryl propped up a whiteboard with suggestions of "who, what, and wheres" to offer up about themselves.

Neither Alex nor Val appeared to be thrilled by the juvenile activity. June would start things off, she thought, to take some of the pressure off them. But then Meryl tossed a red die in their direction—which Val impressively scooped out of the air before June or Alex could catch it.

"Roll to see who goes first," Meryl said.

June was loving this. When was the last time she'd played a game?

"Always lucky when it comes to gambling," Val said, with clear sarcasm, in response to the being the highest roller. "Runs in my family."

She momentarily glanced at the whiteboard's introduction suggestions. "My name is Val. Caruso. My dog is Cash. She's a Brussels Griffon and not a pug mix like everyone always asks. I'm single, never married, no kids, not even plants. I'm from New York—"

"Where in New York?" Alex asked.

Val did not appreciate being interrupted. "Queens," she said, with bite. "I'm currently between jobs—"

"But where did you work before?" Alex interrupted again. "What's your field?"

"I'm in sales," Val said, which could mean a lot of things, and based on the sudden tension, June wondered if she sold something illicit. Val did have a certain roughness about her.

Val continued, going down the list of Meryl's suggestions one at a time. "I first realized the park needed a renovation when I saw Meryl go face down in the mud, which I may never be able to unsee. And I chose this subcommittee because . . ." Val paused. "Honestly? Because June did." She looked directly at June now, but she seemed to still be speaking to Alex. "She's been the nicest to me since I arrived at the park, so I thought I'd like to get to know her better, while taking part in a good cause."

How flattering! June thought. "I'd like that too," she said, and then felt immediately silly for the excitement in her voice.

"You're up," Val said to Alex, in a way that sounded like a dare.

What was happening between these two? Did they already dislike each other for some reason?

"I'm Alex Miller and I hate games, but I have a special hatred in my heart for get-to-know-you games and icebreakers of any kind. My dog . . ." Alex's voice cracked. "I'm about to adopt a dog named Bruce. He's a beagle." Directly to June, Alex said, "I'm thankful to have him." Then she turned to Val. "I'm divorced, no kids, not even plants. I am also from New York. Manhattan."

"Originally?" Val asked.

"I've been there forever."

"But you weren't born there."

"No," Alex said. "Not technically."

"So, technically, where were you born?"

"Pennsylvania. What does it matter?"

"I'm just trying to play by the rules," Val said.

"I'm sorry," June interjected, finally. "Have you two met before?"

"No," they replied in unison.

"Where was I?" Alex continued, but June found it difficult to listen, unsure what to make of the strange tension between Alex and Val.

She looked around the room, at the other subgroups breezily yukking it up, and was overcome by the sense that the two women before her were about to invigorate her life. For good or bad, June couldn't say, but either way, Silas surely would not approve. He preferred her to always stay just as she was when it came to everything from her hairstyle to her taste in food to the people with whom she associated. But June felt a change was coming, and it was going to be big.

"June," Alex said. "It's your turn."

"Right." June beamed a smile at her two peculiar new acquaintances, ready for whatever mayhem she sensed they carried with them. *Bring on the chaos*, she thought, *bring on the fun. Mix up my world like a cocktail in a shaker.*

After all, wasn't that what friends were for?

CHAPTER 6

Keeping a dog quiet while on stakeout would have been impossible had Val not discovered the magic wand called a bully stick. Nothing Val waved at Cash's brachycephalic face worked as well for hypnotizing her. The fact that the sticks were made from and smelled like the penis of a bull was not the deal-breaker Val would have assumed. Her concern was more about how many of these hard, high-protein shafts Cash could devour before she puked. Consensus online was no more than one a day, but the rods came in different sizes—from a thin six inches, to a girthier eight, to an ultra–long lasting, ribbed-for-her-pleasure twelve-inch Magnum. Given the minuscule dimensions of Cash's mouth, Val went with the modest sixers, which she believed freed her to exceed the one-a-day standard.

It was now four p.m., Cash was halfway done with her second bully, and Val was growing weary of staring at the lackluster front of Alex's apartment complex, which had the transient, stop-on-the-road quality of a three-star Econo Lodge.

The earlier part of the day had at least been more exciting.

Val started the morning watching June's house, and by lunchtime Alex had come knocking. June bounced right out the door with Willow in tow, and the three of them piled into June's Mercedes-Benz SUV, looking like a lesbian-friendly ad campaign targeting homely alternative families. They seemed comfortable with each other, at ease, and shared an effortless symmetry in their facial features that one tended to find on television. Neither of them dressed in an elaborate or showy style, or wore much makeup, and yet even in plain-Jane jeans and simple shirts in neutral colors, they each radiated the type of magnetic vibe that could carelessly capture a heart or sell you a car.

Val followed June's truck all the way to Bumblefuck, where a long driveway led to a secluded stretch of land.

Even with binoculars, Val couldn't see squat from the road, and her exact location had baffled Google Maps. She waited almost an hour, then followed June's car all the way back here, which was a happy surprise because now Val knew where Alex lived, or at least where Alex was pretending to live. But the real kicker was that they got out of June's truck with two dogs instead of one.

The midsize, tan-and-white Snoopy-looking dog could only mean one thing. Alex was in this—whatever *this* was—for the long haul. Val still didn't know what to make of Alex's decoy wallet and fake ID, and running a search on her license plate only added more question marks. The Toyota Camry she was driving was recently bought and registered to an anonymous LLC.

Cash lifted her head from her bully stick, looked at Val, and let out a deep-throated, pizzle-stinking burp; *pizzle* being the word used to describe what bully sticks were made of when in polite company.

"Everything about you is disgusting," Val said in reply to the burp.

Cash carried on with her chewing, nonplussed.

Bringing a dog on surveillance was less than ideal, but the single time Val had left Cash home alone, she apparently lost her mind and barked the entire time. Val wouldn't have known about the incessant barking, as she was not there to hear it, but one of her neighbors described the disturbance in a terse note taped to her front door.

Poison-pen letters were easy enough to ignore. It was not as if it had been composed of magazine-cutout letters or threatened anyone's life; however, it was uniquely menacing in that it contained an attachment—the apartment building bylaws and code of conduct. The rules regarding pets and noise disturbances were highlighted in yellow.

Whoever went to such trouble as to print out these pages—or worse, already had them on hand and ready to notate—was not to be messed with. Val would have been less rattled by a direct encounter with a gun-toting thug, which in her experience was never as difficult to handle as one might think, but a personality with this level of careful meticulousness scared her out of her wits. Even the yellow-highlighted lines were bone-chillingly straight.

And so, Val started bringing Cash everywhere rather than leaving her at the apartment. It was a plus that she was discreetly portable. She could be stuffed into a jacket, much like a stolen loaf of bread, except that Val was sneaking her into stores instead of out of them.

Cash was now nearing the end of her bully stick, and Val was bored out of her mind. She was about to head out for a much-needed break when Alex's apartment door opened.

June and Willow and Alex and her new mystery dog made their way, like a big happy family, to June's truck.

Val strapped Cash back into her car seat and readied herself to follow them.

She tailed June, turn for turn, to Rockville Pike, to Wisconsin Avenue, to—Val should have known. Even Cash recognized the shopping center they pulled into as home to PetSmart. She was up on her hind legs, pawing at the side window.

"Smart girl," Val said, with such automatic, cringeworthy parental pride that she was immediately embarrassed for herself.

She pulled into a parking spot a few rows back from June's Mercedes.

"Is the pet store to animals as McDonald's is to humans?" Val asked Cash. "You can smell it before you can see it?"

Together, Val and Cash watched June and Alex gather their dogs and stroll into the store.

On the bright side, Val wouldn't have to sneak Cash into PetSmart, as pets were not only allowed but encouraged to shop alongside their humans, free to choose their own chew toys and kibble or compare prices on the latest styles of onesies. But Val carried Cash in her arms anyway.

"You have to earn the right to walk freely on your leash," she said when Cash resisted.

Last time they were here, Cash had dragged Val around the store, sniffing and inhaling every morsel on the floor, wiggling her ass at every person who walked by, and overall making a wild nuisance of herself. If Val set her on the ground now, there was no way she wouldn't blow up their spot.

June and Alex went to the bedding section first. Val watched them, phone in hand with its camera at the ready. All she needed was to catch some intimate physical contact between June and Alex—nothing crazy like them suddenly making out in the cat food aisle; one telling touch would be enough.

Val captured a few shots of them laying out various poofs and pillow loungers for Alex's dog to try out—and Willow, too, because who could stop her. It wasn't much, evidence wise, but at least beds were involved, which Val could maybe hard-sell as lurid somehow. *The couple who dog-beds together, people-beds together?* It was a stretch, but Silas was getting antsy for some return on his investment, and Val wasn't about to lose this cash cow now. Not after all *she'd* invested. Her apartment was beginning to look like a canine boardinghouse, for Chrissake.

Alex decided on a shag fur donut cuddler, and Val chose to ignore how and why she knew what the eff a donut cuddler was.

Next, Alex and June proceeded to collars, harnesses, and leashes—which, if Val wanted to make an argument for lurid, what aisle had more sadomasochist vibes than this one? She nudged her phone to keep it awake, but she was having a hard time juggling it in one hand with Cash under her other arm, wiggling with all her might to escape. If only Val could stash her somewhere for a while, to be hands-free.

"Oh my goodness." Up came a woman reaching for Cash without consent. "What kind of pug mix is this? Is he a Bugg or a bullpug? Or wait, let me guess, a Frug? A poxer? I don't see pugshund or Pugalier. But maybe a Pughuahua . . ."

Val resisted the urge to just give Cash over to this stupid woman and get back to work. Instead, she rebuffed her without an answer, turned a corner for better cover, and tried to shield Cash's non-pug, puglike face from public view.

An aisle away from where June and Alex were deliberating on retractable versus standard leash styles, Val forged a sightline between two extra-large packages of wee-wee pads.

Bruce was the name Val heard when Alex commanded her new dog to sit. And would you believe that son of a bitch just sat? Meanwhile, Cash was chewing a hole into Val's shirtsleeve in an attempt to free herself via gnawed-off limb.

Before Cash drew blood, Val grabbed some kind of hoof from a display shelf and shoved it into her mouth like a ball gag. Cash promptly spit it out onto the floor.

"Can I help you with anything?" A salesperson approached with caution.

"We're good, thanks." Val moved along, crossing the aisle in a dash for cover behind a display of cat towers—but the split second of exposure was all Cash needed to spot June and catch scent of Willow. She let out a high-pitched war cry that pierced the air before leaping from Val's arms.

June and Alex, along with everyone else in the store, turned to find the source of the horrific sound.

"Fancy meeting you here!" June said, with zero suspicion. But Alex narrowed her eyes at Val. Her annoyingly well-behaved dog, Bruce, finally pulled on his leash, determined to get his Snoopylike snout into Cash's privates. The two of them commenced a sniff fest so impassioned that poor Willow could hardly get a nose in, but as the elder in the group, she took it in stride.

"Uh-oh, Willow," June said. "Looks like Bruce found a new, younger girlfriend."

Gross, Val thought, scooping Cash back up. "She's not ready for a relationship," she said to Bruce.

Alex appeared flustered, unsure of what to do when she commanded Bruce to sit and he basically told her to fuck off.

"I've never seen him act like this," she said.

"Don't worry." June gave Alex a comforting tap on the back that Val would have killed to get a shot of on her phone. "He's just being a dog."

"So, you did finally break down and get one," Val said to Alex. "And here I thought you were just going to keep showing up at the park dogless."

"Speaking of the park," June said. "We're heading there right from here."

"You planning to follow us there as well?" Alex asked.

June looked away, presumably to avoid whatever conflict was about to ensue, but Val couldn't properly spar with Alex while Cash was going berserk in her arms, so she set the dog back onto the floor.

Bruce immediately play-bowed, jubilant. Willow let out a happy bark that Cash ignored. She was too busy wagging her little nub tail for Bruce, pawing at him like she wanted to wrestle.

"By the looks of these two, I may not have a choice," Val said. "To the park it is."

"We still have some things to pick up." Alex observed Val's empty hands, save for her phone, and the absence of a shopping cart or basket.

"Me too," Val said. "This was an emergency trip for one thing and one thing only. We ran out of bully sticks, didn't we, Cash?"

"Oh no, never," June chimed in as Val's unknowing accomplice. "Never get caught bully stick–less. Alex, make sure we pick up some of those."

We, Val noticed she said, and not for the first time. June and Alex were already speaking in *we*'s.

It wasn't easy separating Cash and Bruce, but they managed it. Val let Cash continue along on her leash, like a normal dog, as she made her way to the treats aisle, where Cash got her mouth around a chicken foot that Val had to yank free by the toe.

"Who thought it was a good idea to put these things at ground level?" Val wondered aloud.

Bag of bullies in hand, she dragged Cash to the checkout counter.

Outside, back in the car, she set Cash on the front seat and trained her phone's camera on the store's exit doors. She refused to leave without at least one halfway-decent shot of June and Alex's couple's trip.

"What do you think, Cash? How long would you say they've been banging?"

Cash surprised her by climbing onto her lap. Back feet on the steering wheel, she pawed at Val's waist.

"What's gotten into you?" Val brushed her hand over her jacket to see what Cash was nosing at and—what the heck?

Out of her pocket Val pulled one skinny, sinewy chicken foot.

"Did you steal this?" She turned to Cash, whose chest bulged with pride.

The dog had managed to not only pilfer the item while Val's attention was elsewhere, but also slip it onto her person without her noticing. She couldn't have learned this from watching Val. The only reasonable explanation was that it was her natural-born, God-given instinct.

"Thatta girl," Val heard herself say in her father's voice. She scratched at the back of Cash's neck, then handed over the booty. "You earned it, little one. Good job."

Meryl Bryant, now the head Friend and de facto leader of Hamilton Dog Park, was first to notice Bruce at Alex's side, setting the tone of his welcome to a zealous, matronly delight.

"Isn't he darling?" She cradled Bruce's chin in her palms. "Have you ever seen a more dignified face than this?"

Kennedy, Meryl's number one helper bee, agreed. "Absolutely darling, so dignified. I'd vote for him for mayor."

Kennedy reminded Alex of the sillier girls at her Swiss boarding school, the ones who played second fiddle to the right-of-succession class favorites, showing up to lectures in full makeup and try-hard ensembles alongside actual royal princesses wearing sweatpants.

And then there was Ava, who was just plain ridiculous, putting a tiny doggy tiara on her poor Pomeranian's head. Her reaction to Bruce was merely lukewarm, which only made Alex dismiss her further.

"You doing okay?" June asked, perhaps sensing Alex's sudden animosity.

Alex nodded. What a day it had been, her first as an actual dog owner. She could not have gotten through it without June's help, arriving at Terri's empty-handed and singular, and leaving with someone that would be part of her forever. The gravitas had been overwhelming. It was what Alex imagined new parents must feel like after the birth of a child—entering the delivery room as a couple and exiting as three. Alex had only ever known the opposite, going into a hospital with a person who never came back out. This was better, no doubt, but equally life-altering. It was up to her now to keep Bruce alive and healthy and happy, when she could barely do those things for herself. Alive, sure, so far, and healthy in body but not in mind, but don't even talk to her about happy. Or productive, for that matter. What if caring for Bruce became one more thing she failed at?

"You're awfully quiet. You just soaking up the atmosphere?"

Why are you here? Alex wanted to reply to Val. *Why are you always just appearing places?*

It didn't mean much that Alex had an aversion to Val, considering how little she liked most people, but her distaste for this nosy, pushy woman in red lipstick and a black leather jacket was growing more intense by the minute.

She could have killed her when she showed up at PetSmart.

After the countless hours Alex had spent alone staring at dog supplies as a kid, dreaming about and planning for the pet her parents would never grant her, it had felt special to be at the pet store with June, Willow and Bruce at her side. Long-lost memories and feelings had come rushing in—and the smells. How was it possible that every pet supply shop smelled the same? Whether it was in New York, Pennsylvania, London, Paris, or Switzerland. The continuity of this scent, lingering over chew toys and rawhide bones, was probably the steadiest throughline of Alex's childhood and adolescence. Now, in adulthood, it was a full-circle moment. Alex finally had a dog to buy things for—and she wasn't all by herself. She had June beside her. This was where Alex had been mentally, sharing this significant moment with June, when Val had to show up and ruin all of it.

"No interest in taking part in the group debate over the best pet salon?" Val asked Alex.

"Huh?" Alex replied, just as she heard Kennedy say to Ava, "Whatever they're doing with Popcorn's coat, it's working wonders. Her fur looks absolutely resplendent!"

"They do great work at Fetching," Meryl agreed. "But I'll only take Paisley to Fur Baby Organics, her skin as sensitive as it is, and I just don't trust all those toxic chemicals." She turned to June and said, after a heavy pause, "No offense to Silas."

June smiled sunshine rays in return, as if to say *none taken*.

Val, though, didn't let the comment pass. "Why would Silas be offended?"

No one acknowledged her uncourteous prying by explaining that Silas was a toxicity expert. For years he'd worked as a manager in the Office of Pollution Prevention and Toxics at the Environmental Protection Agency, which was tasked with evaluating chemicals and their risks, with the goal of preventing pollution before it got into the environment.

Meryl didn't own up to the sharp edge of her dull comment, but to Alex's ears it was unmistakable. She must have known what Alex did about Silas's reputation as a man willing to have his palm greased. At Reed Industries, when Alex's father didn't want a warning label to restrict the use of the company's new pesticide, he said, "the pot required sweetening." Whatever the euphemism of choice to allow businessmen in locked rooms to avoid uttering the word "bribe," the connotation was the same: Silas Kennerson was the person to see.

It was a boon for the industry when Silas was promoted to acting director of the New Chemicals Division. Who better to run the office in charge of imposing limits on dangerous substances than their own inside man?

Alex assumed it was pure greed that drove Silas to urge more noxious chemicals onto the market than he prevented, but with further investigation she realized that he was just as much in it for the power. Nothing enhanced a post-agency job prospect quite like being in the good graces of big industry. Whatever Silas wished for next—a presidential cabinet post, perhaps—would be his for the taking. Which was why he needed to be stopped now, before he grew too big to break.

That was where June came in.

As Silas's wife, June could access his personal files, bank statements, copies of emails or text threads that Alex could then package together and pass to her contacts to be used by the legal system.

For this reason, Alex had moved to a new state, taken on a whole different persona, and brought her target's spouse into the fold—but June was turning out to be not just any spouse. Frigging June. Thanks to her, Alex's issues with Silas were becoming even more personal than they already were, and she was beginning to worry about what would happen to June if she did manage to bring Silas down.

"Hear ye! Hear ye!" June wedged herself between Alex and Val, pretending to ring an imaginary handbell. "I hereby call a meeting of the Friends of Hamilton Dog Park Sponsorship Committee."

"Right," Val said. "We did all let ourselves get roped into that nonsense, didn't we?"

"That's the spirit," June said. "I was thinking of going out on the town this Saturday, popping into a few shops, seeing if I can secure some sponsors. Either of you care to join?"

"I'm free on Saturday," Alex said.

"Same," Val said. "But I'll need to bring Cash."

"I was counting on that." June took out her cell. "We'll need her cuteness to melt some hearts."

By Val's facial reaction, one would have thought she'd smelled spoiled milk. "It's more like I'm just tired of getting noise complaints."

"Don't try to play tough, Val Caruso," June said. "It's okay to not like being without her."

"Yeah, no," Val said, annoyed, but June didn't pick up on it.

"You love her. You can admit it." June nudged Val playfully with her elbow.

Val fast-twitched forward, startling June. Alex, too, thought June was about to be knocked to the ground. Her pulse rate spiked.

But Val stopped herself. "Sorry." Her face and neck blushed red. "Automatic reflex to your elbow."

"I'm the one who should be apologizing." June went to comfort Val with a pat on her arm, but wisely changed her mind.

Alex recognized a flight-or-flight response when she saw one, a mind too quick to alert the body to danger.

"Do you do martial arts or something?" sweet June asked.

"In fact, I do," Val said.

But did she really? Or was her instinctive trigger response the product of post-traumatic stress?

"Military background?" Alex asked.

Val shook her head. "Just plain old civilian grappling."

"Well, I won't be sneaking up on you in any dark alleys, that's for sure. Here—" June handed Val her cell phone. "Put in your number. I'll text you both, so we'll have a Friends committee group chat. This is going to be fun!"

"Loads," Val said, back to her regular sarcasm, as if someone were twisting her arm.

Why did she annoy Alex so? Was it simply her too in-your-face attitude and blunt style that made everything sound like an insult? Or was it something deeper and more complex? Was Alex's gut trying to tell her that Val couldn't be trusted?

"If you aren't feeling it," Alex said, "we can handle it ourselves."

"And miss out on all the fun?" Val returned June's phone, but it was Alex she was looking at. "Not a chance."

CHAPTER 7

The Shops on Lincoln Road were not to be confused with The Shoppes on Hickory Boulevard. One was an upscale plaza offering an eclectic mix of quaint storefronts and trendy restaurants, while the other had an extra *p* and *e* in its old-timey name. June made sure to clarify the distinction in her text message to Alex and Val, as they were both new to town and couldn't be expected to understand the ins and outs of the area's coded shopping center nomenclature.

Meet me at the SHOPS, she wrote in all caps, *with the non-archaic spelling and home to the best ice cream in Bethesda. We can start at the day spa and work our way toward the reward of chocolate sundaes.*

June couldn't think of a better way to spend the afternoon, and it began just as she imagined it would, with her arriving first at Fern's Day Spa and waiting with Willow out front. Weatherwise, they struck gold, as June knew they would, even though the forecast predicted a chance of showers. Alex and Val arrived within minutes of each other, both right on time.

Fern's Day Spa was not the swankiest locale in town to get a mani-pedi or back massage, nor was it the plainest. Aesthetically, it was a fifty-fifty blend of New Age hippie and modernist yuppie, much like Fern herself. What made the place a perfect contender for a Friends of Hamilton Dog Park fundraiser sponsorship was Fern's white West Highland White Terrier, Harmony, who held court upon a plush blanket on the couch beside the reception counter.

June had never seen Harmony the Westie outside, and she may have never stepped a paw onto the muddy grounds of Hamilton Dog Park, but as the unofficial assistant manager of the spa, the chance of getting Fern's name on a thank-you-from-our-sponsors banner seemed in their favor.

Disappointingly, when June, Alex, and Val stepped up to the reception desk with Willow, Bruce, and Cash, Harmony's reaction was less than harmonious.

"Harmony doesn't like it when she's not the only dog in here," Fern said, coming around the counter to comfort her. The compact but robust dog's almond-shaped eyes were alight with annoyance and her pointed ears were fully erect.

June explained the reason for their visit as succinctly as possible on account of the Westie's barky resistance to being quieted.

Fern's "I'm sorry, but no" was equally swift.

Alex tagged in. "It'll be great publicity and exposure for the shop. If you're not up for a full sponsorship, maybe you'd consider donating something we can raffle off, like a gift certificate for a facial or eyebrow threading."

"We don't know how to thread a dog's eyebrows!" Fern shot back. "Hair straightening, I can maybe see, or a claw manicure, but . . ."

"The services would be for the dogs' people," Alex said with preternatural sincerity. "Not the dogs themselves."

"Ooooh." Fern responded with new clarity. "Yeah, I can do that. I'll put together a nice package for you."

Success! On their first try. Outside, the three of them high-fived.

"How did you keep your shit together so well in there?" Val asked Alex.

"I guess I have a knack for stupid questions." Alex proceeded to the next storefront.

"Good to know." Val followed behind. "I'll make sure to ask you more of them."

June was still trying to get a handle on their dynamic. Annoying each other seemed to be their thing. "You two bicker like an old married couple," she said. "And yet it's Alex and me the park is up in arms about."

Alex and Val nearly tripped over one another's feet.

"What now?"

"Excuse me?" they said.

Oops. Maybe that wasn't the best way for June to bring up the rumor she overheard via loud whisper yesterday at the park, but she did need to bring it up to clear the air—because it had been worrying her somewhat—so better to just be done with it already.

"Have you not heard?" June forged ahead, lighthearted. "The current hot gossip at Hamilton is that we're having a lurid affair."

"You're kidding," Alex said, while Val remained silent.

"I've been known to kid inappropriately," June said. "But not this time."

Alex's jaw was clenched. Her whole face tightened like a fist. "Just because I'm gay and we've been hanging out a lot, they think something sexual must be going on? That's offensive. People are so disappointing."

Alex looked to Val. "What are you so quiet about? Are you part of this?"

Val deliberated before answering. "I may have heard something. I didn't know if it was true."

"Christ," Alex said. She was genuinely upset, and June felt bad about that, but also somewhat relieved, because it was so easy to give someone the wrong idea.

"I'm sure this is my fault," June said to Alex. "I'm careless with my affection. I've been told that in the past."

"That's absurd," Alex said. "Who told you that?"

"Too many people to count," was June's honest reply. And then her mouth went on talking, ahead of her brain, to provide a list. "My closest girlfriend, who had a different definition of girlfriend than I did. A team physio, who insisted I was flirting with him when I thought I was just being nice. I've been called a tease by numerous men, and one woman who I hoped would make the perfect doubles partner. *Don't pretend like you don't know what you're doing*, she said to me. *Don't play dumb.* But I am, unfortunately, really that dumb."

"You're not dumb," Val said. "You're just pretty. And all those people sound like asses."

"For once, I agree with Val." Alex put a chummy arm around June. "You've done nothing but be a good friend to me, and I don't make friends easily."

"With your sparkling personality?" Val said. "Shocking."

"Ignore her." Alex pretended to cart June away. "Three's a crowd. Let's you and me go play some tennis and let Val finish up here on her own."

June was happy to be laughing together, all three of them—even Val. The air was clear, and it wasn't even difficult to clear it, because despite all their snark Alex and Val listened to June when she spoke—unlike Silas, who only heard the things he wanted.

"You're on," June said to Alex. "But I bet we can find a fourth for Val and make it a doubles match."

"Thanks, but no thanks," Val said. "I'll leave the bougie sports to you two. The closest we had to a tennis court in my neighborhood was a concrete handball wall."

"You can keep score," Alex offered. "Did the wolves you were raised by teach you numbers?"

"Enough that I know love equals zero," Val said.

They were having fun teasing one another, and June felt a surge of excitement and hope that she could barely contain. Let the people at the park have their gossip. It was harmless, as long as it didn't reach Silas somehow, but June wasn't about to kill the moment by mentioning that now.

Their next stop was A-One Dry Cleaners, where they were rejected by the grumpy old male owner and told in an aggressive Italian accent to "please take those mutts outside where they belong."

"At least he said please," June muttered, but Val moved forward as if she hadn't heard the man.

"Old-world Italians are my specialty," she said under her breath, before calling out, "This is quite a place you have here. My, my. Robotic garment sorting? Where's the old clothing conveyor jam-packed with wire hangers? And—"

She strode into the employees-only space between the counter and the back room. "What kind of perc machine is that? Look at that touch screen. I feel like I've stepped into the future."

"No perc." The old meanie smiled with pride. "That's what

they call an alternative solvent machine. It's good for the earth. It has its own brain."

"May I?" Val examined the giant washer more closely, while June and Alex stayed put.

"We just had everything renovated," The man bragged to Val. "Only the best new machines. You know dry cleaning?"

"I do," Val said. "But with equipment that's basically nineteenth-century compared to this setup. I bet you're putting out the cleanest clothes in town. Have you advertised all these upgrades?"

The man paused, thought for a moment. He brought his working-man's hands to the hips of his crisp, freshly ironed trousers. The deep furrows in his brow dissipated.

Val continued, "I bet you could get away with raising your prices ten, fifteen percent and it'll only bring in more business once word gets out."

"Huh," he said. "Hmm." He surveyed his kingdom, nodding his head.

"Now's the time," Val went ahead, as if he had replied with full-sentence coherence. "Maybe take an ad out in the local paper. And you know what else?" She sounded like she was about to let him in on a secret. "You might want to think about letting us raffle off a few gift certificates for your top-of-the line services. Get the community to start paying attention to what you've got going on here."

Val had him, that was plain to see. He was already reaching for a pen.

"Of course," Val added. "If you came on as an event sponsor, we'd have your name and business logo plastered onto all kinds of banners and signage. It would be front and center on all our mailings. But you probably don't have the dough for that, considering all the money you must have shelled out for the reno."

June had been standing there the whole time and she still couldn't quite grasp how Val had managed to unravel this tightly wound knot of a man and make a fervent case for his ability to sign on as an event sponsor.

Back outside, Val fanned herself with his big fat check. "I believe my work here is done."

"Way to close a deal!" June applauded. "Good thing you're some kind of dry-cleaning savant. Or was that just salesmanship?"

"I legit have PCE solvent in my blood," Val said. "It was the family business."

"Was?" Alex asked. "So there's no Caruso Cleaners somewhere in Queens?"

Val was a bit taken aback by the lack of playfulness in Alex's tone of voice, and honestly so was June.

"Not since my parents died," Val said.

"Oh my goodness, I'm so sorry." June allowed herself to touch Val's arm for only a second.

"I'm sorry, too," Alex offered, but she didn't sound sorry. "You must have been young."

"Seventeen," Val said. "Car accident."

"You lost them both at the same time?" June wanted to wrap her arms around Val and hold her close; however, judging by the current look on her face, June sensed that if she tried, Val might punch her lights out.

"It was a long time ago." Val motioned toward the next storefront in line. "Shall we?"

As they made their way to the wine and cheese shop, Alex grumbled, "You're not the only one with dead parents."

Val whipped around. "What was that?"

Alex startled. "Not that it's a contest or anything, I was just saying . . ." Alex looked to June for some kind of help. "It came out wrong, but both my parents really are dead."

"You're such a weirdo," Val said.

June urged them toward the wine and cheese shop door. "I'm sorry for both your losses," she said, trying to sound democratic while fighting back the pang in her gut over the absence of her own mother and father from her life.

"Do you still have both your parents?" Alex asked, as if reading her mind.

"Not really," June said. "But they are alive." June pulled the wine and cheese shop door open, then casually added, "We had some disagreements about my marriage and don't really speak much."

Was it June's imagination, or was the split-second expression on Alex's face the same as Val's—that same mix of pity and condemnation June often caught on people's faces when she spoke of Silas, as if they didn't approve of him, or somehow sensed the rockier aspects of her relationship? But that was impossible. Neither Alex nor Val had ever met Silas.

"Shall we?" June gestured for them to enter the shop ahead of her before they could ask any more questions.

June had not been kidding when she said Maddy's Handmade Ice Cream was the best in town. Halfway done with her scoop of Party Cake on a sugar cone, Val was already planning what flavor she'd get on her next visit.

"Do you always order off the kids' menu?" Alex asked, over a plastic spoonful of her snooty, tea-infused Matcha Cheesecake.

"Do you always order the most pretentious flavor available?" Val said.

"Enough, you two." From across the picnic table, where they'd settled to rest in front of Maddy's, June scolded them between licks of Orange Creamsicle. "Your behavior's worse than the dogs' right now."

"That's only because they got pup cups," Val said. "Which, by the way, appear to be nothing more than overpriced cups of frozen pumpkin puree mixed with peanut butter. I could make these myself at home for half the price."

"I've got a recipe I can send you," June said.

Of course she did.

"Will you send it to me?" Alex asked.

"I'll do you one better." June lit up her sunshine smile. "Let's make a batch together."

No way were they having an affair, Val decided. Along with an impressive number of sponsors and raffle prizes, the long day together had also produced that rock-solid conclusion. June and Alex could be icky and gooey-sweet to one another in ways that made Val nauseated, but they were absolutely not fucking.

Maybe Silas was wrongly assuming an affair just like everyone else? Val didn't know much about much, but she would place a high-stakes bet on June Kennerson not being a cheater.

Still, there was something going on here worth her daily rate to unravel.

Alex Miller was not Alex Miller, and every attempt Val had made this week to try to figure Alex out had come to another dead end. Her apartment was rented under the same LLC name as her car, but Val couldn't get through the onionlike layers of shell companies and dummy corps to figure out who the LLC belonged to—which was, of course, the point of an anonymous LLC in the first place.

Val would have to resort to more drastic measures. She was left with no choice.

"I'll need some time to prepare," Alex said, but Val had lost the conversational thread.

"See that, already she's backpedaling," June said to Val. "Care to join?"

"Me? At the pup cup bake-off?" Val said. "No thanks."

"Try to keep up," Alex said. "We've moved on to planning our tennis match. Do you want to be our ball girl?"

"I'll leave playing fetch to the dogs, thanks."

"Alex is just being mean," June said. "You can sit in the stands sipping a Honey Deuce while I run her ragged around the court."

"Give me a week," Alex said. "That's all the practice I'll need and then we can invite everyone from the park to watch me triumph."

This would be perfect, actually. "Sounds like a can't-miss ticket," Val said. "Tell me when and where."

That's right, give me the exact time and place.

Val didn't want to break into Alex's apartment, but if she had to, best to do it when she knew Alex would be busy keeping her eye on the wrong ball.

CHAPTER 8

Alex was burning off some nervous energy in the healthiest, most therapeutically violent way she could—by grappling with a six-foot-three, two-hundred-twenty-five-pound former military man who currently had her in a choke hold—when her cell phone chimed.

It had long been Alex's habit to keep her cell on vibrate or forget it on silent for hours, maybe even days at a time. Then she started this new life and the volume got turned up loud all day and all night. She assigned June a unique tone for calls and texts—a soft, comforting murmur that somehow captured her essence, so that she would know immediately, during any activity, when it was June desiring her attention.

Erin Kelly, Alex's contact at the FBI, also had her own ringtone. Hers was bossy and direct, like Erin herself. This was the sound that rang out now.

Gilad resented the interruption even more than Alex, but he released her from the hold. By now, he knew about Erin—how everything with her was considered time-sensitive, whether it really was or wasn't—so he accepted the alert as a time-out whistle or end-of-round bell.

"She'll be here in five," Alex said. "Let's call it a day."

"You can stretch for five." Gilad tossed a foam roller the size of a tree log at Alex's chest. He was a man of few words, but always made his intentions clear, which Alex appreciated.

It felt good to be back at the gym, breathing in the familiar blend of diffused eucalyptus and sweat, even though it meant having to lie to June about being too busy with "work stuff" to make it to the dog park for a few days. How strange and wonderful it was for Alex to have to account for her whereabouts this way. In just a few short weeks she had made a home of sorts at the park, and in June she had found someone who actually noticed when she was absent.

Missed you at the park today, June might text when Alex didn't show. Or, just before the happy hour, a message might come in saying *Hope to see you soon!*

Wasn't that lovely? Maybe it should have worried Alex somewhat. It certainly made sneaking around more difficult, but if Alex was being honest, she wouldn't trade it for the world.

Still, she needed to be careful. Alex hadn't come all the way to New York just to exercise. The martial arts gym on Madison and Seventy-Seventh also served as the place Alex and Erin met when they needed to discuss their unofficial business. The location was fairly private, because it was a personal training space, but the fact that Alex owned it made it truly secure.

When they set this as their regular meeting spot, Alex disliked having to reveal to Erin that she had bought the building she wanted to work out in, indulgent as it seemed. She could have explained that her longtime Krav Maga trainer, Gilad, needed a new space to work with his students, that his previous landlord had jacked up his rent, that although she paid the bills, it was his to run as he saw fit. But what business of Erin's was it anyway? Let her make whatever judgmental comments she wished; she always had an opinion on something.

It was laughable at this point that Alex and Erin had ever tried to date one another—for about five minutes, when they first met in New York, just after Alex graduated from Wharton and Erin from John Jay College of Criminal Justice—but Erin did have some admirable qualities. If she believed in something, it was with her whole heart, and if you crossed someone she loved, well, good luck. Alex always thought of Erin as the person she'd most want to be with if she accidentally got into a bar fight. She was solid and strong, with a loyal hardiness that could only come from growing up in an Irish Catholic household with three bruiser brothers who worked in law enforcement or firefighting.

Erin's professional focus at the FBI was fraud in the context of corporate crime, but she had a special place in her heart for the psychology of criminal behavior and criminal minds. Diagnosing—and rediagnosing—the enigma that was Alex Reed remained a favorite pastime.

"How's your mental health been?" was a question Erin always managed to squeeze into their conversations, which annoyed Alex to no end. Another was "Have you had any meaningful relationships since we last spoke?"

"I've been doing fine," Alex would reply, and then they could give up on the small talk and get to whatever it was they needed.

One day, about a year and a half earlier, shortly after her father died, Alex threw a monkey wrench into their usual, predictable back-and-forth. Alex had an idea, a vision of a new life for herself in the wake of the loss of her father—a life of service and courage, but she couldn't embark on it alone. She would need Erin's assistance.

When John Reed passed away, he shocked the world (and Alex) by not leaving her his full fifty-percent stake in Reed Industries. She was, however, the sole heir to his fortune. This rendered Alex wealthier than any person should be, but with little to no actual power in the company that bore her surname. She became a figurehead at the quarterly board meetings she continued to attend to this day—meetings where she would learn about whatever new morally repugnant mess the company was making, without being able to do a damned thing about it.

Perhaps Alex shouldn't have been surprised by getting "screwed in the will," as the crasser talking heads on Fox News had put it. In retrospect, she should have seen it coming. Alex kept her opinions on her father's politics out of the public conversation, along with her feelings about her family's history of profit over planetary welfare, but privately, she and John Reed never saw eye to eye.

It was no secret within the family—among her father, her uncle William, and her cousin Brandon—that Alex "struggled." Behind her back, they called her spoiled, lazy, aimless.

The truth was that Alex did lack purpose. She wasn't comfortable with her privilege or her family's legacy, or her role within it. But if she couldn't commit to their mission, what then was her reason for getting out of bed every day?

After John Reed's death, she figured out the answer. She decided to take a stand. Quietly, silently. If she kept her public face neutral, her official role impartial, she could actively work to take Reed Industries apart, step by step, piece by piece. With her inside knowledge of the company's most rotten apples and most egregious offenses—mainly in the realm of environmental transgressions—Alex envisioned herself a turncoat, a clandestine corporate spy.

As long as she maintained her access to the rooms where decisions were made and deals bartered, she would continue to have ears and eyes on all their transgressions.

But she also needed to bring Erin into the fold—someone with bureaucratic power to whom she could hand off her hard-earned evidence, who could file public charges, issue fines, put bad guys behind bars.

Because of Erin's relentless ambition, she was not hard to convince. Alex would do the dirty work, and Erin would do the rest, including taking all the credit.

Alex's ultimate goal was to wrest control of the company from her uncle and cousin, but it would take years to get there. She needed to start small and build a case against William and Brandon over time. Otherwise, the hatchet would always fall on some minion, leaving the head of the dragon intact.

The first mission Alex would embark on would need to be low-hanging fruit. This was how she homed in on a striving and corrupt EPA official by the name of Silas Kennerson.

Since Alex and Erin began collaborating, it was the best they had ever gotten along. And yet, Erin's constant opinions and wry comments on every little thing continued to drive Alex mad.

Earlier this morning, when Erin arrived for their meeting, dressed for work in a navy blue pantsuit and heels, her hair tied up in a no-nonsense bun, she had taken one look at the beagle penned into a makeshift play area and said, "What the heck is that?"

"That's Bruce," Alex replied. "He is a dog."

"You really are taking this vigilante alter-ego baloney too far," Erin opined, "if you named that thing after Bruce Wayne."

"He came with the name," Alex shot back as she led Erin to the small office at the rear of the gym. It was a spartan setup composed of a desk, a few chairs, and some file cabinets, but it served their purposes fine.

Alex proceeded to tell Erin the reason she requested the meeting.

Back on the day Alex had collected festival donations with June and Val, the three of them had walked together to their cars. Alex stopped to admire Val's 1974 Chevy Nova, which was, in truth, awesome, but she also used the opportunity, while appreciating its front end, to glance at the car's license plate and memorize its number.

When she got back to her apartment, she reached out to her contact at the NYPD, who was far less cautious and paranoid than Erin, and asked him to run the plate and a basic background check.

"Her legal name isn't Valerie Caruso. It's Valeria De Luca," he said when he called back. "No active warrants. Various juvenile offenses, nothing major as an adult. Served community service for breaking and entering, three-year probation for assault."

It was validating in a way, being right that Val couldn't be trusted, but Alex was also sorry her instincts had been correct. She found herself coming up with forgivable reasons for Val to lie about her name and be guarded about her checkered past. Maybe she was genuinely trying for a fresh start. People deserved second chances.

None of this had to mean much regarding Alex's intentions with June, or the Silas mission at all, but she still figured Erin should be looped in.

"I don't like this one bit," Erin had said, just as Alex expected she would. "Give me a few hours and I'll do a full vetting. And when I return, you have some explaining to do about the new dog."

Now, Erin was back—same suit, same bun, but this time carrying a decoy gym bag.

She greeted Bruce by name upon entering, nodded hello to Gilad, and high-heeled across the mat flooring, saying to Alex, "To the Batcave, Robin."

She could be such an ass sometimes.

Alex followed her into the office. She opened the mini fridge wedged into a corner, took out two bottles of green juice, and handed one to Erin. "I take it you found something."

Erin unzipped her gym bag and handed Alex a folder. "It's all in there. Summary page on top."

Alex took a seat and paged through photocopies of old newspaper headlines: *Man with Domestic Violence History Accused of Shooting and Killing Wife*; *Queens Man who Murdered Wife Gets 20 Years to Life in Prison*.

On the top sheet of paper, Erin had written a concise and dismal outline: *Father, Gianni De Luca—career criminal; Mother, Rosetta De Luca—in and out of hospitals for mental illness; Father killed mother when Valeria was 17 years old.* She had double underlined the sentence *Suspected involvement with organized crime.*

One glance at the included photographs and Alex had to set the folder down. "This is horrible. These pictures . . ."

"I guess I should have trigger-warned you about the gruesome crime scene photos," Erin said. "My bad."

"She told me her parents died in a car accident," Alex said. "I can kind of understand why."

"She's a con artist. Everything she told you is probably a lie."

Erin uncapped her juice, took a sip, and made a sour face. "My guess is she's working someone at that dog park of yours."

"It could only be June," Alex said. "She's always buzzing around June. But if it's money she's after, there are way richer people she could target there."

"Then it's something else she's after. And you are in over your head." Erin recapped her juice, handed it back to Alex. "You need to let this one go, or find a different way to get to Silas, far away from Val. On the bright side, at least you got a dog out of it."

"I can't give up now," Alex said.

"Don't be silly," Erin said. "Of course you can."

"I've already come too far."

Erin looked hard into Alex's eyes. "Oh no. Please tell me you didn't sleep with her."

"I didn't!"

"But you want to."

"I don't," Alex said. "Believe me."

Of course, the thought had crossed Alex's mind, if only for a moment. Physically, Alex could admit, Val was eye-catching. Her personality, though, was another story.

"Then what is it?" Erin asked. "You want to save her?"

"Erin, enough. Please."

Erin took on the air of a teacher with an insolent student. "I know you think you know what you're doing, but you have no formal training, and Val's associates may be extremely dangerous. I can't with good conscience allow you to continue."

"Like you could stop me?"

"Alex, your crazy is showing."

Here we go, Alex thought.

"Law enforcement isn't some thrill-seeking hobby," Erin chided. "You could get yourself killed. Do you understand that?"

Whatever the reason, Alex, who feared so much, didn't feel the least bit afraid.

"Have you considered," Erin said, "what could happen if Val finds out who *you* really are?"

Alex tossed her empty green-juice bottle across the room, square into the trash can. "That's not going to happen."

"Good hand-eye coordination isn't going to help you with this, dumbass."

"That reminds me," Alex said. "I've got a tennis match to prepare for."

CHAPTER 9

June knew she would lose. As she put on her best old tennis whites, the dress she had worn while lifting trophies overhead, and her outdated but still perfectly broken-in hard-court sneakers, she could feel in her heart that she had already given Alex the match.

The fact of the matter was that June was excellent at tennis, most likely eons ahead of Alex—unless Alex was a total ringer—but she didn't have it in her to show up her newest friend. The first real friend she'd made in years.

Once upon a time, as a junior player, going pro seemed like a possibility for June. Natural talent was said to be there, and she had the physical strength and stamina necessary. The only thing she lacked, apparently, was will.

"You have to be a fighter," her coach used to say. "You've got to be relentless. It's kill or be killed."

June wasn't a killer. Domination made her uncomfortable. Instead of tightening the grip on an opponent who was smashing their racket in frustration, maybe even near tears, June would instead lighten up and start spraying her shots. No need to humiliate someone already struggling, and, on some level, she would start to feel proud of them if they started to fight back and regain their footing.

Even if her competition turned things around and took the lead, somewhere deep inside, June would feel like she had accomplished something more meaningful—on a larger scale, for that person's identity and confidence, and humanity—than winning a silly match that didn't matter much at all when you thought about it.

June supposed this said something crucial about her personality. That she was a weakling at her core, maybe, or that she could be too selfless, to the point of losing sight of herself and being taken advantage of by others. That she struggled with being assertive and often felt powerless to affirm her right to be respected.

Granted, this was not the mindset of a professional athlete, but it made June June, and she couldn't change it, or didn't want to, because it was the kind of person she would rather be in the world. She worried some about those losing-is-not-an-option types who would do anything to prevail, die for it on court if they had to. Were they okay? But then again, she bet none of them would ever be so passive as to find themselves flaccidly enduring a marriage they secretly feared was doomed, so maybe she was the one who wasn't okay.

When Alex stepped on court, June could see she was taking this seriously. Dressed in head-to-toe black, chiseled arms out and proud in a muscle tee, intimidation was what she was going for, but she was stiff warming up, her motion tight, which meant to June that she was too tense to be playing her best.

June never mentioned her former national ranking to Alex. What would have been the point? It was ancient history, and besides, it had only ever spooked people into bowing out of playing her, people who moments earlier were willing to have a friendly go on court. But as the two of them continued warming up, June got the sense that Alex would not have been deterred. In fact, June began to wonder if Alex herself had been ranked.

"Is there something you're not telling me?" she asked, finally, from across the net.

Alex's grin was conspiratorial. "Like what?"

"Did you play in college? Or have a rating?"

"Nah," Alex said. "I never had that kind of commitment."

Alex didn't return the question, which surprised June, until it occurred to her that Alex must have already known. A simple internet query, and it would have all been displayed before her.

June never thought to look people up. Perhaps she was old-fashioned that way, but it seemed like a crass invasion of someone's privacy; a window didn't have to be gawked at just because the blinds were up. Unlike ogling a neighbor through a curtain slit, however, Google searching was—for some reason—considered socially acceptable.

Alex tossed a coin to start the match. Heads, she won and opted to receive. June served her first ball into the net, and Alex heckled her playfully.

The smell of the court alone gave her a blast of endorphins. Her body began moving all on its own, her muscles remembering every detail of instruction so her conscious mind didn't have to.

June's second serve was an ace that left Alex flat-footed.

"Okay," Alex said. "Game on." She got down low, swaying side-to-side, hungry for battle.

How long had it been since June had gripped a racket, swung through a ball? Five years, maybe six? Her relationship with time had gotten warped once she reached her thirties. What had she been doing with herself if not this? Cooking meat for Silas, June supposed, making the bed, and washing out coffee cups. Going to the dog park like clockwork, day in and day out. Getting older. Feeling older.

Meryl and Kennedy had come to watch, as they'd promised they would. Across the way, with a squint though the chain-link fence, was the dog park, where Ava had volunteered to watch Willow and Bruce. It was a generous offer, but it did not offer much peace of mind considering how poorly she monitored Popcorn. To compensate, June asked Mrs. Pearlberg, who had taught Silas in elementary school, to keep an additional, more reliable, eye on the dogs while she and Alex played. And then, to be extra safe, June also asked Regina to call her cell if any issues arose.

Alex didn't appear too concerned about leaving Bruce in someone else's care while she zipped around the court with speed and impressive agility. She was dictating the first set, a break ahead, with absolute brutality in her shotmaking. June knew Alex was in her early forties, but she wouldn't know it by looking at her, especially in her tennis getup. She could have easily passed for thirty-five. By the way she moved on court, maybe even twenty-five.

Alex had said the reason she hadn't played tennis seriously was because she couldn't commit, but June recognized that tiger look in Alex's eyes. She was the sort who morphed into a different form in competition. Girls like this in June's junior days would be all smiles and pats on the back in the locker room; out in the real world they might be goofballs or practical jokers. Then, the moment the ref said *play*, they became unrecognizable, stopping at nothing to dismantle their dear friend turned opponent, piece by piece.

Alex had a body serve that could take off your limb if you didn't move away from it fast enough. Her forehand slice cut like a knife.

Tennis was a uniquely lonely and psychological game. It required precision, mental toughness, the ability to excel under pressure, and the perfect balance between tension and relaxation. With no teammate to help you up when you fell, to say *shake it off, you've got this*, it revealed an individual's true colors like no other sport. And what Alex's game showed June was that Alex was a killer.

Where was her anxiety disorder now, June wondered, as Alex broke her for a second time to win the first set. What happened to her nervous deliberation and low self-worth?

In a way June would rather not admit, Alex was a lot like Silas on the tennis court. Alex was a far better player, fundamentally, but in mentality they were eerily similar. They even displayed some of the same obsessive or superstitious habits, like not stepping on lines when walking on or off court and refusing to make eye contact during water breaks.

When they first got together, June and Silas had stopped playing after only a few matches because the disconnect between his talent and drive made for some ugly scenes, and when June began throwing games it only insulted him and made him angrier.

"I hope you're not going easy on me," Alex said just before the start of the second set.

June felt her cheeks blush. She was, just a little.

"I told you I quit tennis and went with soccer, right?" was June's reply. "Now you understand why."

Then June really did start to play poorly. Just like the old days, down another break in the second set, her mental chatter drifted toward how well her opponent was playing, how Alex wanted and deserved the win more than she did.

This would have been the point in a team sport, like a soccer match, when a coach might sub her out, or the captain would come say something encouraging or funny, and, just like that, she'd care about winning again—for the team. To make them happy, to make them proud.

June needed a team. Someone else, other than herself, to fight for.

When she gave up tennis for soccer, she immediately excelled as the ultimate "team player," surprising defenders with passes that any other forward would have taken themselves as a shot on goal. She led the league in assists every year she played. Assists were June's glory, and the selflessness that hindered her entire tennis career became her superpower.

This taught June a valuable lesson. Being part of a group was more conducive to her personality than being alone. Which made it sadly ironic how alone she had found herself in her daily adult life.

But here she was hanging out with her new friend, who could be a bit inscrutable at times and a tad socially awkward, and who, even in the short time they had known each other, had displayed some high highs and low lows that were concerning—but June was not one to judge. It wasn't like she was a model of mental health and emotional moderation. After all, June was the one throwing a no-stakes tennis match because she found winning embarrassing.

Meryl and Kennedy cheered extra loudly for Alex when she dove for the net to save a drop shot, skinning her knees bloody in the effort.

"I've got some Band-Aids in my purse," Meryl called out, but Alex waved her off. Nothing could distract her from the task at hand, certainly not blood running down her shins in two horrific streaks.

Alex also made no mention of—or perhaps hadn't noticed—Bruce's constant howling from the edge of the park. It was a distinct, moribund sound, unmistakable. He was obviously in distress, but June felt it wasn't her place to comment on it if Alex chose not to.

Then June's cell phone rang.

Well, it took you long enough, June wanted to say to Regina but didn't. She simply relayed the message to Alex that Bruce was having an issue with their separation.

"He won't move from the gate," June explained. "He's crying out for your attention. He sees where you are but doesn't understand why."

Alex suggested they try to finish the match quickly, but June instead offered Alex a handshake.

"I forfeit," she said. "I was going to lose anyway."

There was a dead racoon in the middle of the road. Driving along Beekman Avenue, on her way to Alex's apartment, Val gasped at the sight. She swerved her tires around it, clutching her heart.

Her heart hurt. Physically. Not metaphorically, in some poetry kind of way. Even though, as a kid, Val and her father used to play an I-Spy game on car trips, calling out roadkill much like this one, and at the time, Val had felt the grislier the better. She would laugh and howl, *Eeew that one was really gross! Did you see the eyeballs, Dad?* feeling nothing but delight.

Years of playing that game made it so Val couldn't help but notice a dead animal on the pavement, conditioned as she was to catch the sight from any corner of her eye, same as she would the pale green of paper money or the shine of a lost quarter.

One nice thing about the dog park was that no one gave a crap if you were unmarried or childless, a big talker or cryptically quiet, a little bit kooky or a lot—as long as you were a person with the capacity to love an animal. Even at this, though, Val didn't measure up. Worse, she just didn't get it—the weird obsession the park people had with their pets, the way they projected onto them the most unlikely human characteristics. *Buster refuses to wear blue, his favorite color is green. Bella insists I leave MSNBC on for her when I leave the house.* Yeah, okay.

Animal-loving in general struck Val as hypocritical when it came to anyone but the strictest vegans. In her mind, you shouldn't be allowed to have it both ways, celebrating your dog's birthday with pupcakes while also serving hamburgers and hot dogs.

And so, it came as a shock just now that her heart could ache, even momentarily, for something as familiar and ordinary as a flattened raccoon. The reason, which came to her in a flash, was even more alarming. The little furry body and whiskery face, the tiny paws. It may as well have been Cash splayed out in the road. All Val could see in this random wild animal's violent demise was her dog.

Or *the* dog. The one that wasn't really hers in the sense that people meant it.

"The dog" was how Val's mother used to refer to the mixed-breed terrier Gianni had once brought home from God only knew where—one story went that he won him in a card game. Val had called the dog Cuddles, but she was the only one to ever use the name. To her parents he was only ever "the dog," or "that filthy animal," or "that hairy mutt."

Cuddles wasn't trained or well-behaved, but he was smart. Within days of joining their family, he wisely refused to eat any food Rosetta set out for him, seemingly in fear of being poisoned. That right there was good instinct. And, even though he was supposed to be an "outside dog," he would often find ways into the apartment that baffled the rest of them. That winter was especially cold, a few nights with the temperature dropping so low that Rosetta had to grant the filthy animal an overnight stay indoors—or else the neighbors might "get on their asses." But they needed to be careful to not spoil him, Rosetta told Val specifically, "or else he might start to think he's a real dog." Val took her mother to mean that Val herself would also not be spoiled, or else she might start to think she was a real kid.

Then, one day, Cuddles was gone. When Val asked where he was, Gianni told her he gave the dog to a friend who lived on a big farm where he could run and play. *What friend?* Val wanted to know. She had never heard of them knowing anyone with a farm. Was it here in Queens? Could they go visit? Gianni was never one to be patient with questions, so, finally, he said, *Go ask your mother*, which Val did. Rosetta told her the dumb mutt had run away.

Rosetta had been "forgetting" to close the gate since Cuddles had arrived. *You did it on purpose*, Val had said, but accusation was the wrong choice when it came to Rosetta. The response young Val received was swift and stung her cheek, bringing immediate tears to her eyes. Conversation over.

Val forced her mind back to the present as she pulled into a parking spot not too far from Alex's front door.

A major bonus of Alex pretending to reside in a second-rate apartment complex was how easy it was for Val to blend in with the residents. Nobody here was going to ask too many questions.

The door locks were child's play. Literally: Val had learned to pick dead bolts on the same model. She wore a ball cap low on her forehead to obscure her face, but there wasn't a camera in sight, or out of sight, as far as she could tell. If that weren't enough, she also had all the time in the world. Tennis matches tended to run long, and even if Alex and June's didn't, she should still have as many as forty minutes to spare, considering the humble square footage before her.

Where to begin? Val started with the obvious hiding places for items people didn't want found. The back of the nightstand drawer, under the mattress, behind picture frames and in between books on the shelf. Closets could be veritable carnivals of skeletons, but not this one. Nothing, nada, zilch.

Fine. Second-tier searching was where things started to get fun, knocking for false wall panels and loose floorboards. Val had been at this all her life. The likelihood of someone coming up with a place to stash booty that she hadn't already thought of was little to none.

Val had left Cash home alone to conduct this reconnaissance mission. She taped a preemptive note on her apartment door that read *Be right back! Sorry for the noise.* So, this search had better yield results and quickly.

Knock, knock. What was that hollow sound on the outer left side of the bed frame?

Wouldn't you know, when she felt around its perimeter, her fingers discovered a thin seam on the underside of the wood.

Alex had tricked out the bed in her rental unit? Not bad. Val admired the effort as she popped off the sideboard and discovered a treasure trove. Papers mostly, a few bottles of pills. Then a thick folder on Silas Kennerson.

Ha! Val gave herself a pat on the back. Was anyone better at their job than she was?

She took a moment to page through the Silas folder. Lots of

numbers, diagrams, and charts that didn't register with her, but she got the takeaway, which was that Alex was trying to figure out if the man was a crook.

As for the pill bottles, well, well, well. Hello, controlled substances, antidepressants and anti-anxiety meds—all prescribed to the name of Alexandra Reed.

Reed? Alex Reed. Aaalex Reeeed, now why was that name familiar?

Val looked the name up on her phone, revealing a scroll's worth of page links about Reed Industries.

A fuzzy image came to mind. The all-day news channel on full blast back when Val was working a job at the Riverside Senior Center. On screen, a gray-haired man and his adult daughter, above the caption: *John Reed, billionaire industrialist, dies leaving sole heir.*

Val knew about John Reed, of course, for his ultraconservatism, outsized political influence, and general villainy, and she was familiar with Reed Industries as a synonym for everything wrong with America, and she was vaguely aware of the daughter—but it just now all came together and struck Val in the head like a meteor.

Holy Mary Mother of God. Alex Miller was Alex Reed.

In a way, it made perfect sense. Alex's perfect teeth and skin, stylish haircut, and patrician features mixed with her discount store wardrobe and generic car. Only now could Val put her finger on it—Alex looked like a rich person trying to pass as a regular person.

Val should go, get out of here now. Who knew what kind of security someone of Alex's means might have? But there was another paper-filled folder stuffed into the bed frame, and this one—wait. This one had Val's own name on it. Her real name.

June couldn't help but notice Alex's reluctance as she followed her from the tennis courts to the dog run, still with her racket in hand. She was clearly displeased their match had to be ended early. But at first sight of Bruce, she softened a bit.

The moment they passed through the gate, Bruce jumped on Alex, manically happy to have her back and refusing to leave her side.

"He's feeling anxious," June pointed out to Alex, as if it weren't obvious. "You can understand that, can't you?"

A shadow fell across Alex's face. "Are you saying I made him anxious?"

"What? No, of course not." June laughed, but that did not help.

All at once Alex became as flustered as Bruce. "I think I should take him home," she said, and then repeated herself. "I think I should take him home right now."

"Why?" June tried to stop her. "He'll be back to normal in a sec, everything's fine. Just show him a little love, make him feel secure."

In saying so, June was trying to show Alex a little love, too, and make her realize she was in a safe space here with June.

But Alex could not be dissuaded. Off she went, the back of her muscle tee wet with equal parts post-game triumph and panicky flop sweat.

Val's heart pounded in her ears as she rifled through printouts of her own life story. Copies of stark official documents, ugly summarized accounts, crime scene photographs . . . and she was a helpless kid once more, her parents fighting as they always did—dishes flying, glass smashing, the threats, the gun. She was ducking behind a piece of furniture when he pulled the trigger. She heard the sound now exactly as she had that day, but the images that followed were fragmentary and illogical. The memories were all there, but in pieces, like her ability to make sense of what she had seen had also gotten blown to bits.

But the feelings came right back. The sheer terror, yes, but also the sense that she had known it was coming and did nothing to stop it. Standing here now, mesmerized by the pages in her hands, Val was too late all over again. Just like in her recurring nightmare, the one where everyone is alive, and has been all these years, and then—*boom*—it happens, and Dream Val's immediate thought is *I had all this time to do things differently, and yet I still did them the same.* Her mother is dead, her is father carted away, and she is the sole witness, with specks of blood on her face and clothes.

How could Alex have this information? These photos? And why?

Val was so caught off guard that she didn't hear the key enter the lock or the door swing open.

CHAPTER 10

When Alex stepped through the doorway and saw a person across the room, she initially thought she had entered the wrong apartment. If Bruce hadn't bolted toward the obscured figure she may have apologized, turned around, and checked the number on the door.

Instead, Bruce was first and foremost in Alex's mind when she charged forward, registering that this stranger, this intruder, could have a knife or a gun and it only took one second for tragedy to strike. Whether she herself lived or died mattered far less than protecting him.

With all her might, the weight of her full body and soul, Alex hurled herself onto the foreign body, slamming them against the wall and then punching, punching, punching.

It was messier and more hysterical than any practice fight with her trainer, and when a fist came flying back at her, hard into her face, it hurt like no rehearsal could have. Alex fell backward, stunned, unable to see for a moment, but when her vision returned—

"You?"

Val was holding the side of her face, at about the same spot that throbbed on Alex's own. Her big brown eyes were wild with fury.

"Fuck you for that folder you have on me," Val said.

Alex ran her tongue over her teeth to make sure they were all still there.

A winding line of red trickled down Val's lips and chin. Alex hobbled toward a box of tissues on a side table, plucked five or six, and handed them to Val. "Don't get blood on the carpet."

"I know who you are." Val accepted the tissues. "And you can afford to buy the owners a new one."

Oh shit, Alex thought.

With the drop in adrenaline, the pain coursing through Alex's body and the stinging cuts on her hands became unbearable. She went to the freezer to get some ice. Only then did she notice Bruce cowering beneath the kitchen table.

"Great," she called out to Val. "You traumatized my dog."

Val helped herself to an ice pack and tossed one to Alex while Alex tried to comfort Bruce and lure him out. Somewhere on the floor was the cap she had been wearing. Her dark hair was half out of its ponytail. "I should sue you for this." Val dropped into one of Alex's kitchen chairs, looking like a boxer in the corner of a ring.

"You broke into my apartment!" Alex sat across from her.

"I was just doing my job," Val said. She released her hair from its loose tie, letting it fall onto her shoulders.

"What is your real job exactly?" Alex asked. "Tell the truth, and I won't call the police on you."

"I'm a PI." Val relocated her ice pack from her nose to her cheek. "Silas hired me to get evidence of June's affair, which I thought she was having with you, but clearly there is no affair. I might have packed it in and collected my fee at that point, except you are shady as hell and I'm not leaving till I figure out what your deal is."

"Mission accomplished," Alex said. "Congratulations."

"Not even close." Val gestured toward the papers strewn across the floor. "How'd you get all that?"

Stunned into silence, Alex could barely look at those photos another time. Despite the predicament in which she now found herself, she had the urge to reach out to Val and hold her.

Val rose her voice. "I asked you how there is a collage of my worst memories all over your floor right now."

"I have friends," Alex said.

"You do not, liar."

"I have contacts in high places."

"Finally, an honest word comes out of your mouth." Val got up to toss her bloody tissues into the trash. "What do you want from me?"

"Nothing. My target is Silas."

"Then why do you have . . ." Val turned again to the papers on the floor. One of the crime scene photos of her mother's body was lying face up.

"I'm sorry about that," Alex said, and she meant it. She abandoned her ice pack to pick up the whole mess of documents from the floor and return them to their folder. "I didn't know who you were, but I could tell you didn't add up, so I had a contact at the FBI check you out. I didn't mean to—"

"None of that's any of your business," Val said.

"It isn't, I know." Alex sandwiched the folder shut.

Alex had only looked through the folder's contents once, which she almost said, but what kind of defense was that? She didn't need to see those images ever again for them to be lodged in her mind—the battered teenager Val had been, one who watched her father murder her mother in cold blood.

This was the person Alex had just been punching in the face.

"I'm really sorry—"

"Stop apologizing," Val said.

But Alex couldn't help it. She felt differently toward Val after learning the horrid details of her life. She wanted to show her kindness, whereas before she had only found her somewhat crude and vaguely unpleasant.

"Why are you keeping tabs on Silas?" Val asked.

Alex sat back down. "Because he's a corrupt megalomaniac who, despite all appearances, cares nothing about the environment. He needs to be stopped before he gets any more powerful than he already is."

Val smirked. "You have looked in the mirror, right? Alex *Reed*."

"You must be confusing me with my father," Alex said. "Or my uncle, or cousin. I'm the good-for-nothing living a life of leisure with no actual power."

Val contemplated this. "Correct me if I'm wrong, but doesn't Reed Industries have a rap sheet longer than my arm? Aren't they always getting in trouble for environmental violations?"

"Yup," Alex said.

"Doesn't that make you a bit of a hypocrite?"

"Yup," Alex said.

Of course there was more to it than that. That Alex was also a traitor, a mole, going after her own company from the inside, sabotaging her father's legacy in the process. But part of Alex taking on this task meant knowing how to keep her mouth shut. Allowing others to form erroneous opinions about her was part of the job.

Another part Val was missing was the debilitating guilt Alex lugged around every day of her life. Not only for the ungodly amount of money in her name, but for the blood on the hands of those who acquired it.

When Alex's grandfather began building his company, it was not fully understood how much the overuse of fossil fuels contributed to destroying the planet, but it was becoming clearer by the time her father took over and expanded the business tenfold. Their decisions weren't her decisions—Alex was her own person—and yet their fortune was her fortune. She benefited in countless ways from them always putting profit first, from the clothes on her back to the education she received, to the places she'd visited, to the free time and space in her brain to dwell on all of it.

Alex once heard it said that there was no such thing as an innocent billionaire but there was a special place in hell for oil and gas industry billionaires. Maybe this was the hell she was already living in—until she made it right.

If all went according to plan, eventually it would all be gone, every cent and asset, but for now she was complicit.

"Is Silas involved with Reed Industries?" Val asked.

Alex nodded. "They've made some deals in the past."

"Is that why you're targeting Silas specifically?"

It was.

"Silas is only one man, I get that," Alex said. "But he's in a critical role, in a larger system that needs to be dismantled."

"And you're the one who's going to do the dismantling?"

Alex shrugged.

"The larger system you speak of must include Reed Industries."

Alex didn't answer.

Val leaned back in her chair, crossed her arms over her chest, pleased with herself. "Because if I recall correctly, wasn't there some issue when your father passed away, of him not leaving you the company?"

It surprised Alex that Val would know this detail.

"He didn't not leave me the company," Alex explained. "What he did was not leave me all his shares of the company, which would have given me equal power to my uncle William."

"Who did he give the shares to instead?"

"He split them between me and my cousin Brandon, William's son."

"In other words," Val said. "He didn't leave you the company."

Alex felt her jaw tighten.

"So," Val said. "It's fair to say you have loftier goals in mind, and Silas is just one stepping stone."

Yes. But Silas was a big one as far as stepping stones went.

"Fine, I get it," Val said. "You want plausible deniability, but I can see by your panicked expression that I've hit the nail on the head. You're going after your own daddy's company—good on you. It's not my concern."

Damn right it wasn't.

"Tell me more about what Silas is doing at the EPA," Val said.

Alex relaxed slightly. This was a subject she was more comfortable discussing. "I've got reams of documents on his wrongdoings," she said. "An astounding amount of paper dating three job titles back. Finding a whistleblower at the EPA wasn't easy, but I've managed one—a scientist whose identity I've sworn never to reveal, in return for top-secret information. All this, but I still don't have enough."

Alex tossed her own and Val's melted ice packs into the kitchen sink and went to the fridge. "Want a seltzer?"

"Got anything stronger? My body's killing me."

"How about a seltzer and some Advil?"

"Sold."

Bruce, fully recovered, picked up his ball and brought it to the couch.

"The gist of what Silas is guilty of is simple," Alex said. "He's making unsafe chemicals appear to be safer than they are. His staff at the EPA's New Chemicals Division evaluate the risk posed by a chemical using two quantities—how toxic it's considered to be and how much of it the public would be exposed to. They do this by using a system that's been in place for decades. Until Silas came around. That's when senior staff began minimizing the estimates of a chemical's toxicity, as well as how much of it would be released into the environment. The pressure to do so was coming from the top."

Alex paused on account of Val's confused expression, then explained. "Silas is seeking out ways to approve more chemicals. Because limiting a chemical with warning labels and restrictions makes it harder for a company to sell. He doesn't want to displease these companies by hampering them with regulations."

"Companies like Reed." Val said.

"Among others."

"Is he accepting bribes?" Val asked.

"That's what I need to prove. What I'm certain of is that Silas is already plotting his post-agency job prospects, so he needs to stay on these companies' good sides."

"Think he's eyeing a future in politics?"

Alex nodded.

"Gross," Val said. "And he looks so innocent to the outside world, with those dreamy baby blues."

"He does," Alex agreed. "But he is anything but. I have printouts of emails of him instructing staff scientists to change the wording in their reports. Instead of classifying chemicals whose risk calculation they haven't measured as being *below modeling thresholds*, they're supposed to use the term *negligible* to describe their exposure—which implies there's no cause for concern, when in fact the chemical in question could be extremely unsafe."

Val was beginning to comprehend the extent of Silas's misconduct. "The flopsy-mopsy man is giving people cancer."

"Probably," Alex said.

"He puts up a good front," Val said. "I looked him up after he hired me and read all about his rags-to-riches story, blue-collar parents, pulling himself up by his bootstraps. He can pass for a real golden boy, tough not to root for."

"It's a nice origin story for any politician or crook," Alex said. "It's even true. That version just happens to leave out the part about carcinogens and his insatiable hunger for money and power."

Val's phone vibrated in her pocket. She checked it and said, "Cash is up and displeased. I've got to go before my neighbors call in the National Guard."

"You've got a camera on your dog?"

Val returned her phone to her pocket. "It's not a violation of her privacy rights."

Alex followed Val toward the door. "You won't say anything to June about any of this, will you?"

"I won't if you won't," Val said. "But I have to ask, why do all of this? Going after Silas, trying to take down Reed. What's in it for you?"

A point, Alex thought. *A purpose.* The only way she could think of to make amends.

"What now?" Alex asked, ignoring Val's question. She reached down to pick up Val's cap, which had been knocked to the floor during their scuffle, and handed it to her. "You stay out of my way, I stay out of your way?"

Val returned the cap to her head and reached for the doorknob, then paused. "Unless we work together."

Alex laughed.

"You need me," Val continued, straight-faced. "You don't even realize how much you need me. I'm way better at this kind of thing than you are."

"You want to team up?" Alex asked.

"I want you to hire me," Val said. "Match Silas's rate, plus ten percent. I know you have it."

"I admire your directness," Alex said.

"It's one of my best and worst qualities," Val replied.

Alex was tempted, but unsure. "How do I know I can trust you?"

Val's phone vibrated again. Cash was losing patience. "I don't like you much either," Val said. "But that doesn't mean we can't join forces for this one specific purpose."

Val opened the door. "Sleep on it. But it's the only logical answer. Otherwise, I'm afraid we might kill each other."

CHAPTER 11

Val woke up an hour before Cash started groaning for her breakfast. Her body felt like she might as well have had a hatchet wedged into her scalp and a pile of bricks bearing down her chest. It was the weight, all over again, of what Alex knew. The folder she had, the crime scene photographs.

When Alex looked at her now, tragedy was all she'd see.

Not that Val cared much what Alex thought of her, but she hated having anyone look at her that way. She didn't want to be defined by her misfortune, even if it made her who she was more than anything else.

After Cash polished off her breakfast—a broken-up patty, whose packaging flaunted a composition of 85 percent venison, organ, and bone—Val hid in the kitchen with the water running so she could eat the remainder of last night's chicken sandwich.

One of the only times Cash left Val alone was when she was washing dishes, so that's what she was pretending to do while quietly unwrapping the leftover sandwich from its wrapper and taking cold bites. Warming it up in the microwave would have given her away, so she gobbled it straight from the fridge.

Overall, this was how this whole job was going—Val had been tyrannized by a ten-pound dog to the point of sneaking food in her own kitchen—but later in the morning, during her phone call with Silas, Val said all was great. It had been almost a month since Silas had hired her, and even though she had come up with little evidence, she told him she was homing in on a few people at the dog park with whom June seemed extra friendly, particularly a handsome middle-aged fellow everyone referred to as the Silver Fox.

As far as shakedowns went, Val gave this one a B-plus.

"Is he on that committee she's been talking about?" Silas wanted to know. "Is the committee even real?"

"Oh yes," Val assured him. The lead-up to the fundraiser event was giving her way more opportunities to keep a close watch on June than if they were limited to interacting solely at the dog park. But not to worry, the Silver Fox was volunteering with a different subcommittee.

Silas was appeased and willing to continue paying Val for her services.

Now Val sat at her rental's IKEA desk, the LAGKAPTEN or maybe the VEBJÖRN, thinking again about her surprise encounter at Alex's apartment. Alex's fake apartment. Where it had been bombshell after bombshell, recon folders, a fist fight! And finally, the answer to who Val was dealing with.

Billionaire Alex Reed, what were the odds?

If Val believed in manifestation, she would be sure her father had a metaphysical hand in steering Alex her way. It was his dream scenario, the chance at a high-net-worth long con.

Gianni used to say that a grift was made where predisposition and opportunity met. Here Val was with both.

"Isn't that right?" Val looked down at Cash, who was pawing at her shins. "What did your grandpa teach us?"

"How to game any system," Val said in the high-pitched pretend Cash voice that she had somehow developed over these past weeks.

"That's correct!" Val picked Cash up and waved her paws around like a stuffed animal.

"How to lie and manipulate people," Val said as squeaky-voiced Cash, while actual Cash frowned, tight-lipped. "How to cheat at any competition."

"Excellent," she said to Cash. "You have been paying attention!"

Gianni would be so disappointed in Val now if he knew she was going to let this opportunity pass.

(Was she going to let this opportunity pass? Could she?)

But Gianni was the lifelong con artist, not Val. And how she was raised didn't have to influence every decision she made in her adult life, did it?

Consciously, the answer was no, but subconsciously, Val was less certain. She knew too much psychology to brush off the possibility that somewhere deep inside there was more to her suggesting she and Alex work together than just another paycheck. Val was intrigued by Alex. Alex was unusual, mysterious, strange in ways Val found appealing, but Val also couldn't deny being charmed by Alex's insane level of wealth. It made Val question if she could be trusted around a billionaire.

Val didn't trust herself around guns, so she didn't own a gun, even though her line of work often called for one. Did it follow that she should steer clear of Alex for her own well-being? There were far fewer billionaires in the world than there were firearms, and this was the first one Val had the opportunity to take into hand—so who could say?

Sometimes Val would watch Cash thrash a stuffed animal, mesmerized by the way she'd get the toy in her jaws and swing it to and fro, to break its neck like an unlucky rodent. Cash's nature in action. Before becoming a highly strung house pet, Cash's breed originated in Belgium as ratters. Even with years of domestication, this was the inevitable result—Cash brutally murdering a plush llama until its stuffing came loose. And it was an important reminder that even the cuddliest of pups were essentially wolves in dog clothing. No use denying it.

So, Val wondered, what was her own nature, considering her breeding? To what extent could she be fully domesticated?

That Val could feel empathy, guilt, and remorse was her one saving grace—conclusive evidence that she was not a clinical psychopath, as she suspected Gianni had been—and yet she also recognized that she did not feel those emotions in the same vibrant color as other people. Something inside her had gone dull.

It was a sad reflection of Val's internal life that she was still holding on to the reaction she'd had to that dead raccoon as proof of something. Her humanity? That her heart did in fact work as well as anyone else's?

Val also found herself caring about June. Sweet, sometimes-spacey, often-corny June deserved more in a husband than a man willing to trash the health of strangers and the planet for his own benefit. Normally it was Val's practice to keep an emotional distance from her clients and targets, but this job had clearly gotten to her. It had become two jobs, and she was now double-crossing one of the hands feeding her.

Val got a text from Alex and set Cash back on the floor to read it.

Hi. Any chance you can meet up to talk? Somewhere private and dog friendly if possible?

"Opportunity knocks," Val said to Cash.

To Alex, Val suggested the Hamilton Dog Park. *At this time of day,* she wrote, *it'll be empty.*

When Val went to the front closet for her leash, Cash's ears perked up and her expression turned alert.

"Want to go to the dog park?" Val asked.

In response, Cash went up on two legs and did a pirouette.

Val had read online that dogs could learn about 150 words and signals. Therefore, Cash, who was far more intelligent than average, must have a vocabulary of at least 2,500.

"Dog park?" Val said again. "Should we take an early trip to the dog park? And see your friend Bruce?"

This time Cash play-bowed and wiggled her truncated tail. Then she mad dashed for the front door.

"Now that you know Bruce is a billionaire," Val said to Cash as she attached her harness, "do you like him more or less?"

Cash let out an excited bark that, for better or worse, sounded to Val like *More!*

At twelve p.m. on a weekday, Hamilton Dog Park was a no-man's-land. The morning crowd was long gone, and the after-lunch shift hadn't yet arrived. Val and Alex had the whole field to themselves. With a singular exception.

"Does she actually just live here?" Alex asked Val.

Val followed Alex's gaze to where old Mrs. Pearlberg sat at her regular bench, with Virgil the German shepherd lying down beside her. It was a familiar, reliable sight Val had begun taking comfort in.

Alex seemed to feel otherwise. "It kind of freaks me out how we always see her here, but she never interacts with any of us."

Virgil rose when Cash and Bruce approached, politely allowing them a thorough sniff.

"Maybe she's a ghost," Val replied. "And Virgil is a ghost dog."

"Thanks, that's a big help." Alex attempted a friendly wave and received no response.

"I don't think she saw me," Alex said.

"I think she's a figment of our imaginations," Val said, then moved to a shady spot beneath a tree.

Alex joined her. "Last night was a lot."

"It was," Val said, "but we're moving on. Today's a new day."

"For what it's worth, I destroyed what was inside your folder," Alex said. "I mean, the folder I had on you."

"Good. Now erase it from your memory and stop bringing it up."

"And I agree to your terms," Alex said. "You're hired."

Val held her facial expression at partway disinterested. "I think you're making the right decision," she said without fanfare, but in truth she found she was having trouble now looking at Alex with total neutrality.

All the ways Val could take advantage of Alex shuffled through her mind, one after another, as if she were flipping through a deck of cards. She could start simply, getting access to Alex's apartment, assessing the security situation, planting a few bugs. Eventually, she would gain entry into her bank accounts. Once Val had the full picture of Alex's fortune, the extent of her foundation holdings, dummy corporations, money she no doubt hid offshore—just the thought of it made Val's heart pound.

Alex was not Val's friend, Val had to remember. And, in fact, that she was struggling at all with the idea of conning Alex was no sign of growth—it was weakness. How could Val go on living her quaint, middle-class life after letting a chance like this slip by?

Val had read the books and seen the movies. She understood well the folly of a con artist coming out of criminal retirement for one final job. But continuing to pretend like she could be normal was the real fool's errand. Striving to be a better person on the outside than she was on the inside was exhausting. It was killing her. So, what did she really have to lose?

Val was not her father. But she was her father's daughter, unfortunately. And the truth was, she couldn't ask for a more perfect mark.

"Hiring me is going to be the best decision you ever made," Val said. "But you have to trust me."

Alex watched Cash and Bruce as Val went on. "The thing you most need on Silas, that you have yet to find, is something undeniably incriminating. A back-and-forth in an email, evidence of a secret bank account, anything proving some kind of quid pro quo is going on."

Alex agreed. "Erin, my contact at the FBI, said we'll only get one good shot at an indictment, so whatever I deliver has to be airtight."

How Alex had managed to convince a sworn member of the federal bureau to engage in such illegitimate activity was beyond Val. Though, had she ever known a G-man who wasn't a little bit crooked? If her own slender connection to organized crime had taught her anything, the answer was a resounding no. To this day, her septuagenarian landlord, Maria, kept a handful of law enforcement officers deep in the pocket of her housedress.

"To obtain that level of evidence," Val continued, "we'll need access to all of Silas's online activity, which means installing some malware onto his computer. His work computer at the EPA would be a challenge and way too risky, but I bet if we get into his personal laptop, we'll find something."

Alex stared ahead with a wide smile.

"What?" Val asked. "Do you already know a way to separate him from his laptop long enough to get the malware installed?"

"Look." Alex pointed to Bruce and Cash. "They play so well together."

It was true. Despite their size differential and Goofus and Gallant personalities, they were a perfect match. Gentlemanly Bruce was happy to take the courteous role of lying on his back while getting chomped on the neck by an overzealous Cash.

Val and Alex admired them from afar for a few moments before Val came to her senses.

"Can you please try to focus," she said. "You wanted a plan. This is the plan. We start by tracking Silas, learning his routines and habits, and that'll give us an idea of when we can get to his laptop without him noticing. We already know he commutes to DC every day except on weekends, and I know he carries a laptop with him to and from work. I noticed he had it on him when we first met, a black laptop bag strapped across his chest."

Val stopped there, unsure if Alex was listening. Her sharp green eyes were still on Bruce, who was now trying to get Cash to chase him, but Cash wanted Bruce to chase her. The result was a dance-floor improvisation that should have been set to tango music.

"It seems like this could take a while," Alex said.

"Doing any job right takes patience," Val replied, using one of Gianni's grammatically erroneous go-to refrains.

"I was talking about the dogs." Alex turned to her. "But I'll be honest, I've also never been great at having patience."

"That's shocking," Val said, "coming from a one-percenter."

She hadn't intended for the barb to come out sounding so harsh. But Alex smiled.

It occurred to Val then that Alex didn't mind being given shit for her privilege. It reinforced something about herself she believed warranted punishment.

"You're just jealous that my ancestors were better crooks than yours," Alex said.

"Ouch." Val hadn't seen that one coming. "The truth hurts."

Then both their cell phones dinged.

"Look who it is." Alex held up her phone.

It was June, sending a message to their group chat.

Hey gals! What are you up to this weekend? Silas will be in North Carolina for an EPA conference, and I'll be all by my lonesome. What would you say to a girls-and-dogs trip?

Val and Alex turned to one another in unison. Val spoke first. "Are you thinking what I'm thinking?"

"Martha's Vineyard?" Alex asked.

"For the mission," Val said, in a tone that caught Bruce and Cash's attention. They both turned their heads in Val's direction. "Not you," she called to them.

To Alex, she said, "We know where Silas will be this weekend, and a hotel will present all the opportunity I need to get into his room, try to get my hands on his laptop. This is a gift."

"Right," Alex said. "So we're going to follow him all the way to North Carolina?"

"Not *we*. Me." Val already found the web page about the conference on her phone. "There's a room block reservation link at the Raleigh-Durham Wingate. That's where he'll be staying."

"I thought we were partners." Alex sounded insulted. "I want to come on the mission."

"We aren't partners. You're my client," Val said. "Besides, I can handle this on my own. You can stay back and watch Cash for me."

"I'm coming." Alex insisted. "If I'm the client, then that means you work for me, and what I say goes."

Val started to protest. Alex would only slow her down, or worse, screw up badly enough to get them caught, but she had already endured enough of Alex's stubbornness to recognize when to give in. And maybe it would be fun to have a ride-along for once.

"If you're coming, *boss*," Val said, "you have to promise to stay out of the way. And you're covering all expenses, in addition to buying the plane tickets."

"To Durham?" Alex pshawed. "I'll fly us there myself."

Of course.

"If you insist," Val said.

It would take some getting used to, but yeah, Val could get used to this.

Still, she never knew when to keep her mouth shut. "I like how you're trying to be this environmental crusader," she said, "and yet you're fine with jet-setting around in your private plane, pollutants be damned."

"A quick trip to Durham is hardly jet-setting," Alex replied. "But I take your point. I offset my carbon emissions, not that it's any of your business."

Then Alex added, "But hey, if you want me to book us a pair of seats with Delta or JetBlue—"

"I was just making a point for argument's sake," Val said.

“Because arguing is your favorite pastime.”

“Top five. Along with kicking your ass.”

“You did not kick my ass,” Alex said. “It was a draw.”

“I think it looked more like that.” Val gestured toward Cash, who was standing on Bruce’s exposed belly, whacking him in the snout.

Alex’s face got serious. “Who’s going to take care of the dogs while we’re away? I’ve never left Bruce alone before.”

Val looked at her phone and June’s unanswered text. “Playdate at Willow’s?”

Alex let out a penitent exhale. “I hate lying to June.”

Val offered her a look of sympathy while, in the back of her mind, she imagined what lies it would take for her to scale Alex’s guarded walls. A real look inside was all Val needed. From there, the possibilities were infinite.

“If it makes you more comfortable,” Val said, “you can leave most of the lying to me.”

CHAPTER 12

June watched Willow, Bruce, and Cash wolf down their early dinner.

"Slow down," she said to Willow. "You'll get a bellyache. Good boy, Bruce. See how Bruce chews his food before swallowing it, Willowbaby?"

"Nice try." June gave Cash a pat on the rump when she searched for leftovers in everyone else's bowl. "You're going to have to be a lot faster than that."

Dog sitting for Alex and Val should have been pure pleasure. "It would be my pleasure," June had said to each of them when they asked, meaning it at the time.

Then, after Alex left Bruce, June had a funny feeling in her stomach and in her throat, something like sadness, but not exactly. Later the same day, when Val dropped off Cash, the sensation returned with double the strength.

Was June upset or jealous that they both had better things to do than hang out with her?

She looked at her phone, thought about sending an update to

the group chat, a photo of the three dogs lingering around their empty bowls with expectant faces, hoping for more. The message would say something like *Appetites are fully intact; everyone's having a great time!* But she deliberated long enough to miss the photo opportunity; the dogs had moved on, and three empty bowls seemed too melancholy for a still life.

Instead, June reopened her text to Alex and Val from Thursday, which she now regretted, convinced its cutesy, needy tone had driven them away.

Hey gals! What are you up to this weekend? Ew.

Silas will be in North Carolina for an EPA conference and I'll be all by my lonesome. All by my lonesome? Yuck.

What would you say to a girls-and-dogs trip? June despised the loneliness her message broadcasted when she reread it to herself now, as well as its accuracy.

"You're lonely," Alex had said to her shortly after they first met. The pronouncement had been bouncing around June's mental universe like a wayward asteroid ever since, until she ultimately concluded that Alex was wrong. She may have spent a lot of time alone, but she wasn't, in fact, lonely.

However, the word itself seemed to be stalking June.

Earlier this week, she'd come across an article online that said loneliness was an epidemic. It was as bad for your health as smoking cigarettes, the article claimed; it could even increase the risk of premature death. June found this hard to believe, but a group of reputable doctors and scientists was making the case. *Loneliness is a public health concern*, one of them was quoted as saying. *The consequences of isolation are profound and widespread.*

What was the cure then? June wanted to know. She read to the end of the article to find out that it was—no spoiler alert—cultivating relationships. Having friends, family, someone, anyone. They made it sound so easy.

June had already tried many of the tips these so-called experts suggested. She volunteered, for example, delivering meals-on-wheels to the elderly and infirm once a week and making regular visits with Willow to bring canine cheer to patients at the local hospital. June even dug in the dirt and picked up trash in a community garden in hopes of finding some *community*. All the hours June passed in service to others was time well spent, but none of it had led to any new friends.

When it came to family, June also felt like she was failing. She barely spoke to her parents or sisters these days. It was embarrassing to think of now, how she had allowed so much distance to form between them over the years, but more so because it was all on account of Silas.

June's mother and sisters, and even her father, had all adored Silas at first. Their approval waned slightly when, after only a year of dating, he began proposing to June, over and over, insisting their once-in-a-lifetime love be made official, but June was flattered by the ferocity of his devotion. It was a special connection she and Silas had, and they made a picture-perfect couple—everyone said so.

When they finally did marry a few years later, their wedding was something out of a storybook, a happy, sunny day in Northern California, June a Cinderella to Silas's Prince Charming.

When Silas wanted to move to Bethesda, June's family asked, "But what do *you* want?" As if it were somehow a weakness to simply want what her husband wanted. Did they not understand that Silas and June were soul mates, and this was how soul mates made decisions?

It was June's younger sister who first used the word *controlling* to describe Silas, but June had the sense she was speaking for the lot of them.

"He's ambitious," June had argued at the time. "And he has a specific vision for our future, but he doesn't try to control me."

Now June wasn't so sure. It was a conversation she wanted to have another chance at with her family, five years too late. But as much as she would like to return to them, to say maybe they were on to something, she couldn't. Doing so would require too big a gulp of her own pride. And, yes, she did in fact have *some* pride. Even if it was only making her feel lonelier and more isolated.

All this had been roiling around June's brain when she decided to choose the phrase *all by my lonesome*, as much as it didn't sound like her.

Now look where she'd ended up. Alone, still, only talking to three dogs instead of one.

On the bright side, she did have somewhere to be tonight with other people. Even if it was dog-related, that still counted as human contact, right?

It was a party in June's backseat when she drove up Meryl's long driveway for the next meeting of the Friends of Hamilton Dog Park. Willow, Bruce, and Cash may or may not have known where they were. Either way, they were elated.

Unlike last time, tonight the Friends would gather in the backyard of Meryl's majestic house, around a boardroom-like picnic table on the patio, while the dogs played nearby within a fenced-in area.

June noticed immediately that tonight's meeting was a downgrade in that the only staff present was Meryl's regular help and the snacks had been prepared in-house. Their numbers had also dwindled to a handful of die-hards.

Seated around the perimeter of the rectangular teak table was Regina, low-maintenance mom to Eloise the miniature dachshund, then Ava, high-maintenance mom to Popcorn the Pomeranian, who made sure to nab a seat next to the Silver Fox, i.e., sexy dad to Mollie the golden corgi. On his other side was Karen, working mom to one of the Cavalier King Charles spaniels, followed by Yoshi the shih tzu's mom, whose name June had once again forgotten.

Kennedy stood off to the side in a lightweight linen dress, cooling herself with a foldout fan while trying to look pivotal.

"June Bug," she said, a nickname June had never signed off on. "When you walked in here with all those pups on a leash, I mistook you for a dog-walker."

June merely smiled, unable to decipher whether Kennedy was being friendly or rude.

After some customary hostess niceties, Meryl got the meeting started, and June was glad the small-talk portion of the evening was over.

"Our park fundraiser event is fast approaching," Meryl said. And it was getting more elaborate every day, according to the Hamilton grapevine.

"Let's go around to get a feel for what progress each committee has made," Meryl continued. "The Media and Public Relations Committee will go first. I'm happy to report that I have been lucky enough to get us advance coverage in all the local papers, and a piece on Fox 5 DC prior to. Fingers crossed they will also be there live the night of."

Meryl paused for applause that didn't immediately come, then said, "Feel free to applaud."

Their small group did, loudly, inciting a robust round of dog barking, to everyone's delight.

"And there's more," Meryl continued. "I took it upon myself to handle the catering. Chef Christian Martinez, who you may remember from season forty-two of *Chopped*, will be providing us an elevated barbecue-style meal, with an emphasis on smoked meats and creative side dishes, alongside a three-course dog menu."

This time, the group applauded before Meryl asked them to.

"Who wants to go next?" Meryl asked. "How about the Auction Committee?"

All eyes turned to the Silver Fox, but it was Yoshi's mom who spoke on their behalf.

"We've procured a number of items in the under-two-hundred-dollar range, and a handful of mid-level prizes, including a luxury grooming package from Fetching and a month of daycare from Puptopia. But our pièce de résistance is three free sessions with Dr. Brawn, the renowned pet psychologist."

"Great work," Meryl said, followed by group applause.

Regina and Karen on the Entertainment and Program Committee did not fare so well. They still hadn't hired an emcee or any live performers for the night. Meryl saved them face by suggesting they speak privately after the meeting. To receive their demerits and after-school detention, June assumed.

Next up came Kennedy and Ava's Décor Committee. Kennedy spoke first. "We've decided to go with a sophisticated summer palette for our theme colors: cool pastel tones like soft blues, lavender, and powder pink. Our theme is Summer Barbecue, and guests are encouraged to interpret that as they wish, whether by keeping it classic or going full-on Americana kitsch, but in terms of décor, our inspiration is more East Hampton Estate and less Jersey Shore Cabana. White tents and twinkle lights will be supplied by Darling Decorations, linens from Woven, and handmade centerpieces by TableEscapes."

Here Ava jumped in. "Don't forget to have your pups dressed and ready to strike a pose on the red carpet, where pet pawtographers from Bow-Wow will be snapping entrance photos for a best-costume contest. If you plan on having an outfit custom-made, I can tell you firsthand that Ricky Roybin is booked. Popcorn got his only opening in the next three months."

"What?" Kennedy interrupted. "You got an appointment with Ricky? I thought Chester was his only commission for this event."

"Uh-oh," Regina whispered to June. "Drama."

"Who's Ricky Roybin?" June asked.

The question left the table dumbfounded. Even down-to-earth Regina seemed to know who he was.

"Ricky's one of the most famous designers in dog couture," Ava replied.

"I thought we were doing couture for the humans and theme costumes for the dogs," Yoshi's mom said. "What's everyone else got planned? I don't want Yoshi to be underdressed."

As it turned out, half the group was planning on costuming their dog as a barbecue food item, and the other half had pushed well into canine Met Gala territory.

"Remember, not all our guests can afford designer prices," Meryl shouted over the din. "For their pets or themselves. Which is why we've given them the option to come dressed as a hamburger if they so wish."

Regina looked at June and rolled her eyes.

"The important part is we're on schedule," Meryl said. "And we're hitting our budget goals. Our long-sought-after park renovation is within reach!"

June had yet to consider Willow's outfit, but high fashion would not have been on her radar. Which was probably a good thing? Did people in other places behave this way when it came to their pets? June had been in Bethesda too long now to remember. But one thing she knew for sure was that her onetime family dog, a yellow Lab named Honey, had never once donned an article of clothing more elaborate than a neckerchief, and he lived a happy, healthy fourteen years none the wiser.

"Sponsorship Committee," Meryl said. "Yoohoo."

June snapped to attention. "Yes. We have gift certificates to raffle off from Fern's Day Spa and donated ice cream, including pup cups, from Maddy's. And A-One Dry Cleaners has agreed to come on as a full sponsor."

The applause was merely obligatory now, but it still felt to June like a warm hug.

"Thank you," she said. "It was a group effort."

"Where is your group?" Meryl asked. "Have they abandoned you?"

Was it that obvious? Was the gaping crevasse between her desire for social connection and her actual social connections spread before their eyes?

"Alex and Val had other commitments," June said. "But I'm happy to have Bruce and Cash for the weekend. They've been great company. It's been a pleasure."

CHAPTER 13

Alex had a black car pick Val up at her rental apartment and drive her to the private airfield where the Cessna was ready for takeoff. The puddle jumper, as Alex thought of it, had all the basic comforts of a larger plane in a compact, more efficient package, but its size never failed to freak out the uninitiated at first sight.

"What the hell is that?" Val asked the moment she stepped onto the tarmac. A small leather duffel bag was strapped across her chest.

"That's our ride," Alex said, with intentional nonchalance.

"You expect me to get in that thing?"

"I'm sorry, were you expecting something bigger?"

Val most certainly was, Alex thought. A company plane, perhaps. Something with luxury seats and more space than the average living room, and maybe a staff of attendants carrying trayfuls of champagne and caviar.

"Come on, we're running late." Alex grabbed Val's bag and loaded it into the trunk area, then climbed into the pilot's seat.

"No." Val stood before the passenger door. "No way are you flying this tin can."

Alex put on her headset.

Val looked around like she was unsure if she was being punked. "Are you even allowed to operate heavy machinery? I've seen the medications you're on. Aren't you too anxious to be a pilot?"

"You'd think an anxiety disorder would work that way. But according to my logic, having someone else fly the plane is much more nerve-racking. This way I have full control." Alex fiddled with the buttons on the GPS, then held a headset out to Val. "You look like you could use a Xanax though."

"I'm fine." Val climbed into the passenger seat and accepted the headset. "I just hadn't realized I was going to perish today when I left the house. I would have worn fancier underwear."

Truth be told, when Alex first made the offer, she had meant a piloted company plane, but then she thought of the Cessna. Val would get a kick out of it, she supposed, and maybe she wanted to impress her just a little. Not in the way a corporate jet was impressive. Instead, Alex felt an urge to assert some sort of street credit, a toughness and capability Val assumed she lacked.

This happened sometimes when Alex found herself associating with people outside her social strata. She would become super conscious of their different places on the hierarchy of wealth and privilege and try to do everything she could to equalize it, to show that she recognized her greater access to resources and opportunities as bullshit—and that it didn't define her. That she wasn't soft and oblivious, living in a bubble, but that she had depth, complexity, and she knew how to suffer.

Look, she was trying to communicate to Val, *I don't live a coddled life. I can do things for myself. I am competent enough to fly my own plane.*

"Buckle up." Alex turned on the engine. Maybe it was silly to care so much if Val respected her or not, but here they were.

With their destination set, they taxied toward the runway. Alex checked her magnetos, the propeller, bogged down the engine.

Flaps up, they were good to go. Alex radioed in her best pilot's voice to air traffic control, then turned to Val. "Ready to roll out?"

Val treated the question as rhetorical, and Alex observed that she did not appear the least bit afraid. She wasn't tense or fidgeting. Her eyes were brighter and more animated than usual, and her mouth was slightly open in anticipation. Alex accelerated for takeoff.

Whoosh! A moment later they were in the air. This part never got old. She focused on getting them to altitude, allowing Val to enjoy the sensation of flight in a single-prop plane. From the corner of her eye, she noticed the wonder on Val's face, her broad smile.

"Okay," Val said after a while, "this is pretty cool."

Alex settled into her seat, satisfied. "So, tell me about yourself."

"Yeah, we're not doing that," Val replied.

"Having a conversation?"

"I don't do heart-to-hearts."

"It's going to be a boring hour and a half if we do it in total silence."

Not totally true. Alex loved the unquiet hum of flight, and she was not accustomed to talking while piloting. Other than when she was learning to fly with her instructor, Alex had only ever flown alone. Val was technically her first passenger.

"You can tell me about you," Val said. "How long ago was your divorce?"

"About that." Alex pretended to check her gauges. "It was a lie. I've never been married."

"Great start," Val said.

"I thought it would make me seem more human at the dog park," Alex explained. "If I'd once had someone love me."

Val made a face Alex couldn't read. "I'll give you one thing. When you do say something honest, you really go for it."

"I'm better at extremes than moderation," Alex said.

"So I'm learning."

"I'm also pretty good at being by myself." Alex pulled back slightly on the throttle and watched her RPMs. "Though I've been surprised by how I've already come to rely on Bruce's affection. I didn't know I'd get so much out of having him. Has it been that way for you?"

"I only got Cash for the job," Val said. "Since we're being honest."

"Oh." Alex was at a loss as to what to say next, then asked, "Do you date much?"

"I recently got out of something long-term," Val said. "It ended badly, and before that it wasn't very good, so no big loss."

"I see why you stayed with him as long as you did," Alex joked.

"Funny," Val said, but she didn't laugh.

Alex verified their air and vertical speed and rechecked the GPS.

"I want to know what you're like in your real life," Val said. "When you're not pretending to be someone else. I'm curious about you the way people hate-watch reality television."

Alex wasn't sure, but that didn't sound like a compliment.

"There are so few of you in relation to the rest of the world," Val continued. "Point-oh-one percent. That's who you get to be, and you don't even have the sense to appreciate it."

"Who says I don't appreciate it?"

"How many houses do you own?" Val asked.

"Too many," Alex said.

"See," Val said. "That's a mopey answer. Where'd you go to school?"

"A few places, mostly Switzerland, then Wharton. It's not that I don't appreciate everything I have," Alex said. "It's that I don't know if *anyone* should have so much."

Val got quiet for a moment, took in the panorama, then asked, "What's the best part of being rich?"

"Less to worry about," Alex said, without having to think about it. "But I never got the hang of it myself."

"What's the worst part?"

"This."

"Fair enough." Val stopped there.

"Is it my turn now?" Alex asked.

"Nope," Val said. "Growing up poor is way too common to be interesting."

Alex was interested. She wanted Val to know that she empathized with her, understood she'd gotten a raw deal. Hell, Alex even wanted to help her, but Val wasn't the type to want sympathy or charity. She didn't even care to be friends. People whose time you were paying for were not in it for the relationship, Alex reminded herself. They were in it for the paycheck.

Alex would have to be okay with that. She was still enjoying herself up here in the clouds. As it turned out, flying with a passenger could be better than flying alone.

The Raleigh-Durham Wingate featured all the amenities one would expect from an airport hotel, including extensive meeting and event space, but the EPA Conference on New Approach Methods for Chemical Safety Testing was a blockbuster event, with attendees and presenters from agencies and organizations far and wide. Such a turnout required the massive capacity of the EPA's own campus auditorium at Research Triangle Park, only a ten-minute drive away by shuttle bus.

Alex and Val acquired all these details ahead of time, along with the complete conference schedule, thanks to it having been posted in full online.

From a distant hotel parking spot, in their turquoise-blue Chevy Bolt, Alex watched the last lingering conference attendees board the shuttle bus headed to the EPA campus.

"You wanted to blend in and our car's the color of a Popsicle," Val said.

Alex had insisted on renting a vehicle one of the environmental folks would have themselves chosen, less from an invisibility standpoint, and more to achieve the overall vibe of the role. The Toyota Prius hybrids were already snatched up and Alex refused the Tesla on moral grounds.

"In this crowd," Alex said, "a battery-operated ice pop is less suspicious than a neutral-colored sports car."

If Alex had let Val have her way, they would probably be sitting in a Lamborghini or a Ferrari right now. The kind of car a kid who grew up watching 1990s television thought meant *luxury*. In a way, Alex understood, Val was still that kid, awestruck by flash and the emblems of overconsumption. But who was Alex to judge? She couldn't fully imagine what it meant to want something and not be able to afford it.

Off went the bus of latecomers for ten a.m. registration, which would be followed by an eleven a.m. welcome and day one overview.

Putting away the schedule, Alex turned toward Val and was momentarily surprised all over again by the disappearance of all her cool. Silas knew Val by face, so it was important for her to keep out of his sight, which she obviously knew well enough how to do. Still, to be extra careful, Val had also made a few slight modifications to her appearance, rendering herself difficult to identify on a security camera. Gone were Val's signature motorcycle jacket and scuffed boots. She had styled her dark hair differently, wore thick eyeglasses, and was dressed in unflattering business casual, in taupe rather than black.

Alex had done the same, as Val had instructed, upping it a notch with brown contact lenses and a chestnut-colored wig in the style of Rachel from *Friends*.

"You really embrace any opportunity to wear a disguise, don't you?" Val said upon first sight.

They had made their costume changes in a gas station bathroom. *Like the real deal*, Alex thought. Amid a stopped-up toilet and filthy sink with only a dribble of water when you turned the faucet. She was having the time of her life.

"We're going to a hotel teeming with environmental and energy industry people," Alex explained when Val cracked up laughing at her dramatic reveal. "If anyone anywhere might recognize me, it's there."

"Are you sure about the wig?" Val asked now. "I'm having trouble taking you seriously."

"I've already noticed three women with this same haircut," Alex said. "So maybe you can take a lesson from the rookie here when it comes to going incognito."

They stepped out of the car. Alex clicked on the alarm.

Val scoped the scene. "Do you think the Rachel is coming back? Or did it never leave among the science and industry crowd?"

The two of them entered the sliding glass doors of the Wingate with the confidence of Cagney and Lacey.

"Go wait by those chairs over there," Val said. "I need to make sure Silas left his room."

"I'll do it," Alex offered. "I'll say I'm his wife, or no, I'll be his mistress, who's also his coworker, and not give a name."

It felt poignant, almost adolescent, the degree to which Alex wanted to be seen and accepted by Val as a valuable member of their two-person team.

"I'll let you stand next to me, but you are to remain silent," Val said.

Naturally, Alex was choosing to fixate on someone who was quick to reject everyone and everything. That had always been her way. She blamed her mother.

At the check-in desk, Val asked the attendant to call up to Silas Kennerson's room with a lack of fanfare that Alex found disappointing.

The attendant called. No answer.

Val said thank you and they moved along.

"Great," Alex said. "He isn't in, but how are we going to—"

"He's in room 1001. Leave it to Silas to choose a top-floor suite."

"How do you know that? Just by watching her dial the phone?"

Val stopped walking halfway to the elevator bank. "You do understand this is what I do for a living, right?"

Alex did, but who knew she would be so good at it?

"Now, let's get this over with," Val said. "Follow my lead and stay quiet. You are the lookout once we get upstairs and only the lookout. Don't say or do anything stupid."

Val had them wait a few steps back from the elevator until a uniformed custodian pressed the up arrow. They stepped inside behind him and Val waved a plastic key card in front of the sensor and poked at the tenth floor button repeatedly to no avail.

"Not again. Do you have your card on you?" she asked Alex.

Before Alex could answer, the custodian heroically flashed his card over the sensor and pressed 10 for them.

"Thank you," Val said. "Modern technology."

The custodian smiled and stepped off on the fifth floor.

"Where did you get that key card?" Alex asked.

"It's from my personal collection. I have a complete set of all the chain hotels."

Outside room 1001, Val pulled out a lock-picking kit. A real live set of tiny forks and hooks and tension wrenches—all contained in a convenient fold-up carrying case. Alex delighted in their diminutive power, how something so adorable could wreak such havoc. She tried to peek into Val's cross-body bag to get a look at more tools of the trade.

"What other toys you got in there?"

"Keep your head down and shut up." Val unlocked the door in seconds.

They entered silently.

But there were sounds coming from the bedroom—Silas shouting at someone on his cell phone.

"Shit," Val whispered. "He's here."

"But we had the desk call up," Alex said, panicked.

"Let's bounce." Val reached for the doorknob.

"Look." Alex pointed. There on the living room table, in front of the flat-screen TV, was Silas's open laptop. "How long do you need to upload the thingy?"

"Like two minutes, but we can just come back later," Val whisper-yelled.

What happened next happened quickly. It wasn't premeditated or at all something Alex would normally do. The only explanation was that she got caught up in the moment, and a little bit of a contact high from Val's PI swagger.

"I'll run interference," Alex said. "You handle the laptop. Meet me back at the car." She motioned for Val to hide. "Get behind the kitchen counter. Go now."

Val was about to object but dove for cover when Alex grabbed a lamp from an end table. A second later, Alex smashed the lamp onto the floor.

Silas came running from the bedroom in time to see Alex dash into the hallway. She threw open a stairwell door with him hot on her trail and vaulted down the staircase.

Alex's body took on a life of its own, swinging over a handrail to the landing below. She jungle-gymed down the next set of stairs, drawing Silas further from his room, but giving him no chance of catching her—until a door opened and she slammed face-first into a porter with a mop and bucket.

"Stop her!" Silas yelled.

Alex grabbed the porter's mop with both hands and used it to thrust him backward, but Silas caught up to her now.

He went for her shoulder, but she smacked him away. "Ne me touche pas!" she screamed out in French. *Don't touch me!*

"Voleur! Voleur!" she cried to the porter. *Thief! Thief!* Then, in broken English, she said, "This man was in my room."

Silas put up his palms, took a step back. "I think there's been some mistake."

The porter looked from Alex to Silas back to Alex. He reached for his walkie-talkie. "I'd better call a manager."

"No," Silas said. "It was just a misunderstanding. Ma'am?" He drew his words out slowly and loudly, as if he were speaking to a child from another planet. "WHAT IS YOUR ROOOM NUUMBERR?"

"My ROOOM?" Alex played along. "Aah. TEN OH TWOO."

"Well, there you go." Silas was pleased with himself. "You went to THE WRONG ROOM. TEN OH ONE. MY ROOM."

"No." Alex said. "Oui?"

"Yes," Silas nodded with enough gusto that Alex feared for his neck.

The porter chuckled.

"Je suis désolé!" *I'm sorry!*

Alex returned to the car, heart pounding, body infused with endorphins. She slammed the door shut and said to Val, "Did you get the malware uploaded?"

Val grabbed hold of her by the shirt. "You are fucking insane, you know that?"

Adrenaline surging, Alex realized how close together their faces were. Val's breath felt warm on her face. She could smell the alluring scent of soap mixed with sweat.

For a moment, Alex was certain they were about to kiss.

"I told you not to do anything stupid." Val let go of Alex's shirt.

Or not. "Did you get it done?" Alex asked.

"Yes. Did he catch you?"

"Oh yeah," Alex said.

"Did he recognize you?"

"Not a chance. We're totally in the clear."

"Are you sure you're okay?"

"I'm great." Alex pulled off her wig. "I'm amazing."

"Christ, you had me worried!" Val pounded her hands on the steering wheel ten times over and then let out a walloping *"Woo!"*

It was a sound someone might make when they stepped off a roller coaster or landed a perfect gymnastic flip. Relief coupled with triumph. And to Alex's ears, it was the assurance that she had at last won Val's approval and admiration.

CHAPTER 14

Early Sunday morning, Val stood before June's front door to pick up Cash. She was expecting a worn-out, exhausted pet sitter who would vow to never watch Cash again.

Instead, June was her bright-eyed self, well-rested and as lovey-dovey toward Cash as ever. "I've got a pot of coffee on," she said to Val. "Want to come in?"

Val couldn't resist being invited inside the home June made with Silas.

She stepped through the doorway and Cash ran to her. Had Val been missed? Was Cash happy to see her? She put out her arms.

As if to say *Psych!* Cash zipped around in the other direction, back toward the other dogs.

"Did Cash behave?" Val asked June, ignoring the slight.

"She was her spunky little self," June said. "She ate and slept fine. There is one thing though . . ."

Here it comes, Val thought. "What did Cash destroy?"

"Nothing." June laughed. "She has a bit of a cough. I wasn't sure if that was new or if it's something that's been going on for a while."

When Val was a child, she got sick a lot. Usually it was something upper respiratory, probably on account of all the cigarette smoke. And yet every time Val fell ill, she was made to feel responsible.

Don't you dare get sick on me was a common refrain of her mother's, which came at the slightest clearing of Val's throat, in preemptive fear of yet another unpayable doctor bill. A second refrain was *You're fine to go to school/church/so-and-so's house, just don't say anything about your sore throat/stomachache/fever.*

And so, Val's immediate reaction to Cash's alleged cough during a sleepover with two other dogs was to defend herself.

"I'm sure Cash is fine," Val said. "It's her smushed in nose that makes all sorts of gross noises when she gets too excited. If you're worried about kennel cough, she's vaccinated."

Kennel cough was one of many new terms in Val's vocabulary that she'd rather not know, along with *heartworms, footpad yeast, mange*, and—her least favorite—*anal gland expression*.

It was a good thing Val's parents didn't keep Cuddles for long, considering. No way they would have ever stepped foot into a vet's office. *Not at those prices*, her mother would have said, which was also how Val walked around as an eight-year-old with a broken arm for half a week before her parents finally brought her to get the bone set.

One of Val's more dedicated caseworkers, a soft-featured, round-faced woman aptly named Angel, once described Gianni and Rosetta's way of doing things as living in "survival mode." Ironic, Val thought, considering the day-to-day precariousness of her survival back then. "Your parents are mentally and emotionally overwhelmed," it was explained to Val. "They are just trying to get by with little money and limited education. We see this a lot with the immigrant population."

As Val understood it, living in a state of perpetual survival meant you were so occupied with not dying that you forgot how to live. But even at such a young age, she knew that wasn't the whole story. Lack of language or education wasn't what drove her parents to try to stab each other with steak knives or throw dishes against the wall to make a point. That had to be something else. Plenty of kids had parents who grew up in a different culture and didn't have any money, and most of them probably didn't smash their wedding bands with a hammer or push each other down a flight of stairs.

"Just thought I'd mention it," June said of Cash's cough. "I'm sure you're right that it's nothing to worry about."

June fixed their coffee, letting the subject drop.

"Would you mind if I used your bathroom?" Val asked.

"Of course, but the one down here is a mess. I had to give Willow a bath—long story involving a roll in some stink—and I haven't had a chance to tidy it up yet. Use the one upstairs instead." June pointed the way.

Val speed-walked a quick tour of the second level, taking note of Silas's home office with its multiple file cabinets and double-monitored desktop computer.

After spending hours the night before poring over Silas's every email and hundreds of documents saved to his laptop's hard drive, Val already suspected there might be another device somewhere, or a single-copy paper trail under lock and key—a hiding spot where the real skeletons were buried. This had to be the place.

Back downstairs, once again sitting across from June, Val sipped her coffee and said little, observing the clean lines and generic extravagance of the kitchen and living room, which lacked any sign of June's warm touch.

"What's Silas like?" Val asked, as if the question had just dawned on her from nowhere.

June hugged her coffee mug with both hands. "Silas is a great man, a great husband. He works a lot." She paused. "He works really hard."

Val said nothing, waiting for more, and she was about to get it when Alex knocked on the door, arriving at the worst time to pick up Bruce.

"Now it's really a celebration," June said, inviting Alex inside. "Coffee?"

"Sure. Thanks." Alex shot a look to Val.

The emotional hangover from last night was still lingering on Alex's face, same as Val felt it on her own. June didn't seem to notice. She accepted their falsehoods without question and offered them cake to go with their coffee.

Alex was a skilled deceiver when she wanted to be, fabricating an elaborate story about the New Jersey golf tournament she'd competed in the day before.

All Val said was that she'd had a family commitment. Respecting her privacy, June left it at that. Meanwhile, Alex was reenacting every detailed step she took to sink an imaginary putt on the eighteenth hole.

Val watched Alex lie. Considering the last forty-eight hours, she didn't know what to make of her.

Val tended to be drawn to idiosyncratic, complicated people, and Alex fit that bill, but at certain moments Val also wanted to smack her across the face. Why was Alex hemming and hawing through her days like a tortured poet? She had won the lottery of life, and all she seemed to want to do was be someone else.

Alex was not likeable in the classic sense, or pleasant, or agreeable. She could, however, be surprising. Take the gambit she pulled at the hotel, for example. Val was also flabbergasted by how much money Alex gave away each year. The research Val did after learning who Alex was had been limited by the gauntlet of protections the ultra-rich used to keep their finances hidden, but even her restricted access revealed a person dead set on easing their class guilt with generosity.

Philanthropy, as far as Val was concerned, was a racket—the oldest trick in the book for the rich and powerful to stay that way while patting themselves on the back. And, in general, the guilty rich were a group Val had historically been comfortable taking advantage of. But Alex was trying so hard to be good. Val almost felt sorry for her.

Almost. But, come on. She was a trust fund kid with so few problems she had to make some up. Was there anyone on the planet easier to hate?

"Do you want to hear what you missed at the Friends meeting?" June asked.

"Of course," Alex said.

"Yes," Val agreed.

June refilled each of their cups with hot coffee. "Let me start by asking you a question. Have either of you heard of someone called Ricky Roybin?"

"I haven't," Alex said. "But I have a feeling I want to." She looked at June with reverence and wonder that Val couldn't ignore. There was an innocence to it even as Val knew Alex was using June to get to Silas.

"Tell us everything," Alex said. "Don't leave anything out."

If Val didn't know better, she would assume Alex was the con artist among them.

And June. June was undeniably wonderful. It was hard not to be swept up by her whimsy, but did she really not know more than she was letting on about what Silas was up to?

"Have you ever heard the term *dog couture*?" June asked.

Christ, what had Val gotten herself into?

Keep your head in the game, kid, Gianni would say. *Stay focused. Do not get distracted. Otherwise, you'll end up the sucker.*

June was not a mistrustful person, but she had somehow, in the past few years, grown into a dishonest wife. It had progressed to the point where now, when she told Silas a lie, it was with a serene detachment, as if she were observing herself from a meditative state. The inverse, ironically, was also true. If she tried to meditate for real, all she could see in her mind's eye were her lies.

Her mistake the late afternoon Silas returned from his work trip to North Carolina was one she had made many times before. She had not transferred the day's dirty dishes from the sink to the dishwasher before Silas returned home. This time, however, there were coffee cups and cake plates that demanded explanation.

"Did you have company?" Silas asked.

Dummy! June scolded herself. She'd had so many hours to take care of this one simple chore, or do the washing and drying by hand, then put it all away. But her defense of the error left her lips calmly.

"Two friends came by," June said, because one visitor might be provocative, while two sounded like an innocent gathering of ladies who lunch.

Silas didn't like guests of any sort. The reason, as June understood it, was because he never felt the house was perfect enough and therefore any visitor would only judge him negatively. This struck June as absurd until she got to spend more time with Silas's mother. If June had been raised by that woman, she would have ended up just as neurotic.

Silas's parents were educated but unworldly. They had not traveled. They could not bear what they called "ethnic cuisine with too much spice," or any food that was "non-American."

And to counter his parents' provincialism, Silas went out of his way to appear more world-wise and sophisticated than he was. Trying so hard to separate himself from his parents only added tension to their relationship, wound Silas up tighter, and translated—unfortunately for June—to him being extra anxious and out of sorts when it came to having other people in their home.

If it were up to June, she would have invited guests over all the time, maybe even kept an open-door policy, had the confidence to ask someone from the garden club or a fellow hospital volunteer over for coffee or dinner. But trying to push Silas that far out of his comfort zone wouldn't be worth the fight. For him it would be an emotional roller coaster of dread, followed by an even worse, post-event conviction he or June had somehow shamed themselves. Maybe the bathroom wasn't spotless, or the inside of the refrigerator smelled of food, or the coffee was too strong, or the wine was not expensive enough. Whatever it was, it was always something.

Because the guest issue was so fraught, June and Silas only ever had people over when it was Silas's idea and planned for weeks ahead of time. So, it was not to please him that June said two friends from the dog park stopped by to talk committee stuff, and that it happened somewhat spontaneously, but it was better than telling him the truth.

Silas would have been enraged if he'd known June had taken in two additional dogs for a night over the weekend. She was extra careful in covering her tracks by scrubbing up theirs, vacuuming to make sure there were no non-Willow hairs around, clearing every speck of evidence. In fact, this was probably the reason she had missed the obvious coffee cups and extra cake plates in the sink.

"Was another man in this house?" Silas wanted to know.

June told him absolutely not, it was two women, and he seemed pacified by their femaleness. Crisis averted. She would not be asked follow-up questions about the imaginary affair he routinely believed she was having.

Then he said, "You know I don't approve of you having strangers in the house when I'm not here."

And something inside of June snapped. "You can't keep me isolated from everyone in the world but you," she said. "It isn't healthy."

Silas looked as though he'd been slapped.

June had obviously lost her cool, but he remained eerily calm. "Where did that come from?" he asked.

Where did it come from? It's not like a scolding from Silas was anything out of the ordinary. Perhaps she was feeling emboldened by the lovely time she'd had connecting with Alex and Val after fearing she had alienated them.

"Let me ask you a question," Silas said. "And I expect an honest answer. Have you been unfaithful to me?"

June almost laughed—but she knew better than to ever laugh at Silas. "You're impossible. I'm not cheating on you! You keep such close tabs on me. If I were having an affair, don't you think you'd have caught me by now?"

"Well, don't you sound like a happy wife." A few moments passed. Silas's eyes roved about, as if they were still trying to work out an answer to a puzzle, or maybe find an alternative solution to the one he already had.

June understood that something grave was about to happen, but all she felt just then, despite her dread, was the grand possibility of change.

It had been over a month now since she first considered divorce, when she did a bit of googling, then got spooked that Silas was on to her and shut it all down. Since then, she had not wanted to take that chance a second time. Raising the possibility of a separation was not something to do lightly. There was no going back once the subject was let out of the box. Once she hurt Silas that deeply, he would not recover—and there was no telling what he would do to try to stop her.

But June was desperate to let loose, have fun, make memories—and with Alex and Val in her life, she was finding the courage to do so. It was this energy that Silas must have been sensing.

June waited while he circled the room like a shark in a tank.

"Did you know," he said, finally, "if we ever got divorced, Willow would rightfully be mine?"

June shuddered at hearing the word *divorce* leave his lips.

"It's the law," he continued. "I bought her. She belonged to me before we got married, which makes her, legally, more mine than yours. Isn't that interesting?"

June remembered the day with crystal clarity, when Silas presented her with the three-month-old golden puffball of joy who would grow up to be Willow. They were still in California. She had been working as an assistant coach at Stanford, their alma mater, which Silas resented on account of all of the away-game travel. *We need you here*, Silas had said, cupping his hand beneath Willow's chin. *How could you leave this sweet face?* It turned out, she couldn't.

"But you don't even like Willow that much," June said now. "She drives you crazy most of the time."

"Not true," Silas assured her. "I love Willow as much as you love me."

June hesitated. She would have liked to explain that she did love Silas, but threatening her this way was calling even that into question, making her second-guess her own judgment.

"Please don't bring Willow into this," she pleaded. "If you want to hurt me, find another way."

"If you don't want me to hurt you," he said, "then don't make me."

This was new. Though he was controlling, Silas had never been vicious. He had never truly frightened her, but he was scaring her a little now.

"There shouldn't be anything I could do to make you want to hurt me," June said.

Silas stared back at her in a way that sent a shiver up her spine, and she wondered, was this a normal way to argue with one's husband, or was he being . . . abusive?

But that word felt ridiculous to apply to herself, with all her blessings, and her mostly beautiful life. What did June really have in common with anyone who was mistreated to such a degree?

Then she recalled a story she once heard about how shelters housing abused women were rarely dog friendly, which resulted in many women staying with their husbands against their will for the good of their pet.

Maybe June wasn't in a situation as bad as theirs, but she couldn't bear to lose Willow just the same. And she didn't think Silas would do anything bad to Willow just to make June suffer, but was she certain enough to take the chance?

No, not with the look of determination on Silas's face and the pained aggression in his eyes. And so, for the moment, if she had to appease him for Willow's sake, so be it.

"I'm sorry I had guests over without talking to you first," June said in a conciliatory tone. "It won't happen again. And I didn't mean to sound unhappy. Of course I'm happy, you've given me everything any wife could ever want."

"That's what I like to hear." Silas leaned in and gave June a condescending kiss on the forehead that made her blood run cold. "I'm glad you've come to your senses."

CHAPTER 15

Val hadn't been snowing June when she told her Cash was fine. Val truly believed whatever coughing June thought she'd heard were run-of-the-mill snorts and sniffles.

Then, at three a.m. Val was awoken by a sound. A hacking.

She turned on her bedside lamp, relieved for a moment to find no vomit on her bedsheets, but Cash continued to hack in fits, between bouts of nose-licking, gagging, and failed attempts to clear her throat.

Val didn't know what to do. She tried giving Cash water, tried to look in her mouth, rub her throat. She even inexplicably blew into her nose. Nothing worked. She googled *Dog can't stop coughing*, then *Dog can't breathe*. Meanwhile, Cash honked like a broken tuba. She looked to Val, confused and terrified. Why was this sound coming out of her?

Finally, Val looked up *Urgent care veterinarian near me* and got an address.

"Hang on," she said to Cash while she threw on jeans and a T-shirt and stepped into her boots. "We're going to go get some help."

On the way, Val considered what she would do, what she would feel, if Cash died before she could get to the vet. *You will feel nothing*, she told herself. *She's just a dog. A dog you didn't even want.*

The GPS on Val's phone estimated the route to the urgent care vet to take twenty minutes; Val got there in ten, pushed through the front glass doors, cradling Cash close to her chest, then held her out to the first person she saw wearing scrubs. "My dog can't breathe."

The scrub-wearing woman accepted Cash from Val's arms and fired some basic questions that Val struggled to answer. She could only repeat the obvious, increasing the volume. "My dog can't breathe!"

"We'll have to examine her," the scrub-wearing woman said. "Please try to calm down."

"Don't you dare tell me to calm down!" Val snapped, inadvertently getting in the woman's face.

A different woman came from behind the main desk and shoved a clipboard between them. "You can have a seat and fill this out."

Cash was taken to an exam room while Val remained standing at the desk, scribbling answers as best she could. She signed and dated her name five times over.

"Do you have insurance?" the desk woman asked when Val handed over the clipboard.

Pet insurance for Cash, Val realized she meant. "No," she answered. She didn't even have health insurance for herself.

"She'll need an X-ray and bloodwork to determine what's going on," desk woman said.

"Okay."

"It will cost nine hundred dollars."

"Oh," Val said. "Wow."

You are not your parents, Val reminded herself as she handed over her credit card. *You make your own choices.*

All there was to do then was sit and wait and try to forget all the awful things she read on the internet.

For $900, this dog better survive and cook you dinner after, Val heard her mother say.

Half an hour later, a nurse approached her. Val leapt from her chair. "Is Cash alright?"

"We can't keep her still enough to perform the X-ray," the nurse said. "She's too nervous. We're going to need your consent to sedate her."

"Okay, you have my consent."

"It'll cost another two hundred—"

"Just do it! Do whatever you need to do! You have my credit card number."

The nurse kindly walked away and Val sat back down. She thought about calling Alex or June. June would know what to do.

Val's head was spinning. *What if, what if, what if*, and all this money was now cutting into her wages. But she hadn't really given it a second thought. Was there ever any question? Even now, Val realized, no matter the outcome of the tests, she would do everything in her power to keep Cash alive and free from suffering.

Son of a bitch. She loved this stupid animal. How did she let this happen?

Val was a PI, for heaven's sake. Living a solitary life was practically in her job description, and until now it was what had come naturally.

To soothe and distract herself, Val gazed at the pet-themed posters that served as art on the walls. One was misleadingly cartoonish, with googly-eyed onion heads and chocolate bars with funny faces, with the less jolly title "Toxic Foods for Dogs."

Oh no, Val thought. What if Cash had eaten something poisonous in the apartment? She tried to remember if she'd dropped any onions or chocolate on the floor in the past twenty-four hours. Or any—she checked the poster—grapes or raisins or avocado or candy containing xylitol. Or coffee? She had definitely had coffee. Had Cash snuck a sip?

Val searched for somewhere else to put her attention and decided on an LCD flat-screen on the opposite wall. It was running a slideshow of animal-related health advice interspersed with corny pet humor.

The word *Dogtrovert* appeared onscreen, which a parenthetical labeled a noun. Its definition followed: *a person who prefers spending time with dogs rather than people.*

"Huh," Val muttered to herself, mildly amused. At least this wasn't about poison.

On the next slide, an unmistakably unhappy wrinkly faced dog filled the screen. A caption read: *Zero Socialization, Zero Progress.* It was followed by an anxious looking cocker spaniel pulling on his leash. Beside him it read *Isolation Breeds Insecurity.*

What the heck kind of messaging was this? Was somebody messing with her? Was she hallucinating?

It took Val a moment to realize she had been reading ads for a local doggy daycare. She turned away from the screen.

More than an hour passed before the nurse approached Val again, inviting her to follow her toward the exam rooms. The doctor would speak to her directly, which Val took as an ominous sign.

Her name was Dr. Tait, and she appeared to be younger than any doctor should be. Val sat across from her office desk.

"Cash is resting. She's still groggy from the sedative, but she's doing well. We were able to control the coughing with an oral suppressant, but our testing shows that Cash has a collapsed trachea."

Val gasped.

"It isn't as bad as it sounds," Dr. Tait said. "She's going to be fine."

"A collapsed trachea," Val repeated. "Is it my fault?" She tried to remember if she had ever grabbed Cash by the throat. Did she try to strangle her and forget?

"You didn't do anything wrong," Dr. Tait said. "It's common among the breed. Structural. Something must have aggravated it, causing inflammation. It is progressive, though, and as she gets older, she may need to be put on medication, but what I'm prescribing for now is temporary, to address the cough, alleviate inflammation, and get her back to normal."

Val released a deep exhale, but the knot that had formed in her gut remained. She felt as though she would be nauseous for the rest of her life.

Was this what love was? Val wondered. *This agony? Nausea?*

"Thank you" was all she managed to say to the doctor, and then "I'm sorry" to the scrub-wearing women at the desk on her way out.

Val returned home from the urgent care facility at six a.m. with three medications, a stoned dog, and a thousand dollars in credit card debt.

She lay the elaborate printed instructions for each medicine out on her kitchen table and brought Cash with her onto the couch.

Carefully, she removed the bandage from Cash's paw at the site where they pricked her with the needle.

"Everything's okay. You're safe," Val said, realizing she sounded more like June than herself.

Cash seemed to understand something of her seeming brush with death. She climbed onto Val's lap, curled head to tail like a baby fox, and looked up at Val with a new expression, one that Val didn't fully recognize.

CHAPTER 16

At first, no one answered the door, and Alex began to wonder if Val wasn't home. Then a haggard-looking Val swung the door open.

Alex barely recognized her in sweatpants and a T-shirt. She was a mess, her hair wild, her face pale, eyes red.

"Are you okay?" Alex had to ask.

"I totally forgot we were supposed to meet."

Alex tried to see past Val, into her apartment.

"It's not a good time," Val said, but Bruce had already caught the scent of Cash and was pulling hard on his leash to get inside.

"Try telling that to him," Alex said.

Cash came running to the doorway, and Val scooped her up. "No playing. You have to take your medicine."

"Is she sick?" Alex asked.

The question appeared to take the last of Val's energy out of her. She crumbled before Alex's eyes. "It's been a really long night."

"What's happened?"

Val started blubbering a stream of consciousness about Cash

coughing, and her not sleeping, and urgent care, and medicine she couldn't get down Cash's throat.

"Can I please come in?" This time Alex didn't wait for an answer, and Val—clearly not herself—was too weak to stop her.

Alex stepped inside and looked around the living room of the small apartment, which was separated from the kitchen by a narrow island that doubled as counter space and a sit-down table. It was covered with open pill bottles and stainless-steel spoons dusted in white powder, vials of yellowy liquid, and syringes in multiple sizes.

"Why does it look like a drug den in here?" Alex asked.

"I am not accustomed to having to take care of another living thing," Val said.

"So you've started cooking meth?"

Alex thought Val would laugh, but instead her eyes threatened tears that she immediately shook off.

"This is impossible." Val took a mottled sheet of paper in hand. "It's like a mathematical equation trying to figure out the right way to give her what and when."

She began reading from the paper. "Sucralfate. Give half a tablet by mouth twice daily, every twelve hours, ninety minutes prior to eating and two hours before other medications.

"Then there's the doxycycline hyclate, which is one tablet by mouth twice daily, every twelve hours. But if you recall, the sucralfate, also given every twelve hours, can't be given within two hours of this one. Not to mention, the number of pills I can get Cash to swallow is zero.

"Did you get all that?" Val asked.

Alex said yes.

"Here's my favorite," Val continued. "Prednisolone. Give point-zero-eight milliliters by mouth once daily, every twenty-four hours, for five days. Because if the pills weren't challenging enough, let's also throw in a syringe."

Alex gently removed the paper from Val's hands. "Let me help."

"You're going to tell me to hide the pills in peanut butter," Val said. "But I tried that, and Cash is too smart. She licked off all the peanut butter and spit the pill out onto the floor. I also tried crushing a pill into a powder, but she hated that more. Maybe if we roll up a dollar bill and stick it in her snout, we can get her to snort it like cocaine."

"Sit down, take a breath," Alex said. "What's wrong with her?"

Val slumped onto one of the counter stools. "She has a collapsed trachea. The vet said it isn't as bad as it sounds, but last night it sounded like she was dying."

"Why didn't you call me? That must have been so scary."

Val didn't answer. If the situation were reversed and it had been Bruce in the exam room all night, would Alex have called Val? Probably not.

"Does June know?" Alex asked. "I bet she's a whiz with all this stuff."

"I suck at asking for help, if you must know," Val said. Her exhaustion was making her honest.

"That's probably your parents' fault, not yours," Alex said. "Blame them."

"Have you been listening in on my internal thoughts?" Val asked. "Or did you learn that in therapy?"

"I've had the best psychanalysis money could buy."

"And you're still like this." Val grinned. "I'd ask for my money back if I were you."

"There's the Val I know." Alex looked over the paper in her

hands. "Come on, we can figure this out. What medicine has Cash taken so far?"

"None," Val said. "I told you! And she ate less than an hour ago."

Alex read the instructions again. "That means she can take the doxycycline hyclate and the prednisolone now and in two hours she can have the sucralfate."

It felt good to be the calm and collected one for a change. Alex checked online and confirmed Val was correct that the number one internet-recommended way to get a dog to take a pill was to hide it in peanut butter, but what was Cash's favorite food?

"Bacon," Val said. "She would murder me for a piece of bacon. She also likes cheese. And eggs, preferably scrambled."

"There you go," Alex said. "All we need to do is order some breakfast."

While they waited for their bacon-egg-and-cheese sandwiches to be delivered from the local deli, Alex read from her phone about how to use a syringe to give a dog medicine.

"Put your hand over her nose and close her mouth," Alex read aloud. "Place the filled syringe into the corner of her mouth and release the liquid slowly. Make sure she licks her lips after."

"How am I supposed to make sure she licks her lips?"

"I think that part should come naturally," Alex said.

After three tries, Val decided none of this was coming naturally. She handed the syringe to Alex.

Bruce looked on, aghast, as Alex cupped the back of Cash's head, held the front of her face, and pushed the syringe into her mouth all the way to the back of her tongue. One quick shot of liquid and Cash pulled away, licking her lips.

"Good girl!" Alex said.

"Thank god." Val collapsed dramatically onto Alex, draping her arms over Alex's shoulders.

Alex felt a jolt at the surprise physical contact.

"I can't believe I'm saying this." Val was still holding on. "But I'm really glad you're here."

"Me too," Alex said, even though, as far as praise went, Val's was mild at best.

Still, was this what bonding felt like?

By late afternoon, Alex and Val were lounging on the L-shaped couch with their laptops on their laps, the remnants of their take-out breakfast sandwiches strewn across the coffee table, and the dogs cuddling between them. Val had taken a shower and cleaned herself up, but she still looked like a gentler version of herself in soft pants and a cozy T-shirt.

All the necessary medicines had been administered.

Alex watched Bruce and Cash sleep. Never had she seen Bruce so content, with his head resting against her legs, Cash alongside his belly, and his back paws blanketing Val's feet. He'd managed physical contact with all three of them, as if to say, *this is my pack*.

Alex remembered learning that dogs were pack animals by nature. Domesticated from wolves, they still exhibited some of the ancestral instinct. Pack animals worked as a team, each member with a specific role, united by a common goal. They slept piled on top of one another because it provided better protection from predators and elements—but Alex preferred to think of it as love. She had already grown so comfortable with the nightly warmth of Bruce in her bed that she couldn't imagine him not being there. They were a pack of two. But today they had grown. This was what

Alex imagined Bruce was dreaming about as he snored and smiled in his sleep.

Alex came over to Val's today because they were supposed to compare notes on Silas now that they had access to all of his laptop activity. They each had files and data to go through separately on their own, with the plan of meeting back up to share what they found. Alex hadn't found much at all. Plus, after seeing Val so flustered over Cash, with her usual defenses down, all Alex wanted to do was talk, to seize the opportunity to learn more about the real Val, the one hiding behind her hardened facade.

"Can I ask you something?" Alex disrupted the drowsy silence.

"No," Val said. Just then, Cash coughed in her sleep and Val winced. "So much for all that medicine."

"It doesn't work instantaneously," Alex said. "Give it a chance."

"It breaks my heart every time she does that." Val sat up. "A few weeks ago, I didn't even have a heart. This is why I never wanted a dog."

"I know what you mean," Alex said. "I've already played out Bruce's death in my mind a million different ways."

Val made a face that either meant she had done exactly the same with Cash, or that Alex had just given her one more reason to think she was an oddball.

"I really lost it at the vet's office last night," Val said. "I couldn't stop screaming at those poor women who worked there, and they were only trying to help."

"I'm sure they get that all the time."

Val ran her fingers across Cash's reddish-brown fur. "It hurts so much to care. I hate it. Have you ever had a dog before Bruce?"

Alex cringed at the question. "Never had a dog," she said. "But I do have dog trauma."

"What the hell does that mean?" Val looked up, semi-amused, teasing insults at the ready.

"I wanted a puppy when I was a kid," Alex said. "More than anything, but my mother was all, *You have a stable full of thoroughbreds, you don't need a dog.*"

"I'm sorry," Val interrupted. "But if your idea of childhood trauma is having a bunch of horses instead of a dog, I'm going to have to ask you to leave."

"Then my mom got sick," Alex continued. "And one day she sat me down and said, *Don't worry, if I die, you can get the puppy you've always wished for, to help you feel better.*"

Alex took a sip of cold coffee from her mug to avoid Val's eyes.

"That's some dark shit," Val said.

Alex knew it was. Even now it was confusing. What in the world was her mother thinking, saying that to an eleven-year-old? Did she honestly believe a pet could serve as a consolation prize for the death of a parent?

"The worst part," Alex said, "was that she told me in the meantime I could prepare. So, there I was reading books about all the different dog breeds and training philosophies. I figured out where in my room I'd put a puppy's bed, what treats I would feed it."

"And then your mom died," Val said.

"That she did."

"And you felt guilty."

"Like a monster," Alex said. "As though I'd killed her by planning for it. I swore I'd never get a dog as long as I lived. I couldn't even look at a dog, let alone touch one—"

"That's why you bugged out at the dog park when I shoved Cash into your arms."

Alex nodded. "But look at me now." She brought Bruce in for a hug as evidence of her evolution.

"I underestimated you," Val said. "Maybe you are as broken as I am." She held her hand out for a fist bump.

Alex acquiesced. "You like me better now that you know I also had shitty parents?"

"Kind of." Val smiled. "I have trouble relating to people who were raised well."

Same, Alex thought.

"Were you close with your dad, at least?" Val asked.

"Close wasn't something our family did," Alex tried to explain. "I spent more time at boarding schools and with nannies than I ever did with either of my parents."

These weren't truths Alex usually said aloud, and doing so was making her temperature and heart rate rise. She needed to settle down, take the focus off herself.

"I wanted to ask you," Alex said. "Something I've been wondering about. When you were left without a parent to take care of you, who did? Did you go into the foster system?"

Val lay back down on the sofa, cradling her head in her hands, and stared up at the ceiling. "I was seventeen. A close friend of my parents took me in for the one year I was still a minor. She was our landlady; she owned the duplex we lived in. She let me stay in our apartment."

"Alone? Rent-free?"

"I worked for her. She owned a dry-cleaning business, among other things."

"That explains your performance at A-One Cleaners." Alex sensed there was also a deeper layer of truth beneath the surface, the part Val wasn't mentioning.

"This was Maria Caruso?" Alex asked, even though she was going out on a limb by referencing anything she had gleaned from her background check on Val.

"It's not what you're thinking," Val said.

"You weren't washing money at the dry cleaner?"

"Yeah, we were. And fencing goods, and running numbers, and a slew of stuff you couldn't even begin to imagine. But Maria was good to me, she saved my life, she's my only family."

Alex said she understood.

"I don't work for her anymore," Val said. "Or mess with any of that stuff. All I do now is earn a meager income as a PI."

"It must have been awful for you, growing up like that."

"That's where you're wrong. I had a blast. Even now, my life is constant adventure. I'm my own boss. I'm great. You're the one who hates their life."

Clearly, Alex had struck a sensitive nerve in Val.

"Fucked-up upbringing or not," Val said. "You've still been handed the world and all you can do is complain. Wah, wah, boohoo, my money is dirty. Guess what? We're living in late-stage capitalism, all money is dirty."

Alex took a moment, a nice deep breath. "So, what I hear you saying is that you'd really like to take a ride on the corporate jet."

"What I'm saying is, I'm not a victim of my circumstances any more or less than you are."

"But isn't everyone a victim of their circumstances?"

Val made no response, and her expression told Alex nothing.

"Well, anyway," Alex said. "I don't hate my life. In fact, I've been enjoying myself quite a bit lately."

Val ignored the hint of flattery. "Talk to me about what happens if we succeed in taking Silas down," she said, overtly changing the subject. "He gets indicted, publicly shamed, declawed. Then what?"

"Then I move on to my next target," Alex said.

"With the ultimate goal of?"

"Reed Industries," Alex admitted to Val, finally. "Under my control, out of the hands of my uncle and cousin."

"Then what?"

Alex knew she should stop speaking. This new mission-based identity that she'd fashioned for herself was predicated on secrecy. If the truth ever got out about what she was doing, she would lose all her access and—worse—be rendered useless once more.

"I clean the company up, take it apart," Alex said anyway, leaving out the part about how she also planned to give it all away, Patagonia-style.

Years back, the outdoor clothing company's owner transferred all of its voting stock to a trust, with the goal of using profits to address climate change and protect the planet. All nonvoting stock was transferred to a nonprofit collective. It was a useful example of what Alex had in mind for Reed's future.

"But let's get back to Silas," Alex said. She glanced at her open laptop on the coffee table, with its screenful of Silas's useless computer activity.

Val slammed the laptop shut. "The reason we're getting nothing out of Silas's data," she said, "is because he's got a desktop computer in his home office that he's probably using as an external hard drive. I saw it upstairs at June's when I used the bathroom. He's also got a line of metal file cabinets with little locks on them, so I think there might be a paper trail. That's where the evidence we're looking for has to be."

Alex was more tired by this news than inspired. "I really don't want either of us to steal anything from June's house. Do you think we could talk to her? Tell her the truth? Maybe she'll want to help us."

Val shook her head. "We'd be taking the chance of losing her for good if she found out now that we've been lying to her."

"But I feel so bad."

"It's for her own good," Val said. "She needs to learn the truth about Silas, but she can't just be told. She has to figure it out herself. Nobody wants to be made to feel like a fool."

Alex agreed, but she still had the feeling that she would rather bring June into the pack. The three of them working together would make them all so much stronger.

Four times in quick succession Val's phone vibrated on the coffee table.

"Do you want to get that?" Alex asked.

"Nope."

Another text came in, more vibration. It was driving Alex crazy.

"Then do you mind if I do?" Alex snatched the phone and silenced it. "Why don't you want to talk to—" Alex checked the contact's name. "Sam?"

Val shot up and grabbed the phone from Alex's hand. "Don't you ever touch my phone again. I'm serious."

Alex could see that she was. "Who's Sam?"

"My ex," Val said.

"The recent one that ended badly?"

The alarmed expression on Val's face told Alex it was.

"Is he bothering you?" Alex asked. "Giving you a hard time?" Knowing what Alex did about Val's past, the idea of her dating a violent man didn't seem far-fetched. "Do you have any reason to be afraid of him?"

Val shook her head, but didn't meet Alex's eyes.

"Is he trying to win you back?" Alex asked.

"She is," Val said.

"Oh. She?" Alex stammered. "Right. I'm sorry, I shouldn't have . . ."

"It's okay." Val took mercy on Alex, allowing her to catch her breath. "I could have mentioned it earlier."

"Weird that you didn't."

"Not really," Val said. "I didn't want you to get the wrong idea."

"I wouldn't have."

"Good."

"Two women who date women can be friends, you know," Alex said.

"Or even better," Val replied. "They can be nothing but professional acquaintances."

Alex laughed. "And here I was thinking we were getting somewhere."

"We are," Val said. "We're getting into Silas's home-office file cabinets."

Alex knew Val had been joking, but she was still a bit hurt. She shot a look to Bruce to tell him it was about time for them to head home.

"You're not thinking of leaving, are you?" Val asked with a sly smile. "Because look at the time: It's almost happy hour."

June arrived at the dog park on this picture-perfect summer evening, vowing to say not a word on the subject of her marriage. What could she say even if she wanted to? *My husband is using my*

love for my dog to hold me hostage? Trying to explain it would make her sound insane, so until she figured out her next move, she would continue going through the motions of her mundane life the same as always. But at the park she felt herself moving about preoccupied, and she seemed to not be fooling anyone.

Meryl was the first person to ask if she was doing okay when she joined the group of regulars in their habitual corner. Alex was the second.

"It's just been one of those days," June replied to each of them separately.

She didn't give sidestepping Meryl's nosiness a second thought, but she was less comfortable circumventing Alex.

June wanted to tell Alex the whole story of her recent trouble with Silas, the way one did with a trusted confidant. It may have been premature to consider Alex her best friend, but that was how June already thought of her. June had become close with Val, too, but it was Alex whom she talked to and texted with every day, and she looked forward to telling Alex stuff, even the silliest things, like whatever clown act Willow had performed, or a catty piece of gossip she had overheard. Alex—and Val—entering her life was the best thing to happen to June in a long time—which was the very reason she felt she couldn't tell them about Silas's threats.

To properly convey the reality of the situation, June would need to divulge how long she had been elevating Silas's needs above her own, seeking his approval, accepting blame to avoid conflict, assessing her own self-worth based on how he behaved. Then what would they think of her? June was too ashamed to find out.

"Junebug, hello." Kennedy was wiggling her manicured fingernails in front of June's face. "I asked you, what are you wearing?"

"Hmm?"

"To the gala."

June realized everyone in their circle, including Alex and Val, was waiting for her to answer.

"I'm sure I have a dress in my closet from a wedding or something," June said.

Alex and Val were simpatico. Alex said she had something from a bar mitzvah she went to last year.

"Same here," Val said. "But it was a First Communion."

"What about Willow?" Kennedy asked. "And Cash and Bruce? Of course, Chester will be in a Ricky Roybin original, as will Popcorn, but I don't even want to discuss it."

Kennedy was keeping close tabs on their core group's attire. She rattled off a list she had committed to memory.

"Meryl's Paisley will be wearing a summer barbecue homage to Sarah Jessica Parker's famous Elizabeth Hobbs Keckley–inspired Met Gala gown, which itself was an homage to Mary Todd Lincoln, so it's sort of a triple-homage. Eloise is going to be wearing something in a Regency style that Regina's seamstress mother is designing herself. And Yoshi the shih tzu is coming in a floral gown inspired by Oscar de la Renta's garden collection. No word yet on the Silver Fox's Mollie, or Karen's Cavalier King, and I won't dare approach Edna Pearlberg with the question. I assume Virgil will be naked."

"It's not like he'll be a streaker," Val said. "Dogs were never intended to wear clothes."

"I haven't gotten anything for Willow yet," June confessed as she watched Willow chew on a stick that Bruce and Cash tried desperately to steal away.

"This fundraiser has gotten completely out of control," Val said. "There is no way I'm dressing up Cash."

June looked to Alex. "Is it dumb that I'll feel bad if Willow is one of the only dogs at the gala not wearing something fun?"

Then to Val, June said, "We don't need to get anything over the top or expensive. Just something to show participation."

"In general," Val said, "neither I nor Cash participate in things."

"Then why does it sound like you're about to get roped into going shopping?" Alex asked, smiling.

"Because you both are," June said. "I know just the shop."

This was better, June thought. She was already feeling more clear-headed. *Stay busy*, she encouraged herself, *stay positive. Remember, loneliness is a health concern of epidemic proportions; it could be downright deadly, so keep your friends and keep them close.*

CHAPTER 17

Potomac, Maryland, bordered the Potomac River and lay just outside the beltway. Like neighboring Bethesda, the place had the feel of a high-priced suburb with big lots, large houses, and front lawns that required ride-on mowers. Until today, Val had only driven through or around its rolling hills and gated mansions, but in addition to fine dining, historic parks, and accommodating one of Bravo's Real Housewives series, Potomac was also home to Bitch Please, a luxury boutique that sold designer clothes for dogs.

Driving along River Road, Val passed the Congressional Country Club, bordered by pillars and a white fence. The club was famous for its fancy golf courses and prestigious membership, but Val was interested in the place for its history during World War II, when its hundreds of acres had been leased to the US government to serve as the training ground for the country's first intelligence agency—a covert operation called the Office of Strategic Services.

Right there, Val thought, where today's congressmen and lobbyists still cursed balls in the sand trap, soldiers had trained as spies, saboteurs, and undercover agents. Val craned her neck to get a good look at the grounds as she drove by. She couldn't help herself; she had always been a sucker for a good spy story.

Val pulled into the shopping center parking lot, where Bitch Please was positioned between a café and the chicest new marker of a stylish neighborhood, a non-alcoholic liquor store.

Alex had arrived first and was sitting in her Camry, looking like a secret agent herself, just waiting there, staring straight ahead.

"You ever play on that golf course near here?" Val asked Alex as she pulled Cash from her car seat.

"The Blue Course at Congressional?" Alex stepped out of her car. "Yeah, me and Tiger Woods hang out there all the time."

"I can't tell if you're joking." Val waited for Bruce to get four feet on the pavement before letting Cash jump all over him.

Alex, Val noticed, had begun to stray from her Alex Miller costume of bargain basement clothing, little by little introducing a few of her own favorite pieces. Today she wore a pair of brown leather boots that Val could tell were expensive, and a well-cut pair of jeans that hugged her body in such a way that they must have been tailored specifically to her long leg-to-waist proportions.

"She seems good," Alex said of Cash. "How's the coughing been?"

Val shrugged. "The medicines seem to be doing their job." Val didn't have the words to describe the relief she felt over this fact, so she didn't talk about that.

Every morning when she woke up, and each night before she went to sleep, Val reminded herself how inconvenient it was to have a pet, and that Cash was an especially needy dog. It only made sense, practically speaking, for her to sell Cash when this was over. Her life, after this job concluded, was not set up for a canine companion.

Then she would remember how she felt at the urgent care office, melting in her chair.

Along with the emotions she was forced to feel during the whole vet fiasco, Val was further humbled by the pathetic state she had allowed Alex to see her in.

It was turning out that Alex was alright as far as people went, even for a billionaire. But Val needed to keep her eye on the prize. Somehow she needed to score an invite to Alex's Manhattan apartment, where she could dig for more info and, ideally, plant some surveillance. Only worming her way into Alex's bank accounts would reveal the next step.

"I'm glad Cash is feeling better," Alex said. She looked about to say something more, then stopped herself.

Val wished she hadn't told Alex her ex was a woman during their misguided bonding session on Val's couch. It was a slip, on account of her weakened state at the time. And she never knew how to properly behave when people were too nice to her. But now that Val's head was screwed back on properly, she was furious with herself for sharing that level of personal information with Alex.

Val wanted to draw Alex closer, but not that close. So-called romance scams were beyond her pay grade. Manipulating someone via fake friendship was one thing, but getting physically intimate with a mark was a whole other situation. Val had never done it, and she wasn't about to start now.

Not that sex had to be so sacred. Lord knew Val had let a dozen and one deadbeats have their way with her—men, women, and genderqueers alike. If she had a type, it was someone who was somewhat disinterested, at least a little bit of an alcoholic, and emotionally damaged beyond repair. It was almost as if she couldn't see potential lovers who were kind and well-adjusted. Her eyes passed right over them to the brooding asshole in the corner.

Val's paramours also tended to be broke. For whatever reason, she had never slept with a single person of means. Money and luxury itself she found sexy beyond her control—but apparently not the people who wielded it. Which, historically, made it easy to steal from them with no risk of falling for their bullshit.

"Still no June," Alex said while she and Val walked across the parking lot, their dogs frolicking at the ends of their leashes. "It's not like her to be late."

When they reached the front of the store, Alex peeked inside the window between one display dog mannequin (a doggequin?) wearing a wedding dress and another wearing a tuxedo. "I guess we can go in without her."

"Are you sure? I'm a little scared," Val said, opening the door slowly.

Inside, the boutique was organized by category and then further broken down by style. Formalwear was its own section, separate from casualwear, but from there you could go classic, bohemian, streetwear, vintage, maximalist or minimalist. Val was immediately overwhelmed.

"Wow, look at this." Alex held up a baby-doll-sized cashmere and lace dress that was hand-beaded with pearls. "Only $520."

Val ran her hands over a mini motorcycle jacket made of leather soft as butter. *Oh my goodness,* she thought, *Cash and I could be twins! No, Val, no.* She had to remind herself that she was not that person. "I think we'd better find the sale rack," she said.

They dragged Cash and Bruce toward the back.

Some of the store's categories were baffling. Outerwear was straightforward enough, and swimwear seemed superfluous but entertaining, but within accessories there was actual dog jewelry—fourteen-karat gold necklaces and clip-on Swarovski crystal earrings.

Where Val really lost her ability to cope was intimates, where, in addition to pajamas and robes, there were "sexy" panties.

"Alex?" Val asked. "Why?"

"I don't know, Val. I really don't."

A saleswoman approached to ask if they needed any help. Val resisted the urge to demand an explanation for doggy foreplay-wear.

"What an adorable little Griff." The saleswoman bent down to pet Cash.

Of course this was the place where a Brussels Griffon was recognizable.

"We're just browsing," Alex told the saleswoman. Then to Val she said, "I'm beginning to worry about June. She should be here by now. I'm going to text her."

Alex and June would stay friends after all this, Val predicted. Maybe not right away, but somehow, someday Alex would find her way back to June, and tell her the whole truth. And June, free from Silas by then, with a new lease on life, would forgive her.

Whereas Val would be . . . where? Long gone? Or still buzzing around Alex, years into skimming from some account? Val would need to hammer down a timeline. Figure out how long she could stay in Alex's orbit without getting caught.

"June seemed a bit down the last few times I've seen her," Val said. "Not her bubbly self."

Alex agreed, just as Val caught sight of June pushing through the boutique's front door.

Together, June and Willow were a whirlwind. "Sorry, sorry, sorry I'm late," June said with a nervous tremor in her voice.

Val could immediately see that June was off by her posture, her gait, the way her shoulders slumped. All were so un-Junelike, as if she were carrying a heavy weight upon her back. Up close it was obvious she had been crying.

"Everything okay?" Alex asked her.

June peddled a few common excuses for her tardiness, including that she was a "dummy" and should have left the house earlier.

Alex looked to Val as if to ask *Do we pretend to believe her?*

"June," Val said, modulating her voice to sound more caring and understanding than she actually was. "You seem rattled. Has anything happened that you'd like to share with us?"

Sharing was the word Val's caseworkers or state-mandated therapists would deploy when they were trying to get her to talk about her feelings. It used to enrage her, as sharing implied Val's most personal and brutal experiences were communal, that her pain could somehow be divided among them—an impossibility.

I'm okay was Val's usual answer to the *care to share?* query. To which one social worker in particular would always reply, "I know you're okay, but I'd like to see you better than just okay," enraging Val further.

June, however, responded favorably to the offer to unload, if the tears that filled her eyes could be considered favorable.

"It's Silas," June said. "We just had a terrible argument on the phone. That's why I was late."

"Oh?" Alex sounded overly interested, but June was too busy further unraveling to notice.

"Silas and I haven't been getting along so well," June confessed.

Val had the tingly sense this was headed somewhere she and Alex wanted it to go. "Have you been fighting a lot?"

"It's my fault," June said, not really answering the question. "He's stuck on the idea that I'm trying to leave him, and he'll never let that happen."

"Wait." Alex glanced at Val with unchecked glee. "Are you considering leaving Silas?"

"I don't know," June said. "But even if I wanted to, I can't, because he'll take Willow from me."

"What?" Val and Alex said in unison.

June explained. "If I ever try to divorce Silas, he'll withhold custody of Willow."

"That's crazy," Alex said.

"So, you've actually discussed the possibility of divorce?" Val asked, hopefully.

"Now he'll barely let me out of his sight," June continued. "He's constantly checking in. I told him that he has to trust me, but I need to earn his trust back."

"Or leave him," Alex said, and Val could see the weakening in her expression. No poker face on this one whatsoever.

Val tried to catch Alex's eye, to silently communicate that she needed to keep it together. To June, Val asked, "Is it even true that if you and Silas separated, he could keep Willow?"

June nodded. "Because he bought her before we were married, by Maryland state law she's considered his dog. Plus I'm afraid he'll, well, I'm not sure what he would do to Willow once he got control of her, just to spite me."

"That's not a reason to stay with him." Alex's wheels were turning. "You can fight it. We'll fight it, together. Do you have a good lawyer? I can help set you up with an excellent lawyer."

"Take it easy, Alex." Val needed to stop the runaway train. She could almost see Alex's next words forming on her tongue, the offer to pay for June's legal services, forgetting herself entirely. "Let June talk."

"Excuse me." There was a tap on Val's shoulder. The saleswoman, who had appeared at Val's side, pointed downward. Cash was chewing the hem of a pink dress encrusted with rhinestones.

Val picked Cash up and returned the dress to its place on the rack. "Maybe we should take this conversation elsewhere," she said to Alex and June.

"But we still need outfits for the dogs." June wiped the tears from her face.

"Who cares? Here." Val headed to the clearance rack and grabbed a half tuxedo that looked like it would fit Bruce. She tossed it to Alex.

"It's classic," Alex said. "I like it."

"June, how about this?" Val plucked out a lace-and-sequin-topped party dress with a bow at the waist and a layered tulle skirt. It was perfectly lovely, except for its color, which Val believed could be described as brat green. "It's summery, no?"

"I think I know why this dress is on clearance," June said. "And why there are so many of them." She checked the price tag. "Sold."

The only item on sale small enough for Cash was a satiny red-and-white-checkered bandana that reminded Val of a fancy picnic napkin. It would have to do.

"Just be glad I'm not forcing you into a gown," Val said to Cash. "Or that Hawaiian shirt and those silly sunglasses. Or, worse, some dumb food costume like a half-eaten baked potato."

At the checkout line, Val took Alex aside. "Watch yourself, remember your cover."

"We have to tell her the truth about Silas," Alex said.

"No. We don't."

"If she only knew," Alex whispered, "that he hired you to spy on her. Along with everything he's been doing at the EPA? The truth will give her the courage she needs to leave him."

"We can convince her to cut him loose without you blowing us up in the process," Val whispered back. "Let me take the lead."

The saleswoman finished ringing up June's purchase and June turned to them, bag in hand.

Alex said, "There's a coffee shop next door with outdoor tables. Let's go sit down there to talk."

"I feel like I've already done enough talking," June said. "Too much."

"So has Alex," Val said.

Alex went into the pink-macaron-colored café while Val and June sat out front with the dogs. As far as Alex could tell, the place was suffering from an identity crisis, part posh coffee shop, part candy-coated bakery, with a third left over for green-juice-drinking health nuts. She exited with a cappuccino for June, a black coffee for Val, a double shot of wheatgrass for herself, and an impulse-buy croissant that nobody asked for.

Outside, Val was distributing "stay quiet" treats to the dogs while June poured them a travel-bowlful of water from her Yeti bottle.

June was talking about how she already felt better, and that she'd overreacted to her argument with Silas.

Alex doled out their beverages and sat. "So you were considering separating from him, but now you're walking it back?"

"I'm having a hard time knowing for sure what I want." June kept her eyes cast downward on her cappuccino.

"We're here for you," Val said before Alex could. "Let us help."

June let out a heavy exhale and then laughed. "It feels kind of good just to say these things out loud."

Val offered June a gracious smile. "Then say more."

Alex wanted to tell June everything right then, about her own connection to Silas, and Val's connection to Silas, to put a stop to all the lies. But Alex also recognized how much she wanted to help June free herself, and she couldn't do that if June stormed off right now—which was the risk of confessing.

Alex swallowed down her bitter wheatgrass shot.

She did her best to remain quiet as June spoke openly for the first time about what went on behind the closed doors of her marriage. Silas's excessive jealousy and accusations, his manipulation and constant criticism, his insistence on having his way, and how he tried to isolate her from friends and family. But even as June vented, it was clear to Alex that she remained unable to see just how awful Silas's behavior was. She made excuses for him, conjured up sympathetic explanations, forced herself to look on the bright side and only see the best of him.

As Alex watched sweet June, who wore an adorable sky-blue sundress with a ladybug print, struggle to say a single negative thing about Silas without immediately apologizing, she wished she could cry out, *He doesn't appreciate you! He is a human bushel over your light. Cut the bastard loose!*

But no one could hear that about a person they loved, not even June, whose heart Alex pictured as bigger than average.

"I feel like I'm complaining too much," June said. "Like I'm being ungrateful."

Alex had to look away. She watched two teenage boys trudging along the sidewalk in the distance. One of them bounced a basketball as they walked, and the rhythmic sound of ball against pavement gave Alex something calming to focus on while June ran down a list of Silas's better qualities.

Alex tasted blood. She had inadvertently chewed through her lower lip. Because even though she understood June's detachment from Silas must happen on its own timeline, and that she could only support her and pray she got there soon, Alex still wanted to kill the man.

The teenagers had disappeared from view, but Alex could still hear the echo of their basketball as she returned her gaze to June's face, which was pink with emotion.

Alex noticed that Val was being uncharacteristically quiet, letting June divulge the secrets of her marital strife, urging her on with only a nod of her head or a murmured *mm-hmm*. She had become attractive to Alex in a way that surprised and confused her a little. Alex often couldn't distinguish between being drawn to someone because she wanted to sleep with them or because she wanted to be more like them—and this could definitely be a case of that. But she was delighted and relieved to learn that Val's ex was a woman. Maybe a little too much?

"I should get back home," June said. "I still have chores that need doing before Silas returns from work."

"Do you want us to come with you?" Val asked. "For company, or protection?"

June declined, which left Alex and Val alone at the table with Bruce and Cash at their feet.

"I applaud your restraint," Val said, once June was out of earshot. "I honestly thought you were going to break and blow my cover, along with your own."

Alex didn't mention how close she had come to doing just that.

"What kind of man," Val said, "uses a dog he doesn't even like as a bargaining chip?"

"June has way too much sympathy for him," Alex said.

"June has too much sympathy for everyone."

"You say that like it's a bad thing."

"In this case, it is." Val sipped her coffee. "People give Silas a pass because he puts up a good front, but you know who else you can say that about? Con men. Sociopaths. The worst of the worst."

"You speaking from experience?"

"If my father taught me anything it's that everyone thinks they have good instincts, but anyone, literally anyone, can be conned."

Alex considered this. She disagreed that everyone thought they had good instincts. She herself, for example, recognized her own terrible judgment, how she was easily influenced and often acted without thinking things through.

"What do you look so sad about?" Val asked. "June wanting out of her marriage is just one more reason to double our efforts. Think about it. What better way to emancipate June from Silas than sending him to jail? We have to get into those file cabinets."

"I really don't want to break into June's house," Alex said. "There must be another way."

"If you can come up with one, I'm all ears," Val replied, in that cocky way she had, certain Alex wouldn't be able to outthink her.

But Alex had been mulling over an idea. "There's an event coming up," she said. "The first week of July, something Silas will most likely be at. It's this annual gala thrown by the Station Institute, in Manhattan."

Val was half listening and half picking at the croissant on the table between them. "Right," Val said. "Your people. Can you believe there was once a time in my life when *gala* was not a term in common rotation? Not long ago, either."

"The Station Institute folks are not my people. They were my dad's people, and they're giving him a posthumous award. I wasn't going to show, but what if . . ."

Val washed down a hunk of croissant with her coffee. Her attention was mildly piqued. "Go on."

"What if I go and try to get Silas to say something incriminating. I can wear a wire or something," Alex said. "I assume you know how to do that kind of thing?"

"You assume correctly. But what makes you so sure he'll be there?"

"It's his crowd," Alex said. "And besides, I can check the guest list ahead of time. It's my own dead, founding-member father who's being honored, after all."

Val downed the last of her coffee. "Not bad, partner."

Alex couldn't stop from smiling.

"But getting what we need from Silas will take more than a simple wire," Val said. "I'll have to take a trip to Queens to get some of my equipment."

"I'm ready when you are, partner."

"Funny." Val swept croissant dust from the table onto the ground, where the dogs tried to catch it on their tongues. "You're not coming with me."

"Even funnier is that you think you can convince me otherwise." The chance to see where Val really lived was too intriguing to pass up. So much about a person could be gleaned from their living space, and with someone as withholding as Val, it might be Alex's only chance to observe a part of her she'd never outright reveal.

Alex looked to the dogs, who were still scavenging for crumbs beneath the table. "Hey Bruce, do you want to take a trip to Cash's city apartment?"

Cash responded first by jumping up onto Alex's lap.

"That was definitely a yes," Alex said to Val.

CHAPTER 18

Val never intended for Alex to be standing in the middle of her living room on a random afternoon in June, where she rarely, if ever, invited anyone. But here they were. The summer sun was blaring through the dirty windows, making the temperature inside the small apartment about ninety-six degrees. Val turned up the window AC unit to full blast, but it would still take an hour to cool things down. Cash and Bruce ran around sniffing every corner, panting from the heat, snorting at Val's belongings, while Alex took in the modest space.

It was a typical Queens row house, two stories, narrow with a pointy roof, and semi-attached to a row of similar homes. Val wondered if Alex had ever been in a row house before, or if she had ever been in the borough of Queens before. Inside, the apartment was nothing special. A long, slender floor plan with the kitchen, bathroom, and dining room in front, the living room in the middle, and the bedroom at the rear, but with windows on three sides, the place got a decent amount of light. Val lived on the second floor. Maria, Val's landlord, lived on the first floor and was thankfully not home.

"It looks less like a PI's headquarters than a regular apartment," Alex said, sounding let down. "Is there another room?"

Maybe Val would regret this. She might already regret it.

"The only other room is where I sleep," Val replied. "Most of the work I do takes place outside the home. What were you expecting?"

"I don't know, a few computer screens, some cool gadgets maybe." Alex perused the bookshelf like she expected one of the hardbacks to be the decoy latch that would swing the whole thing open like a door. "Maybe even some weapons?"

"Sorry to disappoint." Val shook off her jacket and tied her hair back.

She was messing with Alex. Of course Val had cool gadgets and weaponry. That's why they were here. But did Alex really expect all that stuff to be displayed out in the open?

"We came to get equipment, didn't we?" Alex was eyeballing Val's linen closet like it might be the secret entrance to the Batcave.

The dogs redeployed to the bedroom to have a circular zoomy contest on top of Val's bed.

"Before we move ahead," Val said. "Do you understand how dangerous it will be for you to wear a wire and get face-to-face with Silas at the Station Institute event? If anything goes wrong . . ."

Alex waved off Val's concern as she knew she would. Despite all of Alex's anxiety, or maybe because of it, there was something abandoned about her, something uncontrolled. Under certain circumstances she could be extremely reckless.

"Okay," Val said. "If you're sure you want to go ahead with this." She reached into her pocket and shook her key ring free, then unlocked the large but unassuming sideboard that her parents used to refer to as the "china cabinet," even though it never once housed a single piece of china.

Val opened the sideboard's two heavy wooden doors to reveal its inner shelving and drawers, neatly packed with spy tech of various sorts, from old-fashioned bugs to the latest electronics and surveillance equipment.

"I knew it." Alex's eyes glimmered. She reached inside.

Val smacked her hand away. "No touching." She selected a few choice items. "Do you wear glasses?"

"Contacts," Alex said.

"Have the people at this party ever seen you in glasses?"

"Sure, why?"

Val plucked a pair of eyeglasses from the shelf, then closed the cabinet's doors.

She turned to Alex. "I'm going to train you on how to properly use this stuff, under one condition."

"Anything," Alex said.

"You have to take me to see your apartment. Where you really live, here in New York."

The excitement drooped from Alex's face. "Anything but that."

"That's the deal," Val said. "Take it or leave it."

Fair was fair. If Alex got to see Val's personal space, it was only right that the favor should be returned.

Val's heart throbbed with anticipation.

"Fine," Alex said.

Val climbed out of Alex's Camry and wrangled Cash and Bruce while Alex handed her keys to the parking garage attendant.

The sun setting had cooled the evening somewhat, but not enough. Val's T-shirt was stuck to the small of her sweaty back.

"Here we are," Alex said.

Val wasn't sure if Alex was speaking to her or to Bruce, as it was Alex's habit to talk to Bruce as if he were another human along for the ride. Not that Val couldn't relate.

Val looked up. The building, set against the electric blue summer-night sky, was somewhat underwhelming. Its limestone surface was in desperate need of a power wash, and the canopy awning at the entrance was faded and weather beaten. One would hardly guess this was the home of some of the wealthiest, most powerful people in the world. But wasn't that often the way of the gruesomely rich? Appearances were just one more thing they didn't need to try for.

Alex led them inside through the unextravagant lobby, up, up, up, in an elevator that, with the swipe of a fob, opened directly into a private vestibule, where Alex unlocked a secondary steel door with a traditional key.

Val was still getting a handle on the fact that the elevator opened directly into Alex's apartment as Alex rushed her and the dogs through an art-filled entry hall and past a mahogany-paneled library.

Alex unclasped Cash and Bruce's leashes and signaled for Val to enter a large living room. The dogs took off running to explore however many other rooms were left to discover.

Alex stood aside, allowing Val to take it all in. Two long sofas faced one another across a low table, accompanied by a few casually positioned armchairs. To the left, cornered by windows, was a grand piano. To the right, a fully stocked wet bar.

Alex took off her jacket and tossed it over a chair. "I didn't decorate this place. Half this stuff was my dad's. I was just too lazy to get rid of it when I took the apartment over. Can I make you a drink?"

Val could have really used one, but she said, "No, thanks. I'm fine."

Alex went ahead anyway, uncorking a bottle of red wine that probably cost the equivalent of one of Val's more lucrative jobs.

There was a thud in a far-off room, followed by the pitter-patter of two sets of paws. "Bruce's tail already took something down," Alex said, nonplussed.

Val could see it already, how Alex fit into this space, whether it was decorated to her personal taste or not. This was her natural habitat.

"Imagine Bruce's surprise," Val said. "All this time thinking that one-bedroom hovel you've been staying in was his forever home. Meanwhile, he's got all this space to romp around in."

Val didn't mention the flip side of Cash's realization earlier that her—Wait. Was Val calling it a *forever home*? And when had the term *forever anything* entered her lexicon? Either way, the point was that both of Val's apartments, real and fake, were humble, to say the least.

"I don't even have a dog bowl here yet." Alex grabbed what looked like an extremely expensive piece of vintage glass décor, maybe a candy dish? Who really knew when it came to the lay objects of the affluent? Alex filled it with water from the sink behind the bar and set it on the floor near the doorway.

Val did her best to acclimate to her surroundings. Of course the ceilings were high, the furniture elegant, the artwork priceless. In Val's previous line of work, one had to learn how to be comfortable around wealth—but here, now, she felt in her body the gaping chasm between the rich and superrich. She had not seen the Colosseum in Rome or the Taj Majal or even the Grand Canyon, but she had heard that in the face of such magnificence people experienced a sense of awe, an expansion in their chest, a lifting of spirit. That was how this apartment made Val feel. This was her wonder of the world.

Val walked toward the floor-to-ceiling windows to admire the view, imagining the feeling of dominance that came with living in a place like this, from where you could literally look down on people all day. She was self-aware enough to recognize the cognitive dissonance between her loathing of Alex's wealth and her overwhelming desire to possess it, but the awareness did nothing to stop her heart from beating faster or the sweat forming on her brow. The feel-good hormones surged through her veins, rousing the reward centers of her brain, whether she could justify them or not.

Alex handed her a crystal glass half-filled with a deep ruby wine. "I can feel you judging me."

"For what?" Val asked. "Having the most amazing apartment I've ever seen? I hope you know you're going to give me a full tour."

Val needed to see more, all of it, every inch.

"It's shameful." Alex took a seat on one of the sofas. "I should've already sold this place or, like, given it to someone."

Alex's shame made her too generous, too giving. Val remembered the look on Alex's face when June was talking about leaving Silas, how obviously Alex wanted to solve all of June's problems for her. It was palpable—Val could almost reach out and touch it—how badly Alex wished to be someone else's savior, to abate her deep-seated guilt.

It was all too much. Val was failing to keep her wits about her. She was getting lightheaded.

Ask any con artist the most basic trick to scamming someone and they'll say, *Get them under the ether.* As Gianni explained it to Val, the ether was a heightened emotional state that made it hard for a person to think clearly or make a rational decision. It was exactly where you wanted someone if you were trying to sell them a sham sweepstakes or fake gold coins—and you got them there by finding their emotional trigger.

If Val were trying to induce ether in Alex, for example, she might ask about her fraught relationship with her father, the untimely death of her mother, or push her further into feeling even more guilty about her unearned privilege. And once she got Alex talking, Val would then throttle up on those complicated emotions until all of Alex's logic went right out the floor-to-ceiling window.

Instead, it was Val whose head felt like it just hit the clouds.

Val took a seat beside Alex and set her drink down on the table, already too drunk for alcohol. Then, immediately changing her mind, she stood back up and asked to use the restroom.

Alex pointed the way. There was a half bath just across the hall.

Val shut herself inside and took a few deep breaths. How did the bathrooms of the wealthy always smell like lavender or sandalwood or whatever? Did their shit literally not stink? And the toilet paper. It must have been two-hundred-ply. Where did they even find it so soft and thick? Did Alex have it special-ordered? It was basically an entirely different product from the single-ply, sandpaper-rough toilet tissue Val grew up with, which, like the milk in the fridge and the cereal in the cabinets, was generic and in short supply.

Val washed her hands with Alex's silky liquid soap, dried them on her plush towel.

She returned to Alex feeling somewhat better and also slightly worse.

"You know," she said, in spite of herself, "all I ever dreamed of, when I was a kid, was to be rich."

"And now?" Alex asked.

"Now I want to know what kind of car you drive. Because it isn't a Toyota Camry."

Alex cracked the tiniest smile.

"Fine." Val course-corrected. "Tell me whichever one car, of the many you own, that you've got parked down in the garage of this building."

"The Porsche," Alex said. "A 911 Carrera T."

"How fast does it go?" Val asked.

Alex finally allowed herself to break into a full grin. "Fast."

CHAPTER 19

Alex judged her reflection in her bedroom's full-length mirror. Her ensemble, a black pantsuit and crisp ivory button-down shirt, was understated rather than festive. The exact look she was going for.

As Alex had told Val back when they were preparing for this night, she didn't wear eyeglasses often, but she did so frequently enough that this new pair wouldn't draw much attention. It was a plus that she had once been widely photographed wearing a similar style at her father's funeral. Those she had worn because it was easier to cry in glasses than contact lenses, though they turned out to be unnecessary, as she had never come to tears. This pair she wore for the video camera embedded in its frame.

"Look at me," Val said, examining Alex up and down. She slipped a ballpoint pen that was also a recording device into Alex's front jacket pocket.

In the mirror, Alex turned left and right. "From every angle it's almost invisible."

"What does it matter?" Val said. "It's only a pen. It even writes like a regular ballpoint in case someone asks to borrow it. Just make sure you get it back."

Alex loved these new toys, the glasses, the pen. This may have been the most fun she'd ever had in her adult life.

Two weeks ago now, when Alex first brought Val here to her home in New York, she had been concerned. Would Val tease her endlessly or seethe below the surface? Would it make Val only feel worse about her own living style and its limitations? Would it stir a dangerous jealousy? Nothing positive could come from it, that was certain, which was why Alex never had guests.

Instead, what Alex found on Val's face, in her demeanor, emitting from her very pores, was pure, unadulterated joy.

The moment Val asked about the car, Alex knew she would be tossing her the keys. When Alex said, "Want to take her for a spin?" it was not so much a question as it was a leap of faith.

Whether it was wise or prudent to let a near stranger set sail in an extremely fast prized possession ceased to matter. The potential risk was well worth the reward of seeing Val's flushed face when she returned, her accelerated breath, the smile that came through her entire face. "This baby turns on a dime," she said.

It was true, the car did, but when was the last time Alex noticed? Even with an automobile like that, she usually drove responsibly. Unless she was in a particularly bad mood, in which case, look out. But Alex wasn't ever doing donuts in a parking lot as she suspected Val had.

Alex loved her Porsche, but she simultaneously hated what loving her Porsche said about her. She wished to be unaffected by the trappings of wealth, immune to the indoctrination of advertising and capitalism, and she could list every which way she was a hypocrite when it came to her privilege, at least for now.

Val, on the other hand, was unconflicted when it came to wanting more because she had never had enough.

Neither position was completely in the right. Somewhere in the middle, Alex supposed, was where the correct answer should be found, if there was a correct answer to how much a person was entitled to desire.

Alex was fully aware of the effect her wealth was having on Val—and it made Alex happy, because she liked Val, and she wanted Val to like her back. It was that uncomplicated.

Val was fun, exciting, and she lived the kind of life Alex could only dream of. So, wasn't it symbiotic? Each of them getting something she desperately lacked. The pleasure of a monied lifestyle for Val, and the gratification of companionship for Alex.

This wouldn't be the first time Alex bought someone's company and attention—she had been doing so all her life. It came with the territory of being Alex Reed. And anyway, Alex was set on giving her entire inheritance away. It would take time to do so, but the reality was that she would not be this wealthy for long. So why not have one last hurrah? Val might drift away once Alex could no longer enable her to see the world from such great heights, but Alex was at peace with that. She had to be. Otherwise, she would continue to be lonely and alone from now till then. What would that prove?

"Are you paying attention?" Val asked.

Alex hadn't been.

"This is serious," Val said. "What you're about to do is illegal. And even if you get Silas on tape saying something incriminating, it won't be admissible in court."

All of Alex's senses were already buzzing. "Erin knows how to finagle stuff using confidential informants, and whatnot, to get a warrant."

"Fidelity, Bravery, Integrity," Val said, quoting the bureau's motto.

"They do what they have to do to get what they need," Alex said.

"You know that's the same justification the bad guys use, right?"

Just then, Alex's cell phone rang in her pocket, and she knew by the ring who it was.

"I've got to take this," she said to Val and dashed across the hall to a guest room where she could close the door.

"Hello," she said to Erin, phone to her ear. "I'm not screening you, but I'm also not letting you talk me out of it."

Alex was sorry she had ever told Erin about the plan she and Val had cooked up for the Institute gala, or that she had brought Val on to assist with the Silas mission at all.

"You hired a criminal?" were Erin's exact words. Then, "Please tell me she doesn't know about me."

Alex confessed to sharing with Val the tiniest bit about Erin, but not much. Mostly Alex defended Val as an upright citizen and master of covert ops, to which Erin replied, "Of course she is. And she's doing quite the job on you."

"I'm begging you not to go ahead with this asinine plan tonight," Erin said now.

"It's happening," Alex replied. "You'll thank me when I get the evidence that scores you your next promotion."

Erin wasn't buying it. "Whatever's going on in your head right now with this girl, that you're some Agatha Christie spy team like Tommy and Tuppence or a Mrs. and Mrs. Smith—it's a fantasy. It's worse than fantasy. It's horror. You can't trust her. She will turn on you eventually."

"I'm hanging up now," Alex said.

"If you get busted tonight, my name stays out of your mouth."

"You may not have faith in Val," Alex said. "But you can have faith in me. I thought you knew that."

"Okay drama queen, take it easy."

Alex ended the call and returned to Val, who asked, "Who was that?"

Alex said no one because she didn't feel like getting into it. Then she checked her watch. "I should get going. Will you be okay here alone with Bruce and Cash?"

"I can bring them back to Queens with me," Val said. "I wouldn't hold it against you if you didn't want to leave me here by myself."

Alex draped her topcoat over her shoulders. Was she being naïve? Too trustful? Was she supposed to be worried that Val would rob her? That felt absurd at this point. The two of them had a connection, Alex was sure of it, because they were as alike as they were different. And whether Val felt the same or not, Alex was beginning to believe she was a more complete person with Val than when she was alone.

"Bruce!" Alex called out. "You're in charge. Keep Val out of trouble."

Val followed her toward the doorway. "Please be careful."

Alex did her best to project authority as she headed out of her apartment building to where the car was waiting.

On the drive, she tried to not to think of all that could go wrong. Instead, she redirected her attention to the people on the street, the red-orange neon of tavern signs and electric purple of vape shops, two strangers hunched on stools in a deli window trying not to bump elbows. They were the usual sights, rendered slightly more interesting with her own purpose. Alex always did better when she had a clear intention, a goal to reach for. And when in doubt tonight, she would tell herself to simply do whatever Val would do.

Already these past two months, with Val's influence, Alex had noticed she'd been calmer, looser, a less neurotic version of herself. When she was at her worst, Alex's thinking was clouded, her speech slower, and the world passed through her eyes with a sepia tone. Whereas lately life had been happening in real time and in full color. Maybe it should have discomfited her, how easily her mood could be influenced. Was this all she'd needed all along? A buddy? A slight crush?

But tonight would be the true test. If ever there was a social gathering with the power to make Alex anxious, this was it.

As she pulled up to the venue, the crowd gathered out front reminded Alex why she did not usually attend these events. The average Station Institute member was old and cranky. The cantankerous think tank was founded by her father and uncle when they decided that in addition to their outrageous wealth, they should be powerful political influencers. The Institute branded itself as a collective of successful, intelligent businessmen who believed it was their duty in life to lead and guide others by shaping public discourse and government policy agendas. In reality, the group existed to keep money in their own pockets. Undermining the clean energy sector was its actual, unstated mission.

Alex stepped out of her car to a trio of photographers snapping her picture. Whether they were friends or foes, who could say? She shook the hand of a former mayor of New York City—*snap snap snap*, more photos—and a former New Jersey gubernatorial candidate.

Because her father was to be honored tonight with a posthumous award, nobody seemed surprised to see Alex enter the grand ballroom. Members of the Institute and distinguished guests alike welcomed her with open arms as John Reed's surrogate, interpreting her appearance as a gesture of good faith. The wayward daughter was finally stepping up.

High priests of the conservative establishment patted her on the back with approval. That jerk who spent millions to dispute the science behind climate change and global warming. And this clown who was a right-wing conspiracy theorist. And that old buzzard whose sworn mortal enemy was a woman's right to an abortion. There was the half-wit who once said the insurgents who attacked the Capitol on January 6 should have brought more guns.

"It was good of you to come," Alex's uncle William said, appearing at her side to pose for a camera. "He would have appreciated it."

Alex smiled like her uncle's positive reinforcement meant something to her, then excused herself to track down Silas, whom she found in a wood-columned side room that had been repurposed as a cigar lounge. He and Alex's cousin Brandon and a few other big oil VIPs stood in a circle fraternizing and blowing smoke. Alex adjusted her glasses and made her way over.

"Alex! Join the party," Brandon said, then to the huddle of men, "You all remember John's daughter, Alexandra, don't you?"

That got the attention of anyone who hadn't remembered she existed.

"Care for a stogie?" Brandon held out his cigar in what Alex assumed was intended as a joke, an obvious jab at her being one of only a handful of women in the room.

Alex responded the way she thought Val might, by accepting the cigar from him, wrapping her lips around its damp tip, and nudging him aside in the circle.

For a while Alex only listened, waiting for the conversation to shift, as it always did, toward the usual business-related grievances.

Federal overreach, how excessive regulation was sapping the competitiveness out of American commerce.

Alex played her part. "Emissions controls have gotten out of hand." She pointed her cigar at Silas. "They keep this poor guy awake at night."

Always eager to show off his authority and status for his peers, Cousin Brandon seized the opportunity to play big man on campus. "Government would have us by the balls without the right people in the right positions."

Alex added, "And for the right price."

How they all laughed, *ho ho ho, so true!* Bribery was hilarious.

The big-bellied oilman, whose name Alex couldn't recall, fed the fire. "What is the going rate on an EPA official these days, huh, Silas?"

Alex held her breath. She didn't move a muscle for fear of wrecking the audio.

"Too much!" Brandon, the hotshot who had all the answers, spoke before Silas could get a word out.

Silas merely smiled, then said, "You all know how to reach me."

It wasn't much, but it wasn't nothing. Alex was beginning to think she might have a knack for this.

She blew a semi-self-congratulatory smoke ring up toward the ceiling. It wasn't all that fortuitous, really, considering how willing these men were to brag. Alex had been around this type of shoptalk all her life, long enough to understand that it didn't stem from stupidity or even simple carelessness. These men were so accustomed to being untouchable that they lived without fear of punishment. And here, of all places, they were surrounded by only their own kind.

Little did they know Alex was no longer their kind, especially now that she had Val as her partner in crime.

CHAPTER 20

Suddenly, Val found herself alone in Alex's penthouse. Cash and Bruce were there, of course, but they couldn't care less about her when they had one another to sniff and gnaw on. And so, Val was essentially left to her own devices.

The first thing she did was a camera sweep. The apartment had a sophisticated security system, with top-of-the-line surveillance, but Alex had disabled all of it.

She must trust me, Val thought. How unwise of her.

The second thing Val did was shake herself a cocktail. An ice-cold gin martini, dirty, with three olives. Val didn't usually drink martinis, but it felt appropriate for the venue.

Next Val went through every closet and drawer, running her fingers over the fine threading and expensive fabric of Alex's designer clothing—her real clothes, not that scrub Alex Miller's.

Val considered, but stopped short of, trying on Alex's shirts, her beautiful jackets. Doing so would feel a little too Tom Ripley. And anyway, it was Jay Gatsby's shirt collection Val was thinking of—linen and silk, in so many colors and patterns, and throwing them into the air, exultant, all for Daisy's benefit.

Val lay on top of Alex's king-sized bed, arms and legs wide. She could still see the city, the night's darkness and twinkle lights, from her lying-down position.

What a way to live, she thought. To sleep and wake to this panorama.

Alex truly was the perfect mark.

Val retrieved her overnight bag from the guest room. In its hidden compartment lay the listening devices she'd packed with care, the button-sized video cameras, the malware to install on Alex's computer.

Bag in tow, Val ventured into Alex's office. Like the rest of the apartment, it would have once been John Reed's, but it was one of the few rooms Alex had bothered to refashion to her personal taste, a neutral color scheme and modern white shelving. There was no tufted sofa, just a pair of simple armchairs and an elegant table in a contemporary design. Any brass candelabras or medieval paintings were subbed out for artwork and keepsakes from Alex's own travels and adventures—and adventures there were many.

Photographs of the far-flung places she had been to and the daredevil hobbies she enjoyed there lined the wall behind Alex's desk. Here was Alex skydiving, there she was rock climbing, or covered in mud on a dirt bike.

On the opposite wall was a trophy case stocked with awards and blue ribbons. Some were for humanitarian work or charitable acts, but more were for such things as winning first place in some kind of sailing race. That's what a regatta was, right? Something with boats?

The books on Alex's shelves were an eclectic mix of genre and subject and, more surprisingly, language. How many foreign tongues could Alex speak if she was reading Chekhov in his original Russian and Camus in French? Rich people talents were ridiculous. They had so much damn free time to devote to unlucrative activities.

Val moved along to a shelf of yellowed paperbacks closer to her heart—Agatha Christie, Dashiell Hammett, John le Carré. She smiled adoringly at this shared interest.

Then Val returned to the living room, where she took another look around at the sparkling city beyond the windows. After downing the remainder of her martini, she raised the empty glass at an angle between her fingers, the way she imagined a socialite would.

It was time to get to work. Plop went her bag onto the seat of the grand piano. Unzipping it felt almost sensual, like stepping out of a dress. She reached inside and took two audio bugs into her hand, squeezed them in her fist like a pair of dice. Where to? She scoped the room for the perfect spots.

Just then, Bruce came dashing into the room, followed by an out-of-breath Cash, who bounced off Val's shins.

"Yes?" Val said. "Can I help you?"

Bruce sat, short legs firmly on the ground, torso held upright, his gaze attentive.

"Go away," Val said to him. "Go play or lie down somewhere."

Catching on to something interesting happening, Cash took a seat on Val's left foot, as she often did when she didn't want Val to leave the house.

Val shook her off and took a step back, while Bruce continued staring at her, with his big, brown, beagle eyes locked on hers.

Until she'd adopted Cash, looking into a dog's eyes was not something Val had ever done, but once it became a regular occurrence, she was fascinated by the multitude of expressions possible.

With only a glance, Cash could communicate fear, frustration, hunger, needing to take a dump, you name it. And Val had become fluent in this silent language, almost never mixing up one message for another. Which was why Bruce's watery stare was now throwing Val off her game.

Well, this is disappointing, Bruce seemed to be saying. *I thought you had changed, that you were better than this.*

I'm not! Val wanted to reply. *And I don't even know if I believe people can change.*

Down went Bruce's tail, along with Val's spirit.

Cash rubbed up against her leg. She always became Velcro when she got nervous.

Val rattled the bugs in her hand. What was this tightness in her chest? This tremor she felt in her limbs? Could she have been poisoned? She tried to recall what she'd had to eat or drink in the past few hours.

But no. That wasn't it.

This was the feeling of wussing out.

She couldn't go through with it.

Both dogs followed Val as she returned the bugs to her bag, and the bag to the guest room, and then threw herself face down onto the bed. Cash jumped up and onto her back, where she seemed to be holding Val down, just in case. But Bruce was calm and soothing as he snuggled up beside her.

Good girl, his eyes said. *That's a good girl.*

When Alex returned home, Bruce and Cash greeted her at the door, but Val did not.

"Hello?" Alex shouted out.

"In here," Val yelled back. "Whatever you call this room with the piano and the bar."

Alex dropped her overcoat, kicked off her shoes, and walked toward the sound of Val's voice. When she stepped into the sitting room, Val looked up at her from the couch. She was wearing cozy pajamas and reading a book from Alex's shelf. Bruce and Cash raced to return to their places beside her.

"So it went great?" Val asked.

"It went well, not great."

"By that look on your face, it went better than not great."

Alex joined Val and the dogs on the sofa. "Honestly, despite coming away without much in the way of evidence, I had so much fun. You're so lucky to get to do this kind of thing all the time."

"The novelty wears off after a while, but I'm glad you enjoyed yourself."

"I don't want it to end," Alex said.

Granted, she was still high on adrenaline from the night, but the moment the words left Alex's lips she knew that she meant them.

"After we put Silas away," she continued. "And we *will* put Silas away. But after that, I want you to keep working for me. With me, I mean. Together. I need your help if I'm going to take down Reed Industries."

Val smiled and tilted her head to the side in a way Alex was unsure how to read. "I already have a job," she said.

"Sure, sure," Alex continued. Her mouth was working faster than her brain, or maybe it was the other way around. "You can keep taking on other cases if you want. I can help you with those, too."

Val placed a gentle hand on Alex's thigh. "Slow down. How much have you had to drink tonight?"

"Nothing," Alex said. "I'm crystal clear. You can't tell me the idea hasn't crossed your mind."

Val admitted nothing, but Alex picked up on a hint of excitement coming off her. All she needed was a nudge.

"How about if I throw in the Porsche?"

Val appeared to choke slightly on her own saliva. "Excuse me?"

It was no secret that Alex had difficulty with relationships that weren't transactional. Or believing non-transactional relationships were even really a thing. But so what? Big deal. She felt better about herself when she was with Val—that was all that mattered.

"Be my partner," Alex said. "And the Carrera is yours."

After a few seconds of speechlessness, Val cleared her throat and weakly muttered, "I can't take your Porsche."

"You can," Alex insisted. "Think of it as a signing bonus."

"Literally, I can't. I couldn't afford the insurance on that thing."

"You don't need to worry about it," Alex said. "I've got you."

"Alex . . ." Val struggled to get any words out.

She was dumbstruck with glee, Alex was sure. And Alex, too, felt excited. She wanted Val to stay in her life, to be part of her everyday reality. Whatever the price, it was worth it.

Except Val's face changed then. She looked sad, almost, and serious. Oh no, had Alex offended her? She'd gone too far. She always went too far.

"Listen to me," Val took Alex's hands in her own. "Real truth. I'm not a good person."

"Yes, you are—"

"Alex, I—"

Before Val could finish her sentence, Alex leaned in and kissed her. She hadn't known she was going to do it, but yes, she wanted to, and once they started, she didn't want to stop. Until Val was pulling away.

"Whoa," Val said. "No."

"Shit." Alex sat back.

"I can't, I mean I don't—"

"I understand," Alex said. "It won't happen again."

"I think I should go to bed," Val said.

"Okay."

Val left the room, and Cash followed her, leaving Alex alone with Bruce and her shame.

CHAPTER 21

After dinner, Silas resigned to the couch with his laptop. After post-dinner cleanup, he was still there, deeply engaged.

June sat across from him and paged through the new Foggy Dog catalog, while Willow chewed on her stuffed unicorn. June could tell Silas wasn't working by the amusement on his face. He seemed happier than he'd been in days.

"Looking at something good?" June asked him. It was an innocent question, but the moment the words left her lips she worried it sounded like she was prying.

Silas raised his eyes, then turned his laptop around so she could see the monitor. "Only how handsome I am."

"Tell me something I don't know!" June laughed, relieved. Onscreen was a grid of photos.

"Are those from the event last night?" June moved to Silas's side of the couch for a better view.

"They are indeed," Silas said, smiling.

Since their last big argument, June had been treading lightly. She recognized how she and Silas had become enmeshed, that she couldn't always decipher where he ended and she began, that she idealized him, and that a life lived for someone else wouldn't do much to fulfill her.

And yet she didn't know how to stop. Abandoning Silas still felt impossible.

Tomorrow, June told herself, maybe she would act. Or begin to take action. Or begin planting the seeds that could later sprout into action. Perhaps she would make a list, even just a mental list, of different options for her future. June could call her mother, maybe, tell her that she would like to book a flight for a family visit, to see them and speak to them in person. Then June might actually book that flight.

But tonight, all June had to do was get through the evening unscathed and maintain an air of pleasant normalcy.

Silas scrolled backward a few photos to show June one of him posed with some guy she was supposed to know, then forward again to one of him posed with two guys she was supposed to know.

Then, in the background of a different photo, June saw a face that really was familiar to her.

"Oh," she said, surprised. "That's Alex."

Silas furrowed his brow and tilted his head in a way that reminded June of Willow. "You know Alex Reed?"

"Miller," June said. "I'm pretty sure her last name's Miller."

"That is Alexandra Reed," Silas insisted. "The late John Reed's daughter. I talked to her. Quite a character, she was smoking a cigar, which struck me as grossly mannish and inappropriate, but when you're that rich, you can get away with anything."

June was confused. Not as to whether the photo was in fact *her* Alex—of that she was certain, but *her* Alex couldn't possibly be John Reed's daughter. Could she?

“I must be getting her mixed up with someone else,” June said to Silas, but he was already scrolling forward in search of another picture of his own face.

It would go on to bother June all night. Was it possible she had misunderstood something Alex had told her about her upbringing or surname? Perhaps she had zoned off mid-conversation, as she so often did. She really didn’t think so, though.

Before bed, June decided she would ask Alex about it when she saw her at the dog park. Even if it meant embarrassing herself, revealing that all this time, she had been ignorant to this critical aspect of Alex’s character. Alex would have mentioned it if it were true. Otherwise—well, otherwise they had never been as close as June believed—which was an obliterating thought.

Was June that awful a judge of character? It terrified her, the extent to which she could be dense to a situation and misread the world around her. She had placed her faith in Alex and Val, told them things she hadn’t told anyone—but what did she know about them, really? Was she so desperate and lonely that she had gone ahead and pressed herself onto two veritable strangers?

“You did well,” Val said to Alex as she scooped up Cash’s turd with a plastic bag. They had come to the dog park early, to have some time to chat among themselves before the happy-hour droves arrived.

Val was speaking as nonchalantly as she could about the evening before, for her own sake as well as Alex’s, but on the inside she was still freaking out. “You came away from the Station Institute event with nothing super in terms of evidence, but you didn’t screw up, and you didn't do anything stupid, so I'm calling it a win."

"Is that your idea of a compliment?" Alex followed Val to the trash can.

"I'd have no problem sending you out in the field on a mission like that in the future," Val said. "That's my idea of a compliment."

"*You* sending *me* out in the field? So you think you're the boss," Alex joked.

It was the closest either of them would come to acknowledging last night's conversation about sticking together beyond this job.

"In fact," Val continued. "What if you tried again with Silas, just you and him, wearing a wire to a meeting you call on your terms? It's not like he'd turn down the chance to get on the good side of *the* Alex Reed. I bet you could get him to say all kinds of things."

"Now you're talking," Alex said, but she stopped short of reintroducing the subject of her and Val continuing as partners, instead letting it linger silently in the air between them—along with that other thing they weren't mentioning.

They were both doing their best to remain cool. But last night, alone in Alex's guest room, Val lay awake with her mind racing as fast as the Porsche 911 Carrera T Alex was set on gifting her.

What did it say about her that she couldn't plant those bugs, couldn't install the malware? And then she came *this close* to spilling her guts like a Catholic in a confessional booth—when Alex went ahead and kissed her.

Val did the right thing in stopping the kiss, but she waited too long. She allowed herself to feel it.

In the morning, she thought they would need to discuss it, that she would have to explain to Alex why it would be too complicated for them to become involved in any way beyond the professional. But instead, bright and early, they walked the dogs, side by side, and then had breakfast together like it had all been settled and the kiss had never happened. Sure, there were still details to work out, but of course they would continue working together after this job. How could they not when they were turning out to be so compatible?

In the car, Val dozed in and out of sleep while Alex drove them back to Maryland, replaying it all again in her mind. The kiss, but more so the sincerity and hope beaming from Alex when she'd said, *I need your help if I'm going to take down Reed Industries. And, by the way, here, have a two-hundred-thousand-dollar sports car to sweeten the deal.*

Surprisingly, it wasn't Alex's hastiness in offering Val a luxurious automobile that stuck in Val's throat as much as it was her declaration of protective loyalty.

I've got you, Alex had said.

Had anyone in Val's life ever promised as much?

Val looked at Alex now. The early evening sun was casting her in a golden hue that accentuated the contours of her face. It gave her a soft, glowing appearance that nearly took Val's breath away.

"What?" Alex asked, noticing Val staring.

Val had vowed to never fall for a mark, but what if Alex wasn't a mark? And what if Val was just . . . herself?

Just then, June's SUV pulled into the parking lot.

Val and Alex drifted toward the entrance gate to greet June and Willow. Then the three of them made their way to the regular corner.

Val didn't often let down her guard, with good reason, and if she had remained her vigilant self in this instance, she may have been ready for what was coming. But Val was too busy retelling herself the story of her morning with Alex, both of them being overly polite while making coffee and breakfast. There had been a paradigm shift in their dynamic. Even the dogs seemed to sense the energy change in the room.

This was what Val had been thinking about, in a vague, amorphous way, when June said, "Alex, can I ask you something?"

Alex's guard also appeared to be down.

"Go ahead," she said, at ease, her attention scattered between Val and Bruce, who was wrestling with Willow. "Shoot."

As the other regulars had trickled in, they gathered around Meryl, who had some new piece of gossip to share, leaving the three of them alone and in private for the moment.

"Your last name is Miller," June said to Alex. "Right?"

Val froze. She tried to keep her facial expression untroubled and her eyes soft as they met Alex's.

Alex stayed quiet for a moment, which was the smartest thing she could have done, prompting June to say more.

"Because I saw you in a photo from an event Silas was at and he said your last name was Reed."

Alex looked to Val for some kind of help, a lifeline, but Val had none to offer. The goat was already out of the barn, as Gianni used to say.

"Silas was right," June said. "Wasn't he? You're John Reed's daughter."

Alex let her head drop, then nodded.

"Why did you lie to me?" June asked.

It was the obvious next question, to which Alex might have

offered some made-up yet plausible answer. Alex could have said anything really, and June would have likely believed her, hopeful as she seemed for some explanation other than the worst one.

"I'm sorry," Alex said, finally. "Sometimes I don't like people to know who I really am."

Honest, and yet it still could be spun. But Alex, it was plain to see, had lost her will to continue the charade.

"And you know Silas," June said, not phrasing it as a question.

Alex started at the beginning, confirming who she really was—not Alex Miller, a recently divorced DC consultant who was new to Bethesda for a fresh start—but Alex Reed, the well-meaning, but often misguided daughter of the late billionaire John Reed. And, yes, she had lied about that, but for a very good reason.

"Silas isn't the man you think he is," Alex said.

This was when Val knew they were doomed. Alex jumped to finger-pointing far too soon.

"It seems like you're the one who isn't who I thought you were," June said, and Val could feel the pain embedded in that statement, she could see the sorrow in June's slumped shoulders and pursed lips.

If there was anyone in the world who deserved to be treated well, it was June, and yet look at what they had done to her.

Alex tried to explain to June how her own family had personally benefited from Silas's unethical practices and abuse of power at the EPA, but June wasn't hearing it. She was stuck on the fact that all this time Alex had been deceiving her.

"Do you understand how deeply you've hurt me?" June said. "I thought we were close. I thought we were best friends."

Alex's face was red, her neck speckled with hives. She was

visibly sweating. "All of that is still true. My last name is different, that's it."

"That is not it!" It shocked Val to hear June shout. "You've been using me."

June volleyed her eyes, which had heartbreakingly filled with tears, back and forth between Alex and Val, realizing Val had been maintaining a somewhat incriminating silence.

"You knew the truth about her all this time?" June asked Val. "That she's on some kind of manhunt against my husband?"

"I only came clean to her recently," Alex answered for Val. "But here's something else you should know. Val was hired by your husband to spy on you. She's a PI. That's what brought her to the dog park to begin with."

Oh, Alex. Why?

June turned to Val. "Is that true?"

Val forced herself to speak through her shock.

"Silas thought you were cheating on him," Val explained. "And for what it's worth, everything Alex has told you is right. Silas is into some seriously immoral and illegal stuff. But I'm sorry you had to find out this way."

"You don't get to apologize for this," June said, wiping away her tears. "Neither of you."

She marched a few steps forward. "Willow! Come!"

Willow wasn't the only one to recognize the urgency in June's tone. Everyone watched as the usually playful dog dropped what she was doing and rushed to where June was waiting ready with her leash.

"I don't ever want to see either of you again." June clipped Willow's leash to her collar and stormed across the field, toward the exit gate, making eye contact with no one.

It was a different form of June stalking away, one who was assertive and strong-willed, and who, under different circumstances, Val may have applauded for standing up for herself.

Bruce came running to Alex's side, attuned somehow to the alteration in the atmosphere, and Cash followed him.

"This is the worst thing that could have happened," Alex said to Val. "I feel awful."

Val scooped Cash up in one quick motion. "I don't ever want to see you again, either," she said to Alex.

"What? Why?" Alex had the nerve to play dumb, to act like she hadn't just broken the vow of trust between them, dragging Val down with her.

Val hugged Cash close to her chest to keep her from wiggling free as she pivoted toward the exit. "Because you're a snitch!"

CHAPTER 22

Sometimes when June returned home from walking Willow, she would forget to remove her leash from her collar. Confused by this, Willow would freeze in place just in front of the doorway, as if still tethered to something. Even though the other end of the leash was lying freely on the floor, June would have to come back over and release Willow from her imagined confinement.

Leaving Silas, for June, turned out to function much the same way. All it took to liberate her from her shackles was the realization that she could simply just walk away.

Her first step, upon returning home from the dog park, was to go into Silas's office, where she usually never entered. She looked through his desk, tried to open each of his four locked file cabinets. The cabinet drawers weren't difficult to pry open with a screwdriver once it ceased to matter if June would be able to reclose them to appear untouched. It made no difference because she already knew what she would find among the meticulously organized files. Confirmation.

June didn't doubt that everything Alex said about what Silas was doing was true, but she needed to see it for herself, with her own eyes. Otherwise she would never be able to make her next move.

What June found told a complete story, of which she could understand only a portion. Company acronyms, initials, vaguely titled LLCs. This was not the paperwork of crystal-clear, aboveboard dealings. The clincher was a summary page for a bank account in the Cayman Islands that she didn't know existed.

Goose bumps covered June's arms, and her hands shook. She wished to feel relief—she could be certain now that leaving Silas was the right thing to do—but instead she felt nauseated.

This was not triumphant validation, it was more of a shattering confirmation of her misjudgment.

June didn't bother returning anything to its proper place. She left the file cabinet drawers open, papers strewn on the floor.

Back downstairs she called an old acquaintance, someone who used to frequent the dog park until she split up with her husband and moved with her basset hound to Vermont.

Getting the name and phone number of a capable divorce attorney was that easy. It had been all along.

June made an in-person appointment with Jennifer Newman of Newman & Babbitt for the following morning, then made her way to the bedroom.

Willow yelped with premature separation anxiety when June took her suitcase down from the closet shelf and began packing.

"Don't worry," June told her. "We're both going."

On the drive to the hotel, June stopped at the bank and made a large cash withdrawal in case Silas decided to cancel her credit cards.

She left him a note on the kitchen table, which she felt bad about, but it was the only way to escape cleanly. June wrote that she wanted a divorce, she would be staying at a hotel, and not to come looking for her. She added in a postscript that she was keeping Willow.

It may have been reckless, even heartless, to blindside Silas this way. June should have been better at communicating that she was unhappy earlier. But it wasn't until recently, and almost all at once, that she realized it for herself, so how could she have expressed it to Silas any sooner?

Deeper down, there was more to it than that, a truth June could barely admit to herself. If it hadn't come to Silas being an actual criminal, she would likely still have stayed. Even after he threatened to take Willow. Somehow him wronging the world at large, as opposed to just her, counted differently against him. This offense had a clarity to it that transcended June's own part in mucking up her marriage. It held the power to change her mind.

It was undeniable now. Silas was not June's Prince Charming, whom she could never properly appreciate. He was not a great man, or even a good person.

This she could not explain away. *This*, finally, she could not forgive.

Ms. Jennifer Newman, Esquire, of Newman & Babbitt, was a reasonable, rational silver-haired woman whose sentences all sounded matter-of-fact and absolutely not up for debate, which filled June with confidence.

"You can call me Jennifer," she said when June addressed her as Ms. Newman, but she struck June as the kind of person who required a full name, if not an honorific or title of courtesy.

Her degrees lined the wall behind her, along with various awards.

"What was the tipping point?" Jennifer asked, from across her lawyerly desk, which was stacked with case files and decorated with framed photos of her rottweiler, Caesar. "What was the thing that finally made you decide to leave?" Her expression said nothing could surprise her.

Since digging through Silas's file cabinets, June had been unsure of what to do with the information she uncovered. Morally, she understood that she needed to tell someone, but she wasn't sure exactly whom.

June hesitated before going into the story about Silas's abuse of power at his government job. First, she explained that she found out Silas had hired a private investigator to spy on her. Then, almost as an afterthought, she added, "And I found evidence that Silas has been taking bribes."

She left out the part about Alex. She did not explain how they had become best friends, along with the PI Silas hired. It all felt too messy, like June had enabled it somehow, like it was her own fault. For being oblivious to what Silas had been doing right under her nose, for believing she had forged genuine connections with Alex and Val when really she was just being used, for being stupid! Stupid, stupid, stupid. Who would even believe she could be so dumb?

Jennifer Newman advised June that she should reach out to the proper authorities regarding Silas's criminal acts.

Sure, that sounded easy enough. But could a person just phone up the FBI?

Then Jennifer drew up some preliminary papers and scribbled notes on a legal pad as she talked strategy.

"Full custody of Willow," she said. "That's what you want, correct?"

June nodded.

Here Jennifer took off her chic middle-aged-woman glasses, rested her elbows on her desk, and leaned forward. Her gold and silver bangle bracelets made a clanky sound against the desk. "This can be tricky," she said. "While an increasing number of places are enacting pet custody laws, Maryland isn't one of them. Here, our companion animals may as well be a table or chair, or any piece of property. If Silas purchased her on his own before you were married, Willow does in fact belong to him."

Even though June had already discovered this sad fact online, it stung to hear it aloud from a legal professional in real life.

"Would you settle for split custody?" Jennifer asked.

June shook her head. "I'm the one who does everything for Willow, I'm responsible for all her care, doesn't that count for something?"

"Unfortunately, such factors are only relevant in the handful of states with custody laws." Jennifer delivered this news somberly, like the dog lover she obviously was. "But," she said with her more characteristic self-assurance, "we will do everything we can to try to force Silas into a mutual agreement. I'll need you to provide documentation. Veterinary bills paid in your name, receipts from the pet store or groomer, anything you can to prove that you would be the one to provide the best home for Willow following your separation. Show that you're the one with the time and attention to give Willow."

"Silas will never settle," June explained. "This is his only leverage. And if anyone can charm a judge and jury, it's him. You'll understand when you meet him. All else aside, he is extremely handsome and incredibly well-spoken."

"So was Ted Bundy," Jennifer replied in her no-nonsense way. "My job is to bring his ugliness to the surface. And I'm very good at my job."

June wanted to believe her, she truly did, but she returned to the Hilton Homewood Suites in Rockville feeling more alone and depressed than she had ever been.

Even Willow greeted her at the door with an expression that seemed to say *Can we go back to our real home now?*

Their studio suite had all the comforts of a small apartment, with an open layout living area and fully equipped kitchen, but Willow was right. What in the world were they doing here?

June sat on the stiff, uncomfortable couch, petting Willow to calm the both of them, wishing she could reach out to Alex or Val. Then she reprimanded herself for the weakness of that thought.

No, she would not allow herself to get past their betrayal or her own gullibility.

Did it only make her more pathetic, she wondered, that the part of this she was having the most trouble processing was how easily she had been fooled by Alex and Val? More so than the end of her marriage? But she had grown to rely on them and enjoy their company way more than Silas's. June felt linked to them in a way she hadn't experienced since she last belonged to a team.

Even now it was hard to believe that none of those good times had been real.

June wrapped her arms around Willow and drew her close. Some dogs would have pulled away, jumped to the floor, shaken off, but Willow was accustomed to June's smothering. "I'm not letting you go," she said to Willow playfully, even though somber was how she actually felt. "Never, never, never."

Willow licked her face, her ear, her eyeball, making June laugh.

On the bright side—and there was always a bright side, wasn't there?—at least June was finally getting out of her emotionally abusive marriage. She could admit that now—what she'd been enduring for years was emotional abuse. And, yes, maybe she had clung to the first people who helped her feel normal in a long time, and they had turned out to not be who she thought they were, but the breath of fresh air they had brought to her life was what gave her the courage she had now. It was better and more useful to focus on that, rather than her regrets.

"We have to figure out what to do with all the evidence we have that Daddy is a bad man," June said to Willow.

Alex would be able to tell June what to do with it all, make sure it fell into the right hands—she was the one who was so desperate to find that information in the first place—but June couldn't go back to Alex now.

Whatever was coming, June and Willow had to face it alone.

CHAPTER 23

When Val took her suitcase down from the high closet shelf, Cash, who had been sleeping in her donut bed, jumped to her feet and sprinted to Val's side. She stared up at Val and swatted at the case, open now and on the floor at her level, then let out a low growl.

She doesn't want me to leave, Val thought. *Because she loves me.* Then Val reminded herself what a silly, pathetic, and imaginary idea that was.

"Get out of there," Val said sharply, and for once Cash listened.

Val would not miss this place, and it would not take her long to pack. The rental apartment was intended to be temporary all along, a blip, not so different from an unmemorable hotel room. It was a necessity of the job that Val had acquired so many new items in the duration of her stay in Bethesda, but she did not consider them her belongings. The dog dishes and leashes and beds and brushes, the car seat—none of it was really hers. Val came to Bethesda carrying the one single suitcase and would leave the same way, just as she always did. A garbage bag for Goodwill was filling up fast.

An hour ago, when Val's cell phone rang and she'd seen it was Silas calling, she'd known the jig was up. Early on during the call, Val determined that June—surprisingly—had not told Silas she knew Val was working for him. Instead, Silas fired Val for the less-complicated reason that her services were no longer needed.

As was Silas's way with people who weren't June, he was polite and direct. "No hard feelings," he said. "You did your best, but my situation with my wife has changed."

Just like that, Val was free to go, to push Bethesda and all that had happened there into her rearview mirror.

She was relieved there would be no sappy goodbyes. June wasn't speaking to her, and Val wasn't speaking to Alex.

"I must have bought a few more things than I realized," Val said to Cash, on account of how quickly her suitcase was filling up. Also unhelpful was that Cash again decided to sit inside it. But even without the dog taking up precious space, Val could tell she would have trouble fitting everything back inside. She was holding on to too much.

Aha. These were the clothes Val had picked up at Marshalls for the hotel mission with Alex. Surely, they could go into the Goodwill bag. Good riddance.

It shouldn't have stunned Val that Alex would be so quick to give her up to June, that Alex's sense of loyalty, despite her lofty promises, would be nonexistent. It only confirmed what Val already feared—letting Alex get too close would end in disaster.

Val was hired by your husband to spy on you. She's a PI. Alex had spilled it to June so easily. Trust right out the window. Privacy, a secret shared, tossed like yesterday's trash.

What had Val been thinking? She should have known better

than to drift so far away from herself, from the core tenets that had served her well.

The only positive was that Alex's betrayal gave Val an out that was a clean cut. She would take it as a sign, a harbinger of more to come if she stuck around.

Maybe Alex's disloyalty wasn't exactly of epic scale, but it was enough to knock some much-needed sense back into Val. Better it happened sooner rather than later.

And it didn't end with Alex. Val had even been foolish enough to transport a dumb dress from Queens to Bethesda, to wear to the fundraiser gala. That Val had been taking such pains to don a fancy outfit for the thankless people of Hamilton Dog Park was appalling, now that she reconsidered it. It was only a simple black sheath dress—by no means an evening gown—paired with manageable high heels. But still. Who was Val trying to impress? How in the world had she let that group of weirdos get to her? She had somehow forgotten that she wasn't one of them, and that she wasn't a dog person either.

Cash finally got the hint and departed the increasingly full suitcase, then swatted out a few items with her front paw and took a seat on Val's foot. She always had been intuitive to the point of witchy, this dog. But Val refused to read too much into Cash's anxiety.

As though in response to Val's thoughts, Cash extended both front paws skyward, pretending she wanted to be picked up.

Val wasn't falling for it. Cash hated when Val lifted her into her arms. She would immediately try to wiggle free, leaving Val feeling like a sucker.

"All of this is your fault, you know that?" she said to Cash.

One of the items still unpacked was the bandana Val bought Cash for the gala, which Val would have now liked to return, but clearance items at Bitch Please were sadly final sale. She would have to donate it with the rest of this stuff.

It wouldn't be easy, giving Cash up. Val needed to be strong. Flip the switch and get back to her regularly scheduled self. Granted, there were rituals that came with having a dog that Val had grown accustomed to, and odd things about Cash specifically that, over time, she found herself enjoying. The funny baby Buddha way Cash would often sit, or how she would roll around like an otter on top of Val's bed or stretch out long on her back with her paws out straight as rods, which meant she wanted her belly rubbed. Val had even come to appreciate the scent of Cash's fur, how in the mornings, or during a nap, she would smell like warm popcorn. Of course it would hurt at first to let the dog go, but they would both be better off in the long run with Cash in a more suitable home.

Val could take comfort in the fact that it hurt as much as it did—it meant she was a human being with the capacity to love another thing after all. Still, though, better off not to.

A young Brussels Griffon was worth a lot of money—Val hadn't forgotten—but she had been weakened to the point of no longer being able to capitalize on Cash's monetary value. And anyway, how would she even execute such a sale? By putting Cash on Craigslist or Facebook Marketplace? Would she have to resort to some kind of canine black market? Val would much prefer giving Cash to June. It would make her feel less guilty, and Cash already liked her and Willow.

For the second time since June stormed off at the dog park yesterday, Val tried to call her cell.

Again, June didn't answer.

What was Val to do? Asking June to take Cash seemed like a lot to put into a text message, and Val refused to call Alex. Desperate as she was, she would not give Alex the chance to beg for her forgiveness.

Val didn't care that she was overreacting. She refused to consider Alex's position or make excuses for her. Doing so would be moving in the wrong direction because the truth was still the truth. Neither Val nor Alex had been built for closeness or cooperation. They were two lone wolves, no better than wild animals when it came to social connection. They were kidding themselves to think otherwise.

As it turned out, Val couldn't con Alex, but she also couldn't be near her.

Val considered leaving Cash on June's doorstep, but that seemed cruel, and logistically, it didn't hold up. Would she ring and run? How long would Cash be out there alone, leashed to the front door, if June wasn't home?

Testing to see if she could still zip her suitcase closed, Val found she could squeeze in one or two final items. Her gala dress hanging on the closet door would be a wise choice. It was the finest article of clothing she owned, and getting it wrinkled no longer mattered. She tore it from its hanger and was about to chuck it into her luggage when the idea came to her.

The gala. The gala was this coming Saturday night. Val could bide her time, then show up with Cash like all was normal, let her loose in the doggy ball pit or whatever, and take off. Someone from the dog park crowd would take Cash and give her a great home—way better than Val ever could. Then Val could freely disappear off the grid for a while, maybe someplace tropical.

Arf, went Cash, followed by a whimper. She cast her sad gaze up at Val, wagged her nub tail rapidly from side to side. How awful it must be, Val thought, to have no control over your own comings and goings, to be at the mercy of someone else's whims. When solitary independence was everything, and ultimate freedom was the only real power. To think Val nearly let her own be bought.

How had she missed that she was the one being conned all along?

Cash jumped up onto two legs, danced a pirouette, then poked her nose at Val's hands.

Val smiled for Cash's benefit but stopped short of petting her. "You'll see, little buddy. You're going to have the best life without me."

From behind the steering wheel of her Toyota Camry, Alex assured Bruce, who was strapped into the passenger seat, that all was not lost.

"We're not going to let Val and Cash go that easily," she said.

Bruce recognized the approaching building and salivated with anticipation, then barked in corroboration.

Alex wondered how she had ever managed life without Bruce's unconditional support. Last night, when all Alex could do was move from bed to couch to bed, zombified, teary-eyed, and self-loathing—Bruce followed her, stayed with her, with his head on her lap and the weight of his paws heavy on her knees. And when Alex could sit inside no longer and went for her car keys, Bruce found his own leash and brought it to her in his teeth. *Wherever you go, I go*, he was saying.

In her lifetime, Alex had sealed up and packed away a number of relationships, both long and short. With June, Alex supposed the only way forward was to figure out a way to say a proper (if temporary) goodbye, so she could at least detach (temporarily) with acceptance.

The problem was that it appeared June was no longer living at home. This Alex knew because she had driven by June's house multiple times overnight and early this morning and had not once seen June's SUV in its regular spot in the driveway. She must have run off somewhere.

"Well," Alex said to Bruce, "if we played even a small part in convincing June to leave Silas, we could almost call it a win." Almost.

It also helped that despite Alex's current shame spiral (which was excruciating, but Alex had a high tolerance for self-imposed suffering), she believed she might one day be vindicated in June's eyes. Sooner or later, Silas was going to go down, indisputably and in public. Then June would better understand why Alex behaved as she had and—fingers crossed—find her way back into Alex's life.

Val, on the other hand, was someone who could probably maintain a grudge forever. Anyone who had been hurt as brutally as Val had could hold their protective anger close to their chest, like a precious stone.

Alex understood that she had messed up in multiple ways. But she didn't mean to reveal Val's undercover identity to June, it just sort of came out. And Val had basically been working as a double agent anyway, on Alex and June's side, not Silas's, so what was the big deal? But to Val it was apparently a very big deal.

That Alex had not formally apologized for kissing Val was also not helping her case. The humiliating blunder was still hanging around in the background, acting as one more hash mark against her that she was unsure how to erase—but she had to at least try.

Alex pulled into the driveway entrance of Val's apartment complex. Bruce, unable to stop himself, let out a series of loud, high-pitched barks.

"I know," Alex said. "But do your best to keep your emotions in check."

Alex didn't want Bruce to get his hopes up too high. It was possible Val had already disappeared from Bethesda. When Alex drove through late last night, she didn't see Val's Nova anywhere in the large parking lot, but she might have missed it, especially in the dark.

Now, in the light of a new day, Alex didn't bother searching the lot, instead pulling into a parking spot and dragging Bruce along to the building's entrance.

Slipping in when someone held the door for her, Alex headed directly upstairs to Val's apartment and rang the bell.

Cash barked ferociously and Val told her to pipe down. Alex thrilled at the sound of her voice. Val was home. She was still here.

"Go away, Alex," Val said from the behind the locked door.

"You're not answering my calls," Alex said.

"Because I don't want to talk to you."

"I'm sorry I kissed you," Alex said, barely louder than a whisper.

"Oh please," Val shot back. "That meant nothing to either of us, and you know it."

Bruce scratched at the door's wooden surface, unclear on why it remained shut in place.

"I'm also sorry I told June you were working for Silas," Alex said. "I didn't realize I was supposed to keep all the secrets going. I thought it was over."

"It is over," Val said. "You got that part right."

"Val, please. Let me in."

Cash reprimanded Val on her own and Bruce's behalf. Everyone seemed to believe Alex should be allowed to enter the apartment except for Val.

"I'm leaving town," Val said. "Thanks for the memories."

"You can't just run away like this." Alex cringed at her own neediness. She was on the brink of begging, maybe even crying?

"Try me," Val said.

Alex signaled for Bruce to sit, and he obeyed, but Cash continued growling and whimpering.

"You know what I think?" Alex said. "You're scared. Because we're the same, you and me, and we understand each other, and you don't know how to deal with that, so you're using my little flub as an excuse to flee."

"Who told you that? Your psychiatrist?"

"I made a mistake, Val, it was an accident. It doesn't mean you can't trust me."

"We are nothing alike," Val said. "I would never, for example, carry on like this through a locked door. Have some self-respect, will you?"

Okay, that was a little meaner than it needed to be. Alex's tactics were clearly backfiring.

"Fine, I'll go," she said. "But will you at least open the door so the dogs can say their goodbyes?"

A few seconds of silence passed, followed by the click of the latch.

"That was a cheap shot," Val said, stepping outside and closing the door behind her.

"I know, but I was willing to try anything."

The dogs pummeled one another, yelping with relief.

Val had a serious look about her. "Alex," she said, and paused, and Alex knew this wasn't going to be good.

"There's something you need to understand," Val continued. "I'm a con artist. I was designed and built to rob a person like you blind."

"I know," Alex said.

"I was planning on scamming you," Val went on. "All this time."

"I appreciate your honesty."

"You don't sound surprised."

"If you still wanted to scam me," Alex said. "Would you really say so?"

"I don't *want* to," Val said. "But I don't know if I can help it. You make it too easy to take advantage of you."

Alex felt as though she'd been smacked. "Is this about the car? Because that's not what it means when you give someone a gift."

"Sometimes it is," Val said.

"Are you saying you'd rather I was poor and less nice to you?"

"I think you know that's not what I'm saying."

Alex did, but the truth was hard to swallow.

"I wish we could continue working together," Val said, "and be real friends. But—"

"Would you feel differently if I gave it all away?" Alex asked. "Because that's the plan. I'll be redistributing my wealth, and once I get hold of Reed Industries and break it down, I'll no longer be rich."

Val appeared stunned. "All of it?"

Alex nodded. "Don't get me wrong, I won't be destitute. But I won't be like *this*."

"So you'll just be regular?" Val seemed to be trying to picture it. "Normal?"

"Normal might be pushing it," Alex said. "It's still me we're talking about."

Val laughed, her head thrown back. Alex swore she saw something in her facial expression unlock. But a second later, it was gone.

"All the same, I will call the police if you don't exit the premises immediately," Val said. "That is your only warning."

"Val, come on."

"Cash! Get inside." Val opened the door and gave Cash a nudge. Without looking up, she said, "Goodbye, Alex."

Alex wasn't convinced that Val would willingly bring the authorities into any situation, but she returned with Bruce to her car, nonetheless. There she sat, for how long she couldn't say, hands gripping the steering wheel, unable to start the engine. Bruce waited attentively in the passenger seat beside her, watching her, seemingly asking, *What now?*

What now? Alex had no clue.

CHAPTER 24

June thought it was strange to see Hamilton Dog Park at night, lit up and bustling like a bazaar with multiple circus-sized party tents, heavily populated with unfamiliar faces. So many people had turned out in costume or evening dresses or suits and ties in summery hues. Dogs June didn't know charged at Willow for an introductory sniff before disappearing back into the crowd. Some of them were tacos or avocados, one was an ice-cream cone, another was a pineapple. Then there were the frenzied bundles of tulle and lace, fur monsters kicking up dust like runaway brides or heavy-bearded, hyperactive groomsmen in tuxedos with tails.

Someone handed June an orange cocktail in a coupe glass. "Quite a turnout, isn't it? We're lucky it's been dry for a few days. No mud."

Meryl was a sight to be seen in a black-and-white gingham ballgown that was duplicated in miniature for her schnauzer, Paisley, right down to an identical feathery veiled headpiece.

"What is this?" June asked of the cocktail.

"A puperol spritz, the event's signature drink. Basically, it's just a sweeter version of an Aperol spritz, but beware, they're strong."

June took a careful sip while admiring a giant banner dancing in the wind and boasting A-One Cleaners' sponsorship.

"I'm glad you could make it tonight," Meryl said. "How have you been holding up?"

"Oh, you know," June replied, to avoid answering at all.

As she anticipated, word of her marriage woes had traveled fast among the Hamilton crowd. That Willow would be used as a bargaining chip in what promised to be an ugly divorce was too delicious a scandal to ignore.

Regina approached with Eloise, who provided ample distraction in a delicately embroidered, corseted dress that heightened her furry chest—would you call it a bosom?—to a disturbing degree.

"If you were ever curious about what a dachshund would look like as a Regency England prostitute, now you know," Meryl said under her breath.

"Don't you look lovely," Ava said to June.

Ava was wearing a vintage-style bustle gown in Barbie pink with a gathered fabric train in back, fastened with a bow. In her arms, Popcorn the Pomeranian was in a matching gown that boasted a fitted bodice and flared skirt.

"Uh-oh!" Ava turned to the Silver Fox. "Fashion faux pas!"

June then noticed the Silver Fox's golden corgi, Mollie, was wearing the same green dress as Willow.

"That's even worse than two gowns by the same designer!" Ava shouted with delight.

The Silver Fox, looking dashing in a classic black tuxedo, shrugged his broad shoulders. "It was on sale," he said to June.

"Yes, it was," June agreed.

Neither Willow nor Mollie seemed bothered as they snuffled each other's butts.

"We're heading to the play area," Regina said, referring to the section of the park divvied off into what June thought of as a mini Chuck E. Cheese for dogs. There was even a bouncy castle and ball pit.

June said, "Lead the way," while she caught herself glancing, yet again, at the parking lot, and then the welcome area, for Alex or Val. *Just a bad habit*, she told herself, and not one she needed to worry about for long.

If all went as planned, tonight would double as a goodbye party of sorts for June. She and Willow would be gone from here soon enough.

Alex had been to her fair share of galas, even outdoor ones, and those with silly themes, but never had she attended anything as ridiculous as this dog-centric extravaganza that spanned the distance of the entire park, from the tennis courts to the ball field.

She came here tonight gambling on the chance that June might show up, hoping to speak to her one final time. Alex's plan was to make a last-ditch effort at an apology and then beg June to not tell Silas what she had been up to—if June hadn't already. Silas going public about how Alex had been tracking him wouldn't only ruin her reputation, eliminating the possibility of future missions, it could also land her in jail.

For this single purpose, Alex forced poor Bruce into a tuxedo onesie and herself into a cherry-red wrap dress that always garnered her compliments but was as uncomfortable as it was flattering.

Kennedy, wearing an asymmetrical gown with a low front hem and a higher rear hem, greeted Alex and Bruce at the welcome area.

Kennedy's labradoodle, Chester, who Alex knew, was wearing a Ricky Roybin original, and was off enjoying himself elsewhere.

Then Alex spotted June standing in a group with Meryl, Regina, Ava, and the Silver Fox, all dressed to the nines.

Actually, it was Willow Alex saw first, in the loud green outfit June had gotten at Bitch Please, followed by the vision that was June in a yellow cocktail dress—a happy sunshine yellow that only made June's hair appear blonder, her skin glow brighter, and seemed to declare her refusal to be brought down by all the storm clouds surrounding her.

Alex unlatched Bruce's leash, certain he would run straight for Willow, paving the way for Alex to approach June with her own tail between her legs.

"Not that way." Kennedy redirected Bruce. "This way." She took Alex by the arm, guiding her to the red carpet.

"Smile for the camera!" Kennedy instructed, while Alex kept her eyes on June.

Bruce reacted badly to the intense lighting, and worse to the flashbulbs, which also momentarily blinded Alex. She blinked until the stars dissipated, and by then June was gone, absorbed into the crowd.

Bruce snarled at the cameraman. Alex grabbed him by the collar, reattached his leash, and pulled him to a somewhat quieter corner to try to calm him down.

"We won't stay long," Alex promised Bruce. "I need to have one quick conversation and then we can go home."

Bruce appeared dubious.

"I'll get you a pup cup," Alex said, and she could swear he smiled.

"Good boy." Alex gave his floppy ears a scruff. "Should we go find June and Willow?" Alex gestured in the direction she wanted to go, but Bruce pulled the opposite way, back toward the entrance.

"We just discussed this," Alex said. "We can't leave yet."

Bruce pulled harder, with all his might, nearly choking himself in the effort to drag Alex to—

Cash. And Val, looking like a different version of herself in a black dress and heels. Her hair was down, cascading around her shoulders. Was she even wearing makeup beyond her signature red lipstick?

Alex watched as Kennedy nudged Val and Cash to the step-and-repeat. Val was resisting, and Alex smiled involuntarily. She began moving closer to them, to Bruce's relief.

How would Val react when she saw her? Not great, surely. But Alex was prepared to power through any initial opposition. Never in her wildest dreams had she expected to find Val here.

Then, as Val and Cash were being forced across the red carpet, Alex's attention was drawn sideways. Who could say why? Maybe there was a sound or shift in the communal energy that made her turn toward the edge of the parking lot.

"What the hell is he doing here?" someone asked just as Alex caught sight of Silas making his way to the entrance.

Val was on the red carpet getting her photo taken when she noticed a small commotion near the gala entrance. A man, not in costume or dressed up. Just a regular guy in jeans and a black T-shirt, who it took Val a moment to realize was Silas Kennerson.

Val stepped out from under the bright photographic lights and scoped the area. Silas must be here looking for June, but there was no sign of her. Val's eyes rested instead on a tall figure in a gorgeous red wrap dress.

Alex.

When their eyes met, all was forgotten—for the moment. They communicated silently across time and space, understanding mutually that there was no good reason for Silas to be present.

I'll find June, Alex seemed to say. *You take Silas.*

In the next second, Alex took off into the crowd.

Kennedy—in a gown that looked like it was on backward, inside out, and missing parts, but she somehow made it work—was slow on the uptake, trying to urge Silas toward the step-and-repeat, until Meryl appeared.

Always the professional, even in a ridiculous fascinator, Meryl tried to play it cool, keep the peace. She greeted Silas civilly, but he waved her off, continuing forward.

"Sorry, Cash," Val said. "I need to go to work." She tied Cash's leash to a fencepost and trailed Silas in his quest for June.

Val homed in on him snaking his way through the crowd. He appeared hostile, aggressive, with his fists clenched, ready for confrontation.

Far ahead and eastward, Val spotted June in a bright yellow dress that was hard to miss. Alex was talking at her, trying to take her by the arm.

Silas probably saw June, too, but to Val's surprise, he didn't continue after her. Instead, he proceeded through the play area, straight for the doggy ball pit. Pushing past the volunteer who was manning the pit, Silas stomped upon the multicolored plastic balls, scooped Willow up into his arms, and took off in a mad dash.

He had come for Willow, Val realized, not June.

Val chased after him.

Holding a thirty-five-pound dog was slowing Silas down, so Val was certain she could catch him, even in heels. What she would do then, she was less sure. Fight Willow out of his arms, she supposed, maybe use one of her shoes as a weapon.

Others were quick to join the pursuit, perhaps recognizing foul play. Val was vaguely aware of a few running bodies close behind her.

The Silver Fox was incredibly fit for a middle-aged man. He stormed ahead, leaving Val in his dust.

On second thought, maybe she'd better kick off the high heels.

In the momentary pause, Val was nearly taken out at the knees by a bullet-fast borzoi dressed as a lobster, which was when she realized a stampede was forming.

A bulldog in a dinner jacket, a poodle in a summer dress, a bull terrier dressed as a great white shark running so fast its dorsal fin flapped in the wind.

All the dogs from the ball pit had joined the chase. The group at Maddy's pup cup ice-cream truck had also abandoned their places in line to try to catch whatever everyone else was after. Dirt was flying up everywhere, making it hard to see.

Val nearly tripped over a chihuahua that she was fairly certain had come as Dolly Parton, while a Siberian husky wearing a chef's hat nipped at her heels.

Through the melee, Val was able to decipher that she was a few paces behind the Silver Fox, who was a few paces behind Silas and Willow. Silas was leading them to the parking lot, where Val assumed he must have a car waiting.

This was a first for Val. In her long, varied, and often absurd career, she had never before encountered a dognapper.

But wait—was that Willow?

All at once Val realized why the Silver Fox was so motivated to catch up to Silas. It wasn't Willow Silas had in his arms; it was Mollie. Mollie, who had the same golden coloring as Willow, was around the same size, and was wearing an identical green dress.

Dear lord.

In the next moment, Silas appeared to recognize his mistake. He looked down, horror-struck at the golden corgi in his arms. Still running, his attention was distracted just long enough for him not to notice Yoshi's mom, who was arriving with the shih tzu, who was dressed in a pleated floral-print gown. She held a long leash loosely, allowing Yoshi to lunge forward toward all the excitement.

When Silas tripped over Yoshi's leash, he flew into the air spectacularly and landed headfirst, hard on the pavement.

Crack went his cranium on the sidewalk. *Clink* went his shoulder. Then silence.

It was quite the fall, with a comedown of such gory reality that no one even laughed, not even Val, who could find humor in just about anything and despised Silas to boot.

Mollie, thankfully, landed safely upon the ground on all four paws, but was so confused and exhilarated that she took off at full speed in the direction of the empty tennis courts.

The Silver Fox stopped short. Perhaps he was deliberating on whether to tend to the broken man before him on the parking lot pavement or to run after his terrified dog.

Then Val saw the car.

A 1980s Oldsmobile Cutlass Supreme, about the size of an extra-large refrigerator on wheels. Old Mrs. Pearlberg was behind the wheel, barely visible over the steering wheel. Virgil the German shepherd was more prominent, sitting tall in the passenger seat. He let out a loud, emphatic bark.

Down went the Silver Fox, beneath the Oldsmobile's solid steel weight.

The car made no effort to stop. Edna Pearlberg probably never even saw him, just heard the thump beneath her tires.

CHAPTER 25

Silas was in bad shape, but to Val's mild disappointment he was alive. He regained consciousness a minute or so after hitting the ground, where he remained with Meryl and a fortysomething-year-old veterinarian dressed as a bottle of mustard (to coordinate with his pet hot dog), the closest the fundraiser event crowd could produce to a human's MD. He checked Silas's vital signs and offered the surrounding onlookers a thumbs-up.

The Silver Fox did not fare so well.

Dr. Mustard declared him dead on sight, but then proceeded to check his vitals anyway, which were vitally not present.

Val felt terrible about the Silver Fox. Even though he was never the friendliest, and no one seemed to know much about him, nobody deserved to die in a mishap such as the one she had just witnessed. It could have easily been Val herself beneath those Oldsmobile tires, so she owed the nameless tuxedo-wearing dead man a tremendous debt.

It all happened so fast—Silas's nosedive over Yoshi's leash, Edna Pearlberg hitting the Silver Fox. There were a frenzied few seconds where no one knew who was left standing and who was on the ground.

The crowd that had been chasing their runaway dogs came to a halt. They screamed and wailed (which only startled the dog pack further). Val searched the horror-stricken faces for Alex or June's, but neither of them were among this group. They appeared in the second wave of spectators, after the cries of the first had dissipated.

June dashed to Silas's side.

Alex, a few steps behind, appeared crazed, gripping two leashes—an equally wild-eyed Bruce and Willow. Alex scanned the scene before her, searching, searching. Who had been killed? Someone was dead, but was it—

Val watched Alex turn her attention to where Val was standing with her hands on her knees, trying to catch her breath, midway between the two mangled men lying on the pavement. She figured Alex would be relieved to find her alive and in one piece, but she had not anticipated Alex running to her and throwing her arms around her.

"You're okay." Tears fell from Alex's eyes. She would not let Val out of her embrace. Bruce and Willow jumped and barked, tangling their leashes.

Val kept her arms down at her sides and tried to become a piece of cardboard, or maybe a jagged rock. But Alex's body against hers was teeming with energy and heat. She could feel her pulse, and the rapid, white-hot beating of her heart.

"I'm okay," Val repeated, trying to keep her head on straight. Was this supposed to change everything? One near-death experience? Alex seemed to think it rendered her off the hook.

"Thank God," Alex said, squeezing Val tighter.

"Seriously, I'm fine." Val pulled out of Alex's hold, stepped back from Bruce's and Willow's frenetic attention. "I've almost died so many times. This wasn't even that close of a call."

Alex put her head down, sheepish, reacting to Val's dismissive tone. She untangled Bruce and Willow's leashes, then turned to where Silas was lying on the ground with June kneeling beside him. The hem of her yellow cocktail dress was dirtied and mottled, which now seemed emblematic of this whole mess of a night.

"He took quite a blow to the head," Val said. "And landed hard on one arm, which is probably broken, but it looks to me like he'll be alright."

"Goody," Alex said.

Sirens bleated in the distance.

"You should get out of here," Val said to Alex. "You can't be questioned by the police. If your name gets to the media, it'll ruin everything for you, any future mission you want to take part in."

Alex's eyes filled with tears again, as if Val weren't just stating the obvious.

"Go," Val said, more sharply. "Leave your car. Take the back gate at the far end of the park, the one the caterers were using."

"What about you?" Alex asked.

"I can handle myself with the police. Besides, I unfortunately saw everything happen up close. They'll need me as a witness."

"I can stay with you, back up anything you tell the police, or choose not to tell them," Alex said.

"Shut up and just go already! And take Willow with you. I'll let June know she's safe."

Alex finally turned away, pulling the dogs along.

The sirens were getting louder, closer. Val didn't have much time. She shoved her way through the increasingly jam-packed crowd, making her way back to the post where she had left Cash.

When she arrived, Cash was gone. No leash on the post, nothing.

Oh god.

Val looked around. "Cash!" She yelled out. "Cash! Where are you?"

She scanned the grounds, from the buffet tables to the silent auction tent, to the canine play area.

The emcee who had been DJing party music was now trying to enforce crowd control from a mic stand on the stage. "Please walk, don't run. If you've lost your dog, I understand there are volunteers rounding up stray pets and delivering them to the welcome area."

Val had just been to the welcome area, and Cash wasn't there. Besides, no volunteer would be able to catch Cash if she didn't want to be caught. She may have left the park entirely. By now, there was no telling how far she could have run. And with so many busy streets nearby . . . Cash didn't have the slightest clue how to behave in moving traffic. She was impatient, never understanding why she couldn't just proceed through a cross-street of speeding cars.

Oh god. Val felt sick to her stomach.

But what if someone, one of those kindly volunteers, had noticed Cash tied the post, and taken her by the leash to someplace safe? That was possible, wasn't it?

Please let it be possible. Please please, please. I'll never let this dog out of my sight again, Val promised no one in particular. *Just let her be okay.*

Then Val heard a bark she recognized, and the next thing she saw was Cash running toward her, like a little rabbit, dragging her leash behind her.

Val got down on one knee and Cash leapt into her arms. She was shaking as she licked Val's face.

"I'm here," Val told her. "I'm sorry I left you alone."

Cash clung to Val's chest, refusing to be put down.

"I love you," Val whispered into Cash's ear. "You're safe now. I've got you."

Val rubbed soft circles into Cash's back, kissed the top of her head, and carried her back to the parking lot, where an ambulance and several police cars were just arriving.

June was still with Silas, seated beside him lying on the pavement, holding his hand. What could they possibly be talking about?

Silas lay on the cold ground. June felt responsible for his pain, both physical and emotional, even though she had not technically done anything to cause his accident. When the ambulance arrived, she let go of his hand, but he snatched it back with reassuring strength.

"Please don't leave me," Silas said. "Stay."

Whether he meant here, now, on the blacktop of the Hamilton Dog Park parking lot, or in life in general, June's answer remained the same.

"I can't," she said. "I'm sorry, but I can't."

It had slipped, out of habit, her apologizing to him, but it wouldn't happen again.

"It was all for you." Silas tried to sit up, failed at the attempt, and lay back down. "Everything I've done has been with your happiness in mind, to give you the life you deserve."

June wanted to remind Silas that he had just tried to kidnap their dog. She could also make the argument that if his immoral, illegal behavior at work was all for her, then why didn't he share whatever was in his secret offshore bank account?

But why bother? If Silas wanted to continue believing that his behavior was somehow in her best interest, let him.

Then June second-guessed herself. Instead of making the peace, soothing Silas's ego, she forced herself to say something.

"You did what you did for you, Silas," she said. "Because your own image is what has always mattered to you most. And you knew I wouldn't approve, which is why you lied about it. And you tried to take Willow from me to try to control me, manipulate me into staying with you, even though our marriage isn't working. I should have spoken up sooner, that's on me, but everything else—everything you've done and have been doing for so long—is on you. You're not a good person, Silas. You've allowed countless innocent people to get sick, even die, for what? So you could drive a Mercedes? Get a cabinet position one day? I could never stand by anyone with such an utter lack of moral standards."

Silas, unaccustomed to June standing up to him this way, propped himself up on his good elbow and focused his gaze. "I see the stellar influence of your two new friends shining through yet again. You let them change you, June. They've made you ugly."

June almost said, *They have nothing to do with this*, but that wasn't true. They had everything to do with this.

"Who do you think you are?" Silas felt strong enough to raise his voice suddenly. "Ransacking my personal files, trashing my office, and then actually believing you understood something in my private papers? You, who hasn't held a job or handled a financial statement in the whole time we've been married? Ha!"

Silas seemed to forget all about trying to convince June not to divorce him. She had never seen him so furious.

"What's your big plan, June? You think you can outsmart me? Take me down?"

The angrier he got, the more certain June was of his awfulness.

"I've got news for you," he continued. "Whatever you think you found, it's long gone, so now what are you going to do? When it's my word against yours, you've got nothing. You *are* nothing."

Against her will, tears pooled in June's eyes, making it difficult to see. But it was with perfect clarity that she heard Ava's voice behind her say "Dude is so going to jail."

Wiping away the tears, June turned around.

"Yup," Regina agreed with Ava. "Looks to us like you're the ugly one, Silas."

The two of them, along with half the crowd that had formed a few steps away, were filming the altercation with their phones.

"Tell us more about what you've been hiding in your home office, Silas," Meryl called out.

"Or better yet," Kennedy shouted, "June, why don't you tell us?"

Before June or Silas could say another word, the EMTs on the scene went into full action, coming between them. June could finally stand up, wipe the dirt from her hands, step back, and take in her surroundings.

Since she'd crossed into adulthood, real adulthood, she'd had Silas's hand to hold. Who was she without him? What would she think about all day, if not him, his needs, his preferences?

Over the years she told herself it wasn't as if she were miserable, that she was happy enough. Besides, she had made a promise, taken a vow. That had to mean something, otherwise nothing meant anything. All this time and energy couldn't be wasted, she thought. She couldn't begin all over again.

But now she could.

"You're the wife?" one of the EMTs asked, a diminutive but strong-looking woman.

"Not anymore," June said.

"Would you like to accompany him in the ambulance?"

"No, thank you." June took another step away and was embraced by Meryl, Kennedy, Regina, and Ava.

"I'll need you to send me those videos," June said.

"Just wait till I set mine to music." Ava laughed her shrieky, piercing laugh.

"We've got your back," Meryl said. "Whatever happens next." Then she added, under her breath, "I always knew Silas was a real shit. It's about time he gets what's coming to him."

June looked around, searching the crowd for Alex, to whom she owed an apology, or a thank-you, or both.

Alex had acted fast to find June and warn her of Silas's appearance at the fundraiser event. At first, when Alex approached her, June thought Alex was going to explain away her previous misdeeds. But no. Alex was going out of her way to help June, even after she had told Alex to get lost. And while June was still trying to make sense of why Silas had come to the event to find her, and how she should handle him, Alex was the one who thought of grabbing Willow out of the ball pit. Then, with the two of them safe, Alex began searching for Meryl, to alert her to the potential of a scene, an incident of the kind Meryl would certainly nip in the bud. In other words, good-hearted Alex had done everything right.

Silas was lying on a gurney now, about to be shoved into the back of the ambulance and shuttled to the hospital, when the detective caught him for a quick question or two.

Detective Ramos was his name, and he asked his questions in a gentle tone of voice.

June moved closer and craned her neck to listen in on Silas's answers.

"Yes," Silas admitted. "Yes, I accidentally grabbed the wrong dog, but that was because they kind of look alike, and they were wearing the same outfit, and, frankly, I was in a hurry. I meant to take *my* dog, Willow, who rightfully belongs to me, and is legally my property."

"We're in the process of getting divorced," June chimed in. She identified herself to the kind-faced detective. "Custody of Willow hasn't been decided yet, but I'm her primary caretaker."

It was more information than Detective Ramos needed, but June added, "I also would have known which dog was mine if I came here intending to steal her."

"I see," Detective Ramos replied, apparently satisfied for the moment. He left them to go speak to Edna Pearlberg.

The poor old lady. She may have been as much a victim as the Silver Fox in all this. Did she even fully understand what she had done? She appeared to be quite shaken up.

June looked around, not finding Alex and Willow, while avoiding everyone else who tried to speak to her. She was the person of the hour, it seemed. A woman she didn't know, who was wearing a beach ball costume, and was not an official event photographer, held up her phone and was about to snap June's picture.

Val smacked the phone out of the woman's hand. "What the hell is wrong with you?" she said, sounding New Yorkier than June had ever heard her. "The show's over. You can roll yourself on out of here."

With some effort, the beach ball picked up her phone and rumbled off, more annoyed than ashamed, but at least she was gone.

"Thank you," June said.

"No sweat."

"And for trying to save Willow, while everyone thought it was Willow."

Val nodded. "Has anyone seen Mollie?"

June gestured to where the golden corgi was being comforted by Regina, not far from where Ava was being comforted by Kennedy. The death of the most handsome man at the dog park was finally setting in.

"What a mess," Val said.

June gave Cash, who was clinging to Val's chest like a baby monkey, a pat on the rump. "Have you seen Alex?"

"I told her to head out before the cops came. She took Willow with her."

"I'm free to go," June said. "You?"

"Same."

June watched the ambulance exit the parking lot with Silas inside. "Care to follow me to my house?" June asked.

Val nodded.

"And tell Alex to meet us there." June took one long last look at the disastrous scene before her and was overcome with the sense that she was leaving something for good at the dog park tonight.

In a game, when an athlete left it all on the field, it meant they gave their absolute best effort, emptied their entire reserve of energy, and didn't hold anything back. Whether they won or lost, they would go home with no regrets.

For the first time in years, this was exactly how June felt as she walked to her car.

CHAPTER 26

Trudging along Dudley Lane in an evening gown and heels, Alex was halfway to her apartment with a panting Bruce and Willow when Val's Nova pulled up alongside her.

Val said, "Beep beep," with the window rolled down.

First, Alex felt relief because, like the dogs, she was tired and overstimulated.

Then Alex remembered her shame, the humiliation of clinging to Val like her own life depended on it—and being rejected. Again.

Stay tough, Alex told herself. *Try to at least regain some dignity.*

"I'm not supposed to talk to strangers," Alex said.

"Would it be creepy if I tried to lure you in with candy?"

"Yes."

"How about an invitation from June? She asked that we meet at her house."

If Val could have uttered magic words, those were the ones.

Alex opened the Nova's heavy passenger side door and let Bruce and Willow join Cash in the back. When she settled into the front seat, she wasn't sure what to say next.

Neither did Val, apparently. Here they were with a moment to themselves, sweaty and filthy in their eveningwear, hair disheveled, makeup smeared, overall lightly traumatized. It was an opportunity to say literally anything, because the circumstances would have made anything okay, and yet they drove the rest of the way in silence.

When June opened the front door at Willow's excited bark, Alex saw she had changed from her gala attire into a cozy sweatshirt and soft athletic pants. Alex had removed Bruce's and Willow's costumes when she exited the park, and Val had already freed Cash from her checkered bandana. This left only Alex and Val still looking like they just got home from prom in a horror movie.

They stood in June's living room, all three dogs fully and playfully recovered from the evening's events, while the humans remained awkward in one another's presence.

"You should not have lied to me," June said to both Alex and Val, as if they were a single entity. "But I appreciate what you did for Willow and me tonight."

To Alex specifically she said, "I figure I owe you something in return."

Then she led them upstairs.

Alex's heart jumped in her chest. She knew where they were headed. Finally, after all of her attempts to get hard evidence on Silas, she was about to get it.

In the doorway, Val gasped before Alex could. "The file cabinets. They're gone."

June stepped past them into the place on the floor where the cabinets had been. "Silas knew I got into them and saw all his papers," she said. "He must have destroyed everything or moved it someplace else."

"That motherfucker," Val said.

Alex felt her shoulders slump. "This is what you wanted to show us?"

"No," June said. "This."

From her pants pocket, June pulled out a small USB jump drive. "I had a feeling that stuff was kind of important, so I took photos of a lot of it with my phone. There are about fifty pdfs saved on here, including the information to his offshore bank account, where I believe he was storing his bribe money."

"June!" Alex said. "I could kiss you."

"You're a genius," Val added.

"Nah," June said. "I just learned how to be sneakier hanging out with you two."

Alex could hardly believe it. No way would Silas sidestep prosecution with this much documentation.

"This is going to do a lot of good," Alex said. "Lives will be saved. All thanks to you."

June waved off Alex's praise. "You have someone to give this info to, I assume?"

"I do." Alex accepted the USB drive from June.

"Or June herself could be Erin's informant," Val said to Alex. It was the first time Val allowed direct eye contact between them. "June coming forward would shield her from any implication that she had been protecting Silas till now."

Val was always thinking. Always one step ahead.

"Who's Erin?" June asked.

"Erin is my contact at the FBI," Alex answered June, but was looking at Val.

Alex's admiration of Val's mind must have been plain to see. She wanted Val to see it, and to feel it.

June ping-ponged her gaze between the two of them. "Everything cool with you two?"

Alex hoped Val might crack, give in to the moment, and forgive Alex as June had forgiven the two of them. But Val could barely look at her.

"Val friend-dumped me," Alex said to June. "Because I told you she was a PI, which I shouldn't have done, and I apologized for, but now she hates me."

"I don't hate you," Val said, in a way that sounded like a scolding.

Then she softened her expression for June. "I've had a blast getting to know both of you, and I'm glad everything's worked out, but I've got a job and a life in New York to get back to. I'll be leaving first thing in the morning."

June put out her arms and wrapped Val into hug. "I'm going to miss you. Will you stay in touch?"

Val kept her arms directly down at her sides until June released her. "You've got my number if you need anything."

June was never one to be dissuaded by Val's hard shell. "Willow and Cash will need to have a playdate sometime. We'll make it happen. I'm willing to travel."

Val looked down at the floor. Was she even going to offer Alex a proper goodbye?

Just then, there was the pitter-patter of paw claws bumbling up the stairs. Bruce had strayed from his friends to come see what Alex was up to.

"Hi, buddy." Alex scratched behind his soft ears.

Bruce licked her hands and leaned his body against hers, and she immediately felt lighter. The way he play-bowed and wagged his tail made her laugh every time, and he seemed to know it.

It was on account of Bruce that Alex believed she wouldn't sink all the way down to the doldrums in the coming weeks. How could she when he needed to be fed and walked every morning and every night? And given proper exercise and stimulation. And when he adored her unconditionally, with so much vigor.

Alex would be alright. She may have lost Val, and who knew where June would go? But Alex was no longer alone, and she was loved. And she somehow, along the way, figured out how to be happy.

Cash was snoring, lying alongside Val in bed like the small spoon. Val watched the heavy rise and fall of Cash's belly, and it made her feel weak. Tenderized. Like a slab of meat that had been broken down with a mallet, muscle fibers and connective tissues flattened, softer now and easier to chew.

Perhaps vulnerability made a person more palatable, but Val was unused to the sensation and did not like it. She hadn't known it was possible for her to become attached to another living being this way. As it turned out, aside from the time spent trying to convince herself to give Cash away, Val was a far better dog parent than she'd imagined. Keen enough to anticipate Cash's needs, observant enough to recognize her patterns, and emotionally mature enough to show restraint when Cash misbehaved.

Yes, Val loved her, this weird, furry little animal who lived in her house and slept in her bed. She would keep her. And one day, natural lifespans being as brutal as they were, Cash would inevitably die, and Val would be destroyed, and she would have no one to blame but herself.

Why sign that check now? The one that guaranteed tears in a decade's time—if she was lucky. It was a deal only a chump would take. But Val had long since fallen. It was already too late.

It didn't even matter to Val if Cash loved her back or if she just liked being fed and having a warm body to sleep next to. Because, at the end of the day, Cash was still an animal, and excuses would be made. It was that simple.

Person-to-person attachment was way more complicated. Val was a lot to handle. She wore people down. She could be moody, mean, overly negative, and sarcastic. She was guarded and difficult to get close to. In relationships she preferred to always keep one foot out the door.

And yet, the following afternoon when she closed and locked the door to her Bethesda rental for the final time and packed Cash into the Nova with her overstuffed suitcase, the highway wasn't where she was headed.

Val was not needed, nor was she expected, at Alex's apartment. The point of the day's meeting was to introduce June to Erin, so they could discuss the details of June becoming Erin's informant. Val had no reason to be there.

"Moral support," she said in reply to Alex's shocked expression in the doorway, and the valid question, *What are you doing here?*

Alex nodded and led Val inside.

June was already seated at the kitchen table when Val and Cash entered. Beside her, with a stack of papers between them, sat Erin.

Bruce and Willow pummeled Cash as June stood to greet Val. "What a happy surprise!"

Amid her warm welcome, Val noticed June shoot a quick glance at Alex, as if to say *Huh?*

Alex replied with a silent, *No clue.*

Erin remained seated, legs crossed, briefcase at her feet. She wore a blue suit with a white dress shirt, her blond hair up in a bun. Val could have nailed her for a law enforcement agent from a mile's distance.

"Oh good," Erin said. "Another animal has arrived." She offered Val no other salutation or introduction.

Her face was more rugged than Val had pictured and her hands, despite the light pink polish on her nails, were large and thick. This was a woman who could choke a man to death if she cared to, which Val had to respect.

Alex seemed to be watching Val and Erin size one another up, then said, "Should we get back to it?"

The three of them had already started going over the details before Val arrived—what June should expect from coming forward against Silas—so it wasn't long before June took her pen in hand and began signing the various sheets of paperwork Erin slid before her.

Val didn't have much to do but look on, which was kind of a bore, so her mind began to wander, then race. What if she was making a terrible mistake coming back here?

No, she told herself. She wasn't. Because in her own thorny way she had grown to love Alex, much like she had learned to love Cash—even though neither of them was exactly low maintenance.

What a relief, to realize she was capable of it.

June signed the final sheet of paper of Erin's sheaf, and Erin stuffed the pile into a thick brown envelope.

"So, what's next for you?" Erin asked June. "With all the change coming your way, do you have a plan?"

"I think I'll go back home for a while," June said. "Reacquaint myself with my family, then figure out what I want to happen next, wherever that might be."

"You excited to be solo for a while?" Alex asked.

"I won't be alone," June replied. "I've got Willow. Oh, and I almost forgot." She paused, brightening. "I'm adopting Mollie."

"The Silver Fox's Mollie?" Val asked.

June nodded. "She had been staying with Regina, but Regina can't keep her permanently, and it's been weirdly hard to find a friend or family member to take her in, so I volunteered."

Erin clicked her briefcase closed and stood up. "I'll be in touch," she said to June. Then to Alex she said, "We should put a date on the calendar to discuss next steps, post-Silas."

Erin slid one arm, and then the other, into her overcoat and cinched it closed. "Take some time," she said to Alex. "But when you're ready for more action, I've got a lead on something that I think will be of interest. Tons of red tape tying it up. I could use you, if you're up for it."

Alex looked to Val.

Val said nothing, but she didn't turn away. She forced herself to meet Alex's gaze and let herself be seen.

The image of them working side by side filled the space between them.

Erin stopped short of the front door, where Cash, Bruce, and Willow sniffed and pawed at her shoes. "Can you please call off the dogs?"

Alex shooed them out of Erin's way and saw her outside.

"I'm glad you came back," June said to Val. "You and Alex should talk."

Val shrugged. Did they really have to? Wasn't it enough that she was standing here?

Alex stepped back inside, shut the door behind her.

"Why don't I give you some privacy?" June said, to break the silence. She clapped her hands together and called out, "Everyone with four legs, follow me."

From the cupboard, June retrieved a bag of treats, then secured each dog to their leash. "Is it alright if I take these guys to the park?"

"To Hamilton?" Alex asked.

"Yeah." June held all three leashes with one hand. "I'm supposed to meet Regina there anyway, to pick up Mollie. I'll just be a little early."

"June," Alex said. "That would make four dogs you'd be trying to wrangle. Doesn't that seem like a bit much? You can leave Bruce and Cash here."

"No," Val said, in a tone of voice that came out louder than she'd intended. "Why don't we all go?"

No one protested. And, out of what must have been politeness, which Val greatly appreciated, no one acknowledged that she was acting weird.

So they all went to the dog park.

Val didn't expect to see so many cars in the lot when she pulled in. Maybe the perfect weather had drawn everyone out of their houses well before the designated happy hour. The field itself was nearly as crowded as it ever was. Val entered the gate first, because Cash pulled the hardest on her leash, followed by June and Willow, and then Alex and Bruce.

Other than some yellow caution tape shriveling on the ground, all appeared as it always did, which struck Val as profoundly comforting. Even Mrs. Pearlberg and Virgil were in their regular spot.

Let loose from their leashes, the dogs took off running. June forged ahead to where Meryl was yukking it up with Kennedy and Ava.

"There she is," Meryl said, reaching for June.

The group oohed and aahed for a bit over the fact that June was adopting Mollie. Then Regina arrived with Eloise and Mollie in tow, and the collective volume turned up from a seven to a ten.

All the while, Val watched Cash play—probably for the last time here at this park, which had been the center of their lives here in Bethesda.

Val turned to Alex, who'd been quiet at her side. "Do you think Cash and Bruce will miss this place?"

"I think Cash and Bruce can be happy anywhere," Alex said. "Especially if they're together."

"Yeah," Val said. "You're right."

"I am?"

"Seems wrong to break up a bonded pair."

Alex nodded, then finally allowed herself to smile. "I agree wholeheartedly."

"So, where are the good dog parks in New York?" Val asked.

"I don't know," Alex said. "But we'll find them when we get there."

Epilogue

They call it a *rescue* when a dog has been relieved of a neglectful or abandoned situation and given a new home.

Of course, there are some things to consider before you go trying to be a hero to a stray animal. They may have trauma, for example, or temperament issues; there will be vet bills; you may need to invest time in training. Trust will have to be earned. But at the same time, rescues often come with a surprising amount of resilience and gratitude, offering an especially loving and loyal companionship.

After Val and Alex and June became entangled at Hamilton Dog Park, a life was lost—as I predicted—but those three got a second chance at a new way to live.

And before you go shedding tears of mourning for the man they called the Silver Fox, you should have all the facts from the most reliable of sources—me.

I had a front-row view of the whole escapade, seeing as how I was in the passenger seat of my human's car when the Fox came running across the parking lot.

Edna turned to me and asked, "Should I seize the opportunity?"

And I barked, "Yes!" Because one never really retires from being a spy, no matter how old they are, and besides, I knew an inimitable operative like Edna Pearlberg couldn't resist the chance to take out one of the most malicious Russian intelligence agents our country had ever seen.

"It was all an unfortunate accident," the police detective decided. Sweet man.

After all that's happened, will Hamilton Dog Park ever get its renovation?

Probably not, but that's fine by me. All my human and I really need is our one comfortable bench. And now, with the Silver Fox out of the way, we can finally truly relax.

Acknowledgments

Thank you first and foremost to my amazing agent, Kerry Sparks, who has stuck by me through good times and bad, offering advice and encouragement and invaluable support along the way. Kerry, I feel like we've earned this moment together, so cheers to you! I would also like to thank Rebecca Rodd for all her hard work and the entire team at Levine Greenberg Rostan, as well as Dana Spector at CAA and Eric Brooks for their skillful care in overseeing the screen rights to all my books.

Thank you to my brilliant editor, Kate Dresser, whose guidance, wisdom, and good instincts helped me elevate a first draft (or was it the fourteenth?) to the finished novel I envisioned. Kate, I feel so lucky to have you in my corner. And huge, heartfelt thanks to Ivan Held and Lindsay Sagnette, and the incredible team at G. P. Putnam's Sons, especially Ashley McClay, Alexis Welby, Katie Grinch, Brennin Cummings, and Tarini Sipahimalani. Thank you to Carla Benton and Claire Sullivan for their insightful copy edits.

Over the course of writing this book I turned to many dear friends for guidance. My endless gratitude goes out to Megan

Labrise, Beth Parker, Daniela Petrova, Summer Smith, Ryan Chapman, Victoria Comella, Melissa Kravitz Hoeffner, Kathy Daneman, Koa Beck, Amanda Montell, Miwa Messer, Courtney Gillette, Emily Pullen, Emily Moore, and Anna Peele. A special shout-out to Helen Ellis and my beloved Puzzle Posse: Megan Abbott, Dani Koplin, and Kay Wahrsager. And to the friends who've known me the longest: Joanna Greenberg, Amy Badagliacca, Penny and Joe Menicucci, Christine Lavery, Lisa Jusino, Natalia Gibbs-Chiemi and Shellie Citron. I am also indebted to Richard Strauss and Patricia Frischtak for keeping my head screwed on properly.

The seeds of this novel were first planted during the lonely, isolated years of the Covid pandemic. At that time, the best part of every day was five thirty p.m. at the Mattie Stepanek Dog Park in Rockville, Maryland. I would like to thank all the regulars (and their pups!) for making a tough time so much brighter—and for inspiring me to write this book.

Thank you to Tracy at Furbabies of Bethesda. We miss you so much! And my gratitude to everyone at Biscuits & Bath in Greenwich Village for taking care of Pip and keeping her busy so I could actually get some writing done.

Thank you to Norma and David Pennock for all their championing and support. You're the best in-laws anyone could ever hope for.

Sincerest thanks to my family for their lifelong encouragement: Francine and John Azzariti, Michael, Nicholas, and Vincent; Maria and Louis Balsamo, Stephen, Perry, and Diana. And to my father, Frank Perri. Thank you for always being there for me.

To Helen, the love of my life, and the smartest, kindest person

I've ever known. This book would not exist without you. You make everything possible.

Last, but not least, thank you to Pip. There was once a time I did not want a dog, and now I've written an entire novel in my dog's honor. Enough said.

Photograph of the author © Nina Subin

Camille Perri is the author of *The Assistants* and *When Katie Met Cassidy*. She has worked as a books editor for *Cosmopolitan* and *Esquire*. She has also been a ghostwriter of young adult novels and a reference librarian. She holds a bachelor of arts degree from New York University, where she majored in English and gender and sexuality studies, and a masters of library science degree from Queens College. She splits her time between New York City and the Hudson Valley with her wife and their Brussels Griffon named Pip.

camilleperri.com

CamillePerri

CamillePerri